FIVE FATAL I

Louise Mangos

Mana Publishing

Other psychological suspense novels by the author
STRANGERS ON A BRIDGE
THE ART OF DECEPTION
THE BEATEN TRACK

Writing historical mystery as L.S.Mangos
THE SECRETS OF MORGARTEN

For my wonderful mum, from whom I inherited the love of books

1

TRUDY

Present day

When you have a baby, it's not all about the cherishing and nurturing. Don't be mistaken, there's plenty of love. It's just that nobody warns you about the other stuff, the flood of angst filling your soul, the weight of responsibility to do the very best you can for this tiny fragile being you've been entrusted with. The most qualified psychologists can't always work out the mental complexities of birth trauma or postnatal anxiety. And it's even more daunting if you're the mother *and* the psychologist.

Parenting has been way more challenging than I expected four months ago. It started with a nightmare birth, and things spiralled from then, my baby bestowing on me every clichéd challenge in the book.

The part-time project I've taken on at the clinic gives me free time from Benny's colicky crying, and makes me feel worthwhile outside the realms of feeding, soothing, cleaning and sleep deprivation. But I feel guilty every time I experience the relief of being away from it all, knowing my role as a mother should come first.

There are moments when Benny sleeps for more than a couple of hours and things almost feel normal. And last night Harry and I made love for the first time without any of my demons present. There is a glimpse of light at the end of the tunnel.

This morning, Harry brings me a cup of tea in bed before leaving. It's Saturday and he's been asked to visit the site of a new gallery to sign off their architectural plans. He's been working long hours on this, and is proud of the building design. I expect it'll win some prize, perhaps the Stirling Award he's dreamed of since uni. He plans to go straight to the tennis club later for his regular Saturday game.

'Are you sure you're all right with me being away for so long, Trude?' he asks.

'Benny and I will be fine,' I say. 'It's probably the first time I'm saying that in all honesty.'

'I can't avoid the work, but I could always cancel the tennis. Let me know by lunchtime if you change your mind.'

'It'll be fine.' I smile.

He kisses me before leaving. I give him a flirtatious look. We made each other feel good last night. I tell myself it *will* be all right.

Benny is still sleeping. For the first time ever, I have an urge to go and wake him. But I don't. Instead I lie in bed, the warmth of the lovemaking the night before still suffusing the rumpled sheets.

I eventually get up, open the curtains and gaze across the garden to the field beyond. It's a bright summer's morning, not too hot, with fluffy clouds hanging in an azure blue sky. The field of wheat has been harvested, the stubble shining golden in the sun. In the field further out, long grass undulates like an ocean in the breeze.

When Benny finally wakes, I first go down to the kitchen to prepare him a bottle and then feed him sitting in bed, propped up with pillows, letting the waves of grass in the distant field calm me. Benny looks up at me at one point with a frown and I huff out a laugh.

'That's a hint of happiness you can see on your mother's face,' I say as he seeks the teat of the bottle with his mouth, his eyes still on me.

When he's finished, I take him downstairs to the kitchen and put him in the baby bouncer while I make myself a cup of tea. I pull my notes towards me and flick through them, knowing I should go to the office at some stage and write reports for each member of my post-trauma therapy group. But not today. Today is Benny's day.

I run a load of laundry, tidy the kitchen and empty the dishwasher, making a game of everything for Benny's sake, wanting to make this his best day ever. He slept in this morning, so it will be late when he goes down for his nap. He begins to grizzle around midday, so I put him in the stroller to take him for a walk, hoping the movement will send him to sleep.

We wander down the lane past the farm. He's making the familiar grouchy hiccupping noise that usually precedes a full-on screaming fit, and for a moment my serenity falters. I so want things to be perfect. Two horses trot over to the fence near the river and the old grey mare nickers in recognition. I stop and lift Benny out of the stroller. His eyes widen, he stops crying and his tiny fingers reach out to the soft whiskery muzzle. I used to ride this mare in my teens in exchange for helping the farmer's wife deliver milk in the village. I know the horse won't nip, but I place my hand between her quivering upper lip and Benny's fingers as a precaution.

I put Benny back in the stroller and walk up through the Bowes-Lyon estate. Three huge chestnut trees dominate the middle of the field, their gnarled old trunks twisted with tales of my youth. One thick bough is bent down to the ground. I sit on the branch, remembering days of scrambling up into the canopy with my sister. The summers of our innocence before adult responsibilities were ever a thing. I tip the seat of the stroller back and leave the hood open as Benny becomes fascinated by the foliage. His eyes squint when the leaves move to let spots of sunlight shine across his face.

On the homeward stretch, he finally falls asleep. When we arrive, I wheel him into the garden, put a net over the hood and fetch the laundry to hang on the line. A sheet billows and snaps with a sudden breeze, but Benny doesn't wake. I half-heartedly do a little gardening, weeding around the spinach and the radishes, listening to the insects buzzing, the birds singing. I top some long-dead tulips, trim the lavender, and recklessly eat the last of the raspberries that should have been gathered to make a dessert.

I take advantage of this moment of peace and lie down on the grass under the trees next to the stroller. The gentle swaying of the branches casting dappled shadows over my face sends me into a deep sleep.

When I wake, it's because the sun has moved across the sky and is shining directly on my face. My heart is beating; I've had a disturbing dream. There was darkness, violence, perhaps a tussle with someone, maybe blood. I remember red, but that could have been the sun on the insides of my eyelids as I stirred. I try to grasp the reality of finding myself in my garden. I focus on the droning of a tractor in the distance and the sweet fermented smell of freshly cut grass drifting over the hedge with spindles of dust winking in the sun.

I stretch and wonder how long I've been asleep. I haven't slept that deeply for a long time. The sleep of the dead. The darkness of my dream is chased away by the balminess of the summer afternoon. I glance at my wrist but I'm not wearing my watch. I notice dirt under my fingernails.

My gaze drifts up to the stroller. A breeze has lifted the net. I groggily push myself to my feet, hearing the insects humming constantly amongst the other background noises of the rural countryside.

I lift the netting away and push back the hood, exposing the empty blue cushioned seat. I suck in my breath.

Benny's not there.

2

RACHEL

Three years ago

She focused on the splendid symmetry of a single frozen crystal. The rhythmic movement made the snowflake appear bigger and smaller, bigger and smaller in front of her face.

She recalled the darkness of the bar, the pounding music and the musky bodies. She was on her way home when she was yanked from the steps to the bin shed and slammed against the rough wooden planks. His body pinned her there. He tried to kiss her, but she twisted her head away from his foetid whisky breath.

In the distance the bar door opened. Voices and music flooded the night. She opened her mouth to call out, but he pressed his hand over her face. The stale smell of nicotine on his fingers replaced the creosote stink of the shed wall.

She concentrated harder on the microscopic crystal with six fragile arms and a multitude of delicate thorns. She knew this thing of beauty had an infinitesimal flaw at its nucleus, a nanoparticle of dust around which water had condensed in the troposphere, before freezing and falling to his shoulder.

Somewhere deep within her she wouldn't have been aware of nature's violent survival. The fusion of a miniscule seed of dust burrowing inside a tiny drop of moisture. A snowflake in a storm. The potential for perfect beauty, extending its limbs like icy crystals. Clinging to the warmth in the darkness.

A miracle of creation existing only because of one filthy piece of dirt.

3

TRUDY

Present day

I draw my gaze away from the stroller, my throat closing against a rush of panic. The ordered neatness of the flowerbeds mocks me after my recent gardening work, those tailored bushes with bright pink cosmos growing around them. The scent of clipped lavender mingled with the petrichor of freshly-turned soil galvanises me into action.

The backdoor slams against the wall as I rush into the kitchen.

'Harry!' I yell. 'Are you home?' I pause for two seconds. 'Hello?'

I haul in a ragged gulp of air.

'Benny?'

I know he can't possibly answer, but I listen for his babbling noises or crying. I let the silence in the house sink in with the stone of dread weighing heavier in my stomach with each passing moment. I back out of the kitchen onto the patio and race across the lawn to grab my phone from where I left it on the rug. I call Harry's number but it rings and rings until voicemail kicks in.

'Harry! Harry, oh God, please call me. Now!'

I tuck the phone into my back pocket and run down the path leading from the back of the house to the front, onto the road. Our cottage and the farm are the only buildings at this end of the lane. Sometimes walkers park their cars on the side of the road, but there's no one there now.

After turning around several times, desperately searching for any sign of Benny, I run all the way to the hump-backed bridge over the village stream, calling for him. Running. Running. Breath getting shorter. I slide down the silty bank, see the watercress swaying in the clear flow under the brick-lined arch of the bridge and call again.

'Benny!' My voice echoes as though in a cathedral.

Someone must surely hear me? I shout his name louder, and the echo lengthens my call like the tolling of a bell.

Racing back to the farmyard, I bang on the door of the farmhouse, but there's no answer and despair makes my heart beat harder. The tractor passed us earlier on the lane, and their Land Rover isn't parked in its usual place. The only warm bodies in the barn are the young calves in their pens who've been taken away from their mothers. *Think! Why isn't anyone around? Someone must be here somewhere! Someone should have heard me. Why isn't anyone noticing me?*

I try Harry's number again, hoping he's taken a break between games and come back to the bench on the edge of the tennis court.

'Hi, Trude. I've just noticed a missed call from you.'

'Harry!' I say, a jumble of words sticking in my throat.

'My mobile fell out of my racquet bag,' he continues. 'I would have left it under the seat if you hadn't—'

'Did you come home?' I interrupt. 'Did you take Benny with you?'

Harry laughs.

'Do you have Benny?'

'What are you talking about? You're joking, right?'

My voice cracks.

'Benny's gone! He's... disappeared.'

'What the...? Have you called your mum? Checked the farm? Maybe someone stopped by.'

'No... I... We were in the garden. He was right here.' My voice shudders, ending with a sob.

'Have you called the police? I'll be there as fast as I can, Trude.'

I hear him shout to his tennis partner, the sound of the zip on his canvas bag, before the phone beeps and then silence. I call 999.

'Police! Police!' I shout when asked which service I require. 'My baby's disappeared. Benny's disappeared! Someone's taken my baby!'

The woman on the other end talks to me with exaggerated calm, asking me for our address and then repeating it back to me. When I hiccup, sourness rising in my throat, the woman tells me to calm down.

'My baby's gone!' I yell. 'Don't tell me to calm down!'

'The police are on their way, Mrs Greenwood. What you should do in the meantime is recall your exact movements over the past hour or so.'

'I was right here in the garden. With Benny. But he's gone.'

A moan escapes my throat to stop the woman at the emergency call centre adding an accusatory tone to her already patronising one. I am riddled with enough guilt as it is.

'Don't move from where you are now,' continues the woman. 'I'll stay on the line with you until the police get there.'

Don't move?

'But shouldn't someone be out there looking?'

I glance at the flowerbeds, the freshly turned earth, draw in a breath, and let out a sob.

Oh God, oh God, oh God.

4

OLIVE

Two years ago

Olive checked herself in the mirror. There was a mauve cloud on her cheek, those billowy ones, what did they call them again? A bit of make-up would cover it up. He still wanted to take her out, so she'd better hurry up.

Cumulus! That was it. She suddenly remembered from one of the geography lessons at school she hadn't skipped. The barman at the pub had called her Weather Girl last time. She was getting cleverer at covering up the clouds. She hoped he wouldn't notice this time.

She turned her face, looked at the other cheek in the reflection. This one had turned yellow from the storm the week before. Yellow like sunshine. Weather Girl. She rummaged in her toilet bag. *Come on. Come on*. He said he didn't have much time tonight. Wanted it all, for fuck's sake. The sex and the social. Always expecting her to look good. An extra sponge of foundation here, a brush of blusher there.

All fixed up, she looked at herself again and smiled.

When she came out to the tiny living room where he was waiting, she hoped this particular bout of anger was over. Why did these men like things so bloody rough?

Sticks and stones. That was bullshit.

The pain was always a relief after the cruelty of his words.

5

TRUDY

Present day

'The police will be with you soon,' says the woman at the emergency call centre.

I want to throw the phone down to stop her voice, but I clutch it harder, the burn of tears behind my eyes. I look at the head-high garden gate leading down the path to the front of the house, which I've just navigated several times. It's closed, but not bolted. We never bolt it.

'How far away are they?' I ask.

'They've come from Hitchin. Just through St Paul's Walden now,' replies the woman.

My gaze darts about the garden, calculating. Someone must have come in while I was sleeping. I look over the hedge at the back to the harvested field. Try to recall what crop they planted this year. Was it barley or wheat? *Why am I thinking this?* Could someone force their way through the hedgerow? Probably not, it's blackthorn, and there are nettles.

'Are you still there, Mrs Greenwood?'

I give a high-pitched bleat in reply.

'The police have entered the village from the Hitchin end.'

'It'll take them ages to get through the High Street,' I say, knowing that the traffic parked on the side of the road is terrible at the weekend. Nowhere to pass.

'Are you all right, Mrs Greenwood?'

I want to tell her of course I'm not, but before I can speak, Harry enters the house calling my name, and I hear a siren in the distance. I imagine the frantic actions of oncoming drivers, pulling into any space they can along the row of tightly-parked cars on the High Street.

My mind sways between panic and confusion and I wonder inanely if I should get a siren and a blue light to navigate my way out of the village on work days.

'I'm out here, Harry,' I shout. 'In the garden. They told me not to move.'

Harry marches across the patio and onto the lawn, his tennis bag still over his shoulder. I'm rooted to the spot.

'What the hell happened?' he asks. 'How did Benny just disappear? My God, Trudy!'

'I was dozing,' I say between sobs. 'We were together. Here on the lawn.'

I point to the empty stroller next to the rug I was lying on. Harry's gaze pauses at the trowel lying next to the flowerbed before settling on the stroller, his brows creased.

'I woke up,' I continue. 'Saw the netting had shifted on the stroller. Worried a bee or an insect had got in. And... and then... he wasn't there!'

I gulp air, then breathe deeply to try to calm my heartbeat. Tears dampen my cheeks. Harry puts his hand on the top of his head, bites his lip.

'I thought you came back,' I say. 'I thought you took Benny to let me continue sleeping. Oh, Harry! Whitwell's such a friendly village. Can you believe it? Someone has come into our garden and stolen our child! While I was sleeping. Right there underneath the hazelnut tree. Christ!'

My stomach roils with anxiety. I think I might be sick.

'Stolen? Benny? How could someone sneak in here so silently and take a baby?' asks Harry. 'They would have made a noise.

You would've woken up. Benny would've woken up, wouldn't he? What the hell?'

I feel my face crumple. What have I done?

'It's okay, Trude. I'm not *blaming* you. I'm just trying to understand.'

6

DANIEL

Two years ago

A buzzard flew off a fence post, its pale brown body ghosting on the mist. Mottled wings dipped towards a mash of flattened carrion glued to the road. Temptation eclipsed a normally careful perception, and it alighted with tail feathers fanned in excited anticipation.

Sarah was calculating how long the sirloin would take to roast in the oven when they arrived home. She recited minutes per pound, couldn't choose between low or medium heat.

A shift of the eyes. A flutter of lashes. A beat of the heart. A split second. That's all it took. The car swerved to avoid the bird.

Increasing velocity and engine vibration released the oncoming driver's ill-fitting water bottle in its holder on the central console. It bounced off his leg and rolled onto the floor. The driver reached down, searched at his feet near the pedals, fingers patting dried mud, pieces of grit and stale crisp crumbs. As he stretched further forward under the column, his fingers slipped against the condensation on the bottle. The movement hauled the steering wheel imperceptibly sideways.

In a strange line-dance of two vehicles in the middle of a narrow country lane, the head-on encounter was perfectly synchronised.

7

TRUDY

Present day

'Who would have taken him? How did they get back here without you noticing?' Harry asks.

I glance towards the garden gate at the side of the house and bite my lip, a hot well of tears distorting my vision. The sirens are getting louder.

'I don't know. They can't have got very far, surely? I want to go out there again and search, but the woman at the emergency call centre told me to wait here.'

'Did you look through the whole house?'

I nod, the edges of my mouth drawing downwards. 'I... went down the lane too. As far as the bridge over the Mimram. Oh God, Harry. This is a nightmare.'

A movement catches my eye in the flowerbed, but it's the cosmos swaying in the breeze. I think about clearing away the garden tools. They look menacing, lying there next to the freshly turned earth. Why do I feel like I've been through a time warp? Everything has slowed down. I hear blood pounding in my head.

'I'll go and check. You stay here like they said. It doesn't need two of us standing here doing nothing.'

Was that an admonishment?

'They told me to wait here. I'm only doing what I'm told.'

Harry touches my arm, leaves his tennis bag at my feet and runs across the lawn. He pulls the side gate towards him, rushes through and it clacks in its frame behind him, making me jump, even though I was expecting the noise, staring at it as it closed. I feel useless.

The siren is closer now, and I know the police have turned into our road.

Moments later Harry comes back out of the kitchen door with two uniformed policemen and points towards me across the patio. One of them disappears back inside the house with Harry. The other uniformed policeman approaches me, stepping onto the lawn from the patio tentatively as though it might be against the rules. It's not like we have the lawn tended to golf-green perfection. The dry spell over the past weeks has resulted in it looking permanently parched and there are bare patches. In truth he's probably a little worried about what state of mind I'm in. He looks quite junior.

I repeat what I told Harry. I was asleep, awoke, looked into the stroller. No Benny.

The policeman takes a photo of the stroller, then looks upwards. I follow his gaze and catch sight of the other officer passing our open bedroom window. Shouldn't I be there too? Shouldn't Harry be with him? The officer next to me continues checking upwards, above us, to the sky.

'We'll leave the stroller here for the investigation team. Check for prints and all that.'

I nod numbly, assuming he's making sure it won't rain on the evidence, if there is any. The sky continues to display all the positives of a classic English summer. It seems like an insult; the day should now be drab and grey, or heavy with an approaching storm.

'You don't have to stay out here, though, Mrs Greenwood. It may be a while until the investigating team arrives. They'll be here as soon as possible,' he says, seeing my face scrunch up. 'Why don't we go inside and join your husband?'

His kindness makes me want to cry again, but I can tell he's still worried about my unpredictable behaviour.

'Do you think you'll find Benny?' I ask hopelessly.

'We'll do our best,' says the young officer, glancing around, his eyes seeking any object but my face.

He narrows his eyes at the freshly turned earth and a spike of heat rises up my spine. He looks at me for a moment with a furrowed brow and then I follow him into the house.

8

ALAIN

One year ago

He sold the Bechstein for a third of what it was worth. Some might say he was ripped off, but it was no loss for him. He burned Annie's sheet music the day the men from Mozart's Wine Bar took the piano away.

He wondered if the men who collected it were waiters. It needed four of them to manoeuvre the heavy instrument down the narrow stairs, as gently as a giant tray of champagne glasses. He envisioned one slip, and the instrument splintering on the stone hallway of the terraced house. But that didn't happen. They loaded it on a trailer, secured it with rope, and drove away.

He and Annie had hardly ever lit a fire in the brick alcove. The flat was on the top floor, and the flue wasn't long enough. The last few times they'd tried, they ended up with smoke billowing back into the room, especially if a *bise* was blowing from the northeast. But sheet music must have a tendency to flare. It didn't hurt to see the piano music go up in flames. On the contrary, it was a catharsis, as always.

He closed his eyes and remembered Annie's fingers flying over the ivories, melting his heart. He recalled the times they'd had sex on the rug, right in front of the piano.

His dreams floated weakly up the chimney before puffing half-burned, ashy furls out onto the hearth, like the first dusting of winter. Debussy's "Footprints in the Snow".

He fanned the fire, watched orange seeds excitedly racing along the edge and jumping to the next pile of score sheets.

He looked around for something else to feed the flames.

9

TRUDY

Present day

The burly DS is built like a front-row rugby player, his huge thighs threatening to burst from his trousers at any moment.

'I thought Suzy would be here,' I say.

I don't want to talk to this big policeman who, despite his bouncer-like proportions, doesn't instil in me with a sense of security.

'Given you and DS Dawson have a professional and social history, it's against procedure to put her on your case,' he says.

'But I haven't done anything wrong!' I say, wishing my friend from the force was here instead. She would know me perhaps better than anyone in this situation.

I suspect the two uniformed police officers who showed up before this man didn't believe me. Once we'd gone back inside and joined Harry, I followed them as they searched upstairs yet again – *very sorry, Mrs Greenwood, but it's protocol, don't be offended, we have to do it for any missing person.* I kept thinking they might magically uncover Benny in a corner. It felt like an intrusion itself, having these strangers riffle through our cupboards, our drawers, Benny's room, his cot, his toys, even the dirty laundry basket. I kept telling them he wasn't here. How could a baby climb the stairs? They should be out on the streets looking for him!

Outside, their inspection of my freshly-tended flowerbeds in the garden lasted a moment too long for comfort.

The badge on this policeman's jacket says DS David Flatman. I might not be wrong about his rugby-playing history. He has the same tone, bordering on jovial, as the ex-prop-turned-commentator I've seen on TV. I'm sitting in my favourite armchair, the DS on the sofa. Harry paces up and down in front of the fireplace. The DS sucks in his bottom lip, which makes his round face almost cherubic, returning my thoughts to babies. Benny.

'I know my colleagues have already asked, and Mr Greenwood has been making calls, but is it possible he's with any other family member, friend or neighbour?' asks DS Flatman.

I shake my head.

'My mum would be the only person, but we checked and she doesn't have him. Anyway, she would never have taken him *away*.'

Harry sits on the arm of the chair and rubs my shoulder. I couldn't bear to hear the shock and worry in my mother's voice, so Harry had called her. She'll undoubtedly be on her way over now.

'Can you think of anyone at all who might have taken Benny?' the DS continues. 'Maybe a friend stopped by, saw you were sleeping and took him for a walk so you could rest?'

'I... no. I already told the other policemen. No. Oh, God.'

I've almost rubbed the upholstery bare on the other arm of the chair. I continue to pick at a silky thread, pulling and pulling. I can't take my eyes from Benny's area in the corner where a mobile frame spans his play mat, the normally noisy toys motionless and silent.

'Is there anyone at all who holds any grudges, anyone who might have taken Benny out of spite or thought this might be some kind of joke?'

'What? No!' says Harry. 'That's crazy. Who would do that?'

A *joke!* I dwell briefly on the eclectic members of my group therapy, remembering some banter, some attempts at humour in our first sessions together, before dismissing the thought. I chew on my cheek repeatedly until I know I'll have an ulcer there to-morrow.

The policewoman who came with DS Flatman and was told to do a "recce" comes back into the house, talking on her radio. She mentions dogs and roadblocks, and I suck in my breath.

'Could you also find out how far away SOCO is?' DS Flatman asks his colleague. 'And ask how the uniforms are getting on with their house-to-house.'

I put my hand to my chest as the policewoman goes out through the front door, the radio voices fading down the lane.

'We'll need a list of all your contacts. Both yours and Mr Green-wood's,' says DS Flatman, looking from me to Harry.

'Jesus, you think one of our friends would steal our baby?' asks Harry. 'Who would want to take Benny?'

'A kidnap?' I ask, shocked.

'Every angle will be considered,' says DS Flatman.

'Kidnapping's insane! We don't have that kind of money,' says Harry.

I shift to the edge of the armchair, my knee bouncing. I take deep breaths, feel like I'm suffocating. I cross my arms over my stomach, lean over and rock back and forth, staring at the stressed oak floorboards in front of my feet.

The radio hisses at the pocket on the policeman's hip, making me jump.

'Just outside now, Sarge. I think you should come and look at this.' It's the voice of the policewoman.

The three of us stand up at the same time. I rush past Harry to the front door.

'Please, Mrs Greenwood.' DS Flatman holds out his arm as his immense body moves through the hallway. 'Stay here for the moment, please.'

I stand on the step, the breeze blowing from the kitchen out through the front entrance. Somewhere upstairs a door slams. I jump again.

'The windows are all open up there. Airing the house,' I say to no one in particular.

Harry puts his arms around me. We watch DS Flatman talking to his colleague. She's pointing at the path leading to the back of the house. One arm sweeps back and forth. In her other hand she's holding a roll of crime scene tape. The policewoman shrugs and begins unravelling the tape. I stifle a sob.

'Oh God, Trude. This is horrible! Who do you think could have taken him?' asks Harry.

I am grabbing wildly at the possibilities in my head.

DS Flatman walks back to his car parked along the lane. The two police officers confer. The big man gets into the car, talking in bursts to someone else on the radio. Something he doesn't want us to hear.

I bite my knuckles as he comes back to the house.

'Is there any news? What's happening now? Who is looking for our son?' I ask.

'The entire force is aware your son is missing, Mrs Greenwood,' says DS Flatman. 'My colleagues back at the station are putting together a plan of action for a search. We have crime scene officers on their way too. We'll do a house-to-house, question your neighbours. Please don't touch the stroller in the garden or anything in the house for the moment. The thing we need from you is a decent photo of Benny.'

I scan the wall in the hallway. All the pictures of Benny with the family, Benny with Harry and me. Wrapped up, held on laps, wearing silly bonnets. In the end I pull out the one I have in my wallet.

'This one's probably the best. It's quite small.'

'That's okay. We can enhance it. It's good. A full facial. He's a good-looking little lad.'

My attitude towards DS Flatman softens.

'What was he wearing?'

For a moment all I can see is flowers.

'A cream-coloured onesie, nothing distinctive,' I say with a sniff.

'We'll need to ask you some more questions, Mrs Greenwood. Can my colleague make us all a cuppa?'

This must be standard. To calm the parents. The woman officer photographs the picture of Benny and sends it to someone on her phone.

'We'll keep this anyway if you don't mind, Mrs Greenwood,' she says, before going to the kitchen, opening the cupboards and drawers.

She finds mugs, spoons, teabags and milk, and fills the kettle as if it's her own kitchen. She must have done this before.

'Do you think it could be one of those people you're working with on your project?' asks Harry.

The policewoman turns around. Both officers look at me expectantly.

'I've been running group therapy for a few of my former patients,' I explain.

'What kind of patients?' asks DS Flatman.

'PTSD,' I say, my breath shuddering inwards as I feel the heat of tears again.

'Trudy's a psychotherapist,' says Harry. 'She's preparing a study, gathering some data. It's for the British Association for Counselling and Psychotherapy.'

Harry sounds almost proud. But I can't help feeling he blames me for Benny's disappearance.

'What does this study entail, Mrs Greenwood?' asks the DS.

'Um… It's a kind of experimental group. Finding ways to diminish the intensity of spontaneous PTSD memories that occasionally still arise by having people share their different experiences with others. It's to aid ongoing recovery.' I quote almost verbatim the pitch I made to the funding committee for my research paper. I take a deep breath. 'It's a part-time thing. I'm theoretically still on maternity leave. But I don't think…'

'You're probably right, but I'll need their names too, Mrs Greenwood.'

10

RACHEL

Nine weeks ago

'I'm Rachel,' she said, turning her hand towards herself.

Her black-lacquered nails gathered the air, bringing the focus towards the Che Guevara silhouette on her tee-shirt. She wore a ring on each of her fingers and her thumbs. Several mismatched bangles jangled on her right arm in between various coloured cotton and leather friendship bands. Along the inside of her left arm an intricate swirling tattoo of intertwined black roses crept up from her wrist.

Following Trudy's recommendation to look at her own story like scenes from a play, rather than the whole picture, Rachel drew from the fact that she'd been good at drama at school. It had been her favourite subject next to English. These group sessions seemed redundant to her. Her story had already been shared several times on Trudy's therapist couch and examined from all angles. At least that had dulled the personal impact by now.

She was sure these were information-gathering sessions rather than designed for the patients' benefit – *their* benefit. It was all for the paper being written for the shrinks' association Trudy had told them about.

The only useful thing was that she and Trudy had come up with the idea together of including men in this group. Trudy kept checking with Rachel that she was okay with it. They agreed it would benefit both her and Olive by helping them feel comfortable in the company of the opposite sex when they left the refuge, which Rachel hoped would be very soon.

'Would you like to share first today, Rachel?' Trudy asked.

Rachel sighed, then cleared her throat.

'I used to have this trick when I was young,' Rachel told the group. 'When something bad happens, you try to think of something else. Something wonderful. Something completely different from the bad thing that's happening to you.'

Trudy had explained in their one-to-ones that this was Rachel's coping mechanism and she might start with that to share with the group. It was as though Trudy had chosen her to lead the guinea pigs in her project.

Rachel looked up to the high-beamed ceiling. It reminded her of the youth club she used to go to in the village where she grew up. Sneaking cigarettes with Andy Bonham, the first boy she ever kissed, splitting his last stick of Juicy Fruit before her mum would pick her up by 9pm sharp. They were all so innocent back then. Rachel felt like a cigarette now, though she'd given up the previous year.

'Have you ever looked at a snowflake?' she continued.

On the other side of the circle, the man who looked like a real toff snorted. He kept looking at his flash watch as though he wanted to be anywhere but here. Trudy shot him a frown. Rachel ignored him and continued.

'I mean really looked at its design, like under a microscope? It's amazing. Apparently no two are alike. When it snows there are millions of unique crystals falling out of the sky. We learned about them in Mr Chalmers' science class at school. He played this speeded-up film of how they grow from a nucleus. It's fascinating. Worth looking it up on YouTube.'

Rachel straightened her back and bit her lip. The dark-haired man next to the toff was listening to her intently, and then seemed confused when she began talking about the party.

'There was this private party at The Three Moorhens. The whole place had been rented out for an eighteenth. We were all mates, like one big happy family. All connected to this person who just happened to have his birthday that night. It felt so safe. But, hey, *never* assume you're safe.' Rachel paused, gazed around the room. 'I was drinking vodka tonic – all the drinks were free. Hard to believe anyone who was eighteen could afford it. But he lived in a massive house in Gosmore with a swimming pool and three cars, so he could probably afford to buy an entire distillery.

'Anyway, I'd had too much booze, and was wondering whether I had enough money to get a taxi home. As I left the pub, he grabbed me. There's a wooden lean-to for the bins round the back. The bastard got me over there and pinned me against the wall. I should never have worn a skirt. Don't think he would have been able to get into my skinny jeans.'

Olive, sitting next to her, patted her lightly on her thigh. She guessed it was meant to encourage, but it sent a tingle of annoyance along Rachel's leg.

'You know that thing I said about concentrating on something else?' continued Rachel. 'There was a single snowflake on the shoulder of his jacket. I stared at it as he was pounding away.'

Rachel was getting some satisfaction by shocking the men. She surprised herself by being able to talk so much about it in the first session. She would have thought it would take two or three at least. Trudy smiled, her eyes urging Rachel to continue. She would have been thrilled Rachel was performing for her, setting the precedent for the others to follow.

'I heard the pub door open. I tried to shout out, but he clamped his hand over my face, digging his fingers around my jaw so hard it left bruises. I felt something tear inside me so I concentrated harder on that snowflake.'

Rachel paused, took a deep breath. More memories of that lesson in Mr Chalmers' science class in third year came back to her.

She'd been fascinated with the beauty of something that seemed so perfect in nature. Chalmers, though. He was the same teacher who'd split the boys and girls and taught the girls sex education the year before, while Mrs James taught the boys. What messed-up protocol led to that decision? It would have made more sense for him to teach them self-defence.

'Anyway, back to that snowflake. Nature's got a few tricks like that. Tiny cells that join together to form miracles. Some we can hold on to, and some we lose.' Rachel's voice cracked a little.

She placed the palm of her hand on her abdomen as she heard the dark-haired man utter something in French with shock in his voice. She felt a little sick as Olive pressed her thigh against Rachel's, making her flinch.

Was it regret or retaliation she recognised still simmering just below the surface of her bitterness?

11

OLIVE

Nine weeks ago

'Hi. I'm Olive. Been in an abusive relationship. Several, actually, truth be told.'

Olive looked at Trudy, who had one eyebrow raised. She felt a strange kind of satisfaction that she'd managed to keep some of her history from her therapist for all those months. Several abusive relationships. It all started with her father. But Trudy hadn't even got that far in their sessions.

Olive looked at each of these people, crammed in this tiny circle of chairs like some double blind date. Two men, two women, four traumatic histories. And Trudy supervising them all. She was betting there were others in the group with secrets they hadn't told Teacher Trudy.

Not like Rachel, usually so withdrawn, who'd just revealed a massive chunk of her trauma a few years back. Olive had learned about Rachel's rape as soon as they'd met at the refuge. Getting down to the nitty-gritty, as Rachel might put it, she'd had non-consensual sex. But there's no fluffing over political correctness to face the fact it was *rape*. The word rape was *meant* to shock. The act was shocking. But Rachel chose to reconstruct her experience with that magical and mysterious snowflake scenario. Judging by the posh bloke's snort, he thought they were all a bunch of snowflakes.

'The last affair was the longest,' said Olive, thinking the word 'affair' had more intrigue than 'relationship'. Like 'non-consensual sex'.

She rocked gently back and forth as she spoke. Her hands clasped her elbows, clutched against her body. She wanted to sound as confident as Rachel, but couldn't find the words to make her telling of it quite as classy. She wanted to give everyone something to think about, like Rachel.

She'd agreed to do this more out of curiosity than anything. She wondered whether anyone else had had a life as crappy as hers. She already knew about Rachel, but hearing about the others' horrors might have made her feel better. Like watching one of those psycho-thriller TV series where the lead girl's life started out shit, and kept getting worse.

'We met in a skanky pub completely misnamed The Rising Star. Became our local, even though he was totally out of place there. You should've heard him boasting, especially after all those Old Fashioned cocktails we were knocking back.'

She grimaced, as though the taste of whisky was still on her lips.

'Fucker tried to impress me by saying he owns a yacht in the South of France and goes on holiday every winter in the Austrian Tee-roll, wherever that is.'

Trudy cleared her throat. She'd already warned Olive about curbing her bad language.

'He had all these great pick-up lines. Might as well have told me he owned a Ferrari. Gullible. That's what my dad would've said. He was always calling me that. It was ages before I found out what it meant. Thought he was calling me Gulliver. Didn't make a difference though; whatever he called me, he always made me feel like a tiny piece of shit.'

Olive sniffed, drew her finger across her top lip, annoyed that she'd conjured up another memory of her dad.

'This guy, though, it wasn't his neighbourhood, see. No one knew him there. He must have thought he could get away with so much more round our way. Don't get me wrong, I like a bit of rough and tumble. But with Trudy's... help, I now realise he was going too far. Always sorry after he lost his temper. The long and the short of it is, it's hard to tell someone to bugger off when they're paying your rent.'

Olive dug her fingers into the tendons on her wrist. She felt better when she could focus on pain.

'Shame so much shit got broken in my poky flat.'

Olive remembered having to sneak bits of splintered wood down the road after dark to chuck them into the skip outside number 14 after a particularly bad fight.

'The barman in that pub once asked me why the hell I kept going back. He was the only one who seemed to notice the bruises. Or he was the only one who *chose* to notice. People don't understand. You get used to it. When someone like him is the only person you've got.' She paused. 'I was important to *someone*. I still miss that. I know it sounds crazy.'

Olive looked at Rachel, the closest thing she'd ever had to a sister. She was the only one who understood her. Trudy didn't even come close.

Olive looked down; she'd been unconsciously scratching herself again, but she kept going until it burned. The sweet zing of pain soon tipped over to intense discomfort. She'd created an angry pattern of nail marks on her skin. She was fascinated that her old scars still shone ghostly white through the redness.

'Anyway, one night in the corridor at the back of the pub he starts pushing me around a bit more than usual. Didn't often do that in public. Usually kept that stuff behind closed doors. Must've been frustrated that his cow of a wife wasn't giving him what he needed. That night he definitely went a bit far. The barman and his girlfriend picked me up outside the pub later. Bastard must have knocked me out again. I begged them not to call the police. He wasn't known around those parts, and he had his uses. The rent, the drinks, sometimes the groceries. I was pissed off, though. Not just because I couldn't see out of one eye, but the blood from my split lip ruined my favourite cream top. I bought that thing with my own fucking money.'

Olive looked around the circle of faces, every one of them with their mouths at different stages of open. She still remembered the cool of the concrete slab against her cheek, the smell of boot soles and cigarette butts on the pavement, the swish of car tyres through the oily puddles in the road.

'So in the end I'm grateful it was that barman what saved me. I think he fancied me, though he had a girlfriend at the time. The two of them ended up taking me to the refuge. The best thing about that, apart from moving away from that shithole Luton neighbourhood, was meeting Rach. We look after each other, Rach and I. Like sisters.'

She pronounced it 'sistahs' and went to place her hand on Rachel's thigh again next to her. But Rachel crossed her legs and Olive's hand fell into empty space. She snatched her hand back as if she was the one who changed her mind first. She tried to ignore the frown on Rachel's face. She wished she'd had the guts to tell her she'd do anything for her.

Anything.

12

DANIEL

Nine weeks ago

'Good evening. My name is Daniel, and it's been ten months, three weeks, two days and...' he checked his Patek Philippe watch '...three hours since my wife died.'

The young woman called Olive made a choking noise. The other man in the group looked away and mumbled a quiet, *'Merde.'* Daniel winced. Not a good way to start. But he wanted to get his 'turn' out of the way.

He recognised the French swearword. The man had a European look, a dark brooding type. His green eyes were holding back either intense sadness or simmering anger. Probably both. The black-haired girl with the heavy make-up, Rachel, muttered under her breath and Daniel thought she might have said 'posh twat.' He glanced at Trudy, but she didn't appear to have heard.

Daniel was only trying to break the ice by using the stereotypical introduction of addiction groups. Self-help scenarios you probably only saw in films. Sarah used to tell him he often cut a threatening figure, especially when people found out what he did for a living. Mistaking him for the epitome of a city trader. He was hoping to raise a laugh. But black humour wasn't really the thing to start with in a group therapy gathering like this.

It had probably made things worse, and he kicked himself mentally for not thinking harder about what he was going to say before opening his mouth. These people weren't alcoholics or drug users, although thinking about it, maybe they all had that kind of look.

The look of addiction. But Trudy had already told them that's not why they were there. It was all about the trauma. Daniel had probably just made the others think he was an utter arse. An impression which would undoubtedly be reinforced when they found out why he was really there. And it wasn't about the accident.

Remembering the crash, though, brought a spontaneous threat of tears. A burning in the back of the throat. The last thing he wanted to do was to cry in front of those people. Nothing he'd done or planned to do would drag any sympathy from that sorry lot. He couldn't think what had possessed him to agree to the group therapy, this weird sobriquet of self-help.

'There's this irrational part of me that wonders what was going through *his* mind, considering there was a union of souls that day. When they cut the bodies out of the cars, they found a bottle of water on the floor of the man's Escort. He wasn't wearing his seatbelt, but it was half pulled out of its position, as though he'd released it to reach down to fetch the bottle. The steering column severed his spine at the neck.'

Olive, the one wearing a provocatively tight pink tee-shirt, had her fingers over her mouth and her eyes were a little creased. Squeamish or incredulous, he wasn't sure.

'And then there's the envy. That he took Sarah from me. That they left this world together. I know it's irrational, but it's one of the things that got to me. That it was the end of us and the beginning of them. It was one of the reasons I...' His voice tapered before clearing his throat. 'I often fantasise that it was a near miss, the cars stopping a little way down the road from each other. They would have stepped out, the guy apologetic, Sarah ready to give him a mouthful, but then relieved that she'd narrowly escaped an horrific accident. She always looked at the positive side of people, giving grumpy cashiers and train conductors the benefit of the doubt. Feeling sorry for the fact that they might have a sick parent at home, heard a negative diagnosis at the doctor, or lost a pet.'

Daniel bowed his head, then opened his eyes and looked at the two young women sitting opposite him. They were like chalk and cheese. One dark-haired, dark-eyed, the other pale and dirty blonde. And a dirty mouth.

'I imagine them taking each other's numbers, getting together for a coffee. I know she probably wouldn't have started an affair, but I still wish she'd had that possibility. I'd suffer the humiliation of infidelity, if only she were still alive. I think I'd be able to deal with her leaving me more than I've been able to deal with the finality of her death.'

Daniel didn't want to see the differing emotions in each of these people's eyes. Instead he looked at the yellowing walls of the old community hall where they were sitting. Were those nicotine stains? The place could have done with a lick of paint. He sniffed, wanting to concentrate on a different societal breach. But the only smell was the nostril-parching aroma of dust on the silver-painted hot tube radiators. It reminded him of his old prep school. He gazed up to the rafters, his imagination conjuring another picture of Sarah in heaven. Sometimes she was holding her arms out to the children she could no longer reach. And sometimes she was pointing an accusing finger at Daniel.

'You're carrying enough guilt to fill a skip,' said Olive. 'No point in loading yourself with an extra burden where it's not justified.'

Trudy cleared her throat, and Olive squirmed on her seat, pressing her lips together. Daniel was surprised she'd nailed his guilt straight away.

He'd seen some of the faded chalk marks on the road from the police investigation the day he went back to the site of the accident with Jasper and Emma. The angles of the cars. The children had wanted to say goodbye to Mummy. The Family Liaison Officer thought it would be okay for them, but it was most important for *him*. Having the children there would give Daniel something to anchor to.

He leaned back in the uncomfortable tube chair. The plastic bucket seat flexed against his kidneys. It was a strangely satisfying discomfort.

'It comes back to me in fractured pictures at the strangest of times. It's like my mind determines which bits to let me remember, like watching a TV serial out of order. There was a bird of prey. A buzzard, I think. I've often tried to imagine what was going on in its tiny avian brain.'

He traced a line back and forth across the varnish of the wooden parquet strips with the toe of his deck shoe. Flakes of yellow paint from the ancient badminton court lines floated across until they caught in the cracks between the parquet. He wanted to get down there and dig them out with his fingernail. He didn't look at any of the others for the moment. Not even at Trudy. His resolve wobbled. If he made eye contact, he might cry. *Breathe. Control. Breathe.*

'It all happened so quickly, but took an age to unfold in my head. This brown object coming in from the left in my peripheral vision. It was aiming for some flattened animal in the road. I read somewhere that those carrion birds are driven crazy when they see fresh road kill.'

It was the last thing Daniel remembered clearly. That damned bird. It would have felt safe for him to blame the buzzard. But he couldn't. And neither could he blame the driver who'd hit them head on, even though the idiot had drifted into the middle of the lane.

Olive sucked in her breath. 'Fuck. You were in the car?'

Daniel closed his eyes as Rachel muttered, 'Jesus,' under her breath.

'Sarah would have been happy we swerved to avoid it. Always wanting to save the animals, donating to World Wildlife and the RSPB.' He opened his eyes and looked at the dirty-mouthed blonde. 'I wasn't just a passenger in the car, you see. I was at the wheel. It was *me* who swerved to avoid the bird.'

13

ALAIN

Nine weeks ago

Alain pulled his unfocussed gaze back from the ceiling. He'd been daydreaming again, missed the last confession – that's what he liked to call these story-telling sessions. Something about a bird. A car crash? He'd paid attention when the girl called Rachel had talked about snow. He'd expected her to tell them about skiing or the mountains, but instead she'd described one single snowflake so poetically.

She reminded him a little of his sister. Grief stung briefly in the back of his throat with the memory. His bone marrow hadn't been a match for Françoise and neither had anyone else's in their family. The toughest thing he'd ever witnessed was Françoise's slow death from leukaemia. She was so young. Had her life ahead of her. He was always seeking ways to relieve the rage he felt at the injustice. That same rage surfaced when he imagined Rachel being violated. He had to control his breathing, knew what would happen if rage took over. Fire.

Rachel had compared the miracle of the snowflake to the miracle of life. Which meant the bastard who raped her got her pregnant.

Across from him, Olive was fidgeting. It looked as if she wanted to comfort Rachel, but also that if she did touch her, Rachel might break. When Olive lifted her hand to bite on her thumbnail, the inside of her pale arm turned outwards for Alain and the rest of the group to see. Her skin was almost translucent. Regular white spider lines slanted across the blue of a vein. The scars descended from her elbow to her wrist in a perfect parallel ladder.

When Olive caught Alain staring, she took her hand from her mouth and pressed her arms tightly to the sides of her body. Alain fixed a smile to avoid showing fascination. What made someone do that to themselves?

He wasn't really sure why he agreed to this farce. To satisfy Trudy's need for this project, perhaps. It also meant she could keep the police informed about his own ongoing reaction to his trauma. Make them believe he was still suffering. There was some English expression Annie used to say about scratching each other's backs.

'I still don't remember how the fire started in our flat,' he lied. 'I came around when a fireman lifted me over his shoulder like a sack of potatoes, my eyes stinging from the smoke.'

Another half-lie. He'd been drinking, and there were probably tears when the fury took over. He still remembered the taste of cheap red wine backing up in his throat as he was hauled out of the building. So fruity. These English liked their wines with vanilla and blackberry tones.

For the purpose of the group, he needed to concentrate on that rescue. Trudy said the detail was important, to accept the trauma.

'Why don't you just leave, go home to your family – are they in France?' Olive asked.

'I am Swiss. I am *éloigné*... estranged from my family. I have good friends back there, but I can't leave yet.'

He rubbed his thumb and first two fingers together in the age-old sign of money.

'Blimey, I'd much rather be in Switzerland than here.'

Olive probably added her last comment so Alain didn't think she sounded racist. *Why don't you go back where you came from?* He nodded, took no offence. But that was what people were mostly thinking in this country. Immigrant fear was rife.

'No one is sure whether it was the *cendres* blowing out of the fire box or if there was a crack in the stone, how do you say, hearth? By the time I knew what was happening, it was too late.'

Everyone was staring at him. He didn't want to tell a huge saga, and paint colourful pictures for everyone's imagination like the others had. Mostly he didn't want anyone to think he was guilty. The less he said, the less his story could be interpreted. He had the excuse of this not being his mother tongue, so he shrugged, indicating he didn't have anything else to say right now. Keeping things brief.

'I heard about a fire on the terraces on the London Road. Was that your place?' Rachel asked.

Alain nodded.

'It was completely gutted, if I remember rightly,' she continued. 'You wouldn't be allowed to still live there, would you?'

'A friend is letting me sleep in the back of his music studio.'

He'd rather not have stayed with Ron, but he didn't have much of a choice. At least he had a roof over his head now that Annie had left him. After she'd brought him to this country whose lifestyles, habits and politics he didn't understand.

Ron asked Alain if he could help with an event in exchange for staying there. Some kind of kids' Christmas concert. Months away, but something to do with editing images with songs on a movie programme. It was his excuse for the mess of photos, magazines and papers littered all over the place. Alain wasn't interested in getting involved, but he might have had to agree to help Ron with *something*, as his money was running out. Still, it didn't stop him thinking that the best way to sort everything out at Ron's place would be to put a match to it all. It had worked in the past.

14

TRUDY

Present day

I bite my lip, thinking of the members of the therapy group I pioneered. Harry has gone pale and scrapes his fingers through his hair. He doesn't know any of these people; I can't imagine what's going through his mind.

The woman police officer puts two cups of tea in front of Harry and me. She pushes a half-empty bag of castor sugar across the table. Both of us shake our heads. DS Flatman puts three heaped spoons into his own cup. I write down the four names of my former patients in his notepad, and give him the clinic number so colleagues can provide further details.

'Is Benny a good baby? Is he well-natured?' the policeman asks, stirring his tea.

I pause in writing the names he's asked for, the annoying sound of DS Flatman's teaspoon ting-ting-tinging against the edge of his teacup. The clock ticking faithfully away on the wall emphasises the subsequent moment of silence.

'Um, well… He's had a lot of problems with colic since he was born. He's been quite fitful, not a great sleeper. He recently started teething, so that has added to his… fussiness.'

'So he might be a baby who cries a lot? I'm asking because a crying baby will attract attention. It might help us find him faster.'

I nod, feeling like I'm badmouthing Benny. And then a warning bell goes off in my head. I need to rein in the negative comments. I don't want my parenting skills to be in question.

The policeman's phone dings and I draw in a sharp breath as he looks down at the screen.

'Is there anything *we* can do?' asks Harry.

'A search party is being organised in the village and the force will naturally be on duty all night following any leads and looking for Benny. We're arranging road blocks in the wider area so all cars can be checked and we've got officers checking CCTV where they might be on the roads leading away from here. We will do everything we can to get Benny back to you as soon as possible. The best place for you is right here at home for when your son is returned to you. We're assigning a family liaison officer who will remain here this evening. I'll wait until she arrives.'

Harry takes a call on his mobile and wanders towards the living room. I watch him and meanly imagine the stakes are much higher for me than for him. I deserve more sympathy than he does, given the biological circumstances. Then I bite my lip and immediately feel guilty for thinking that.

It could be my mother on the phone, who probably wants to bring some stroganoff or goulash. Comfort food to help keep me and Harry strong while the police search for her grandson.

The two officers finish their tea and each put their mugs in the sink. DS Flatman hands over his notebook with the list of names I've written to his colleague who taps their names into her phone. I stay seated, staring at the pen still in my hand, swallowing back another bout of tears.

The policewoman's radio hisses as she finishes typing the list. Harry follows her down the hallway to the front door.

'I'm just popping to the car,' she says as she opens the front door. 'Please stay with your wife and DS Flatman.'

As she steps onto the path, I hear her tell Harry about how at times like this social media can be useful. She encourages him to post on any of the village groups.

I imagine a horror newspaper headline in my head. I think of the cruelty of journalists, how they seem to have no boundaries when they're looking for a story. I know there will be people who'll blame me anyway. After all, I was supposedly only three feet from Benny when I fell asleep.

Has our world just imploded?

I focus on the names of my former patients still shadowed in my mind from when I wrote them in the DS's notebook.

Rachel Headley
Olive Stanton
Daniel Lockyear
Alain Favre

I stand suddenly, the chair scraping loudly on the kitchen tiles, and finally succumb to the rising bile, rushing past Harry and the bulk of the policeman to the bathroom down the hallway.

15

TRUDY

Nine weeks ago

As I turned out the lights in the hall's galley kitchen, Alain was stacking the chairs next to the makeshift stage. I smiled to myself. The one Swiss in the group seemed to have adopted the tidying-up monitor job. As the rest of them put on their jackets and picked up their belongings, I wondered whether everyone was itching to get away from the group, to be on their own. I hoped at least they'd digest what they'd all talked about during the session so next time they might feel a little more familiar with each other and their issues.

I'd love to have gone to the pub, ordered a double gin and tonic, had a moment to myself before heading home to the chaos of motherhood. But I was knackered, and I was driving. I had a new weight of responsibility on my shoulders.

'Are you all okay for next Monday at 7:30pm?' I asked.

A few positive shrugs, some 'okay's, some nods, but no one said they couldn't make it.

'Send me an email if there's a problem. Otherwise I'll see you then.'

I held the door open as everyone left the hall, and locked it behind me. A gust of wind blew a swirl of leaves and sweet wrappers around my legs. There was a chill in the air. Could summer possibly have been on the turn already? No, the leaves were green, beaten to the ground from a hail shower that afternoon. I didn't want summer to end. It would be another thing to worry about, wrapping my fussy baby in so many layers against the long dark winter.

Rachel and Olive left together, walking in the direction of the refuge. Daniel strode away, head down to his oversized mobile phone. Alain was halfway across the road and threw a jovial *'bonne soirée'* back at me. It was the happiest I'd heard him for a while; he sounded relieved the session was over. He unlocked a battered-looking Toyota parked illegally in the Asda truck delivery lane, and climbed in. It started after a few wheezy turns of the engine.

I suddenly felt a little deflated. It was as though they couldn't wait to leave each other now that they'd met. I should have been happy. It was another sign they didn't need individual therapy anymore.

I was still in two minds about whether I wanted to go home. I tried to quash the feeling of dread about facing domestic baby tasks. This was far from a full-time return to work, but the ability to get away from that shackled duty at least once a week was a tiny breath of fresh air. Harry had been accommodating, promising to get home early on Monday evenings for me to conduct the group. He'd made many concessions in our desperation to be parents, some he would never have complete control over. But now I wondered if it was all worth it.

The guilt seeping in at that very thought soon drove me home.

I kicked off my shoes as I came in the door. The TV was droning quietly with the news in the living room. I almost wished Benny was in there hanging over Harry's shoulder, so I'd know some parenting had been going on while I'd been gone. But then if Benny was sleeping, I hoped the dishes weren't still piled up in the kitchen. Then I bit my lip for even thinking these things. It wasn't like I'd gone back to work full time. Harry and I had both agreed on which of us, and when, would be the main breadwinner.

Harry was on his own in the living room, not really looking at the telly, but scrolling through something on his iPad and writing notes on a document next to him. A new wave of guilt hit me for my thoughts. We'd never addressed how he truly felt about fatherhood considering the fertility issues came from his side. I'd made sure he was the one who'd made the ultimate choice on the sperm donor data.

'Oh hey, Trude, how'd it go?' he asked with a smile.

'Pretty good, actually. I was a bit worried at one point, thinking there was some resentment and a change of heart with some of them. But it worked out.'

I threw my bag onto the armchair and shuffled out of my jacket.

'The best thing was that each of them was able to speak about *something*. I was initially worried about stage fright, about clamming up. But they were all surprisingly forthcoming.'

'I guess the first group meeting was always going to be your greatest challenge,' he said.

I nodded.

'I thought none of them would want to talk too much about themselves. But they opened up way more than I expected. Overall there wasn't much interaction, but I hope that'll increase in the coming weeks.'

Although the group was no longer officially on the clinic's active files, there seemed to be something that bound them. That they'd all been my patients at some time.

'No issues with the male-female dynamic?'

'The two men have never met. And although Rachel and Olive are hardly the best of friends – at least in Rachel's mind – it seems appropriate that they're at least familiar with each other in case of tension. I vetted them carefully before committing to this. I made it clear when I asked for their help for the project that there isn't the same client-therapist agreement as there'd be at the clinic despite all the ethics forms we had to fill out. I'm curious to see whether this whole exercise will help any of them. It could set a model for future post-trauma therapy, especially where sexual abuse has been an issue in the case of the girls. It's also reignited my excitement that a published paper may come out of it.'

'It's great you could connect with work again. Benny's milked up. Washing up's done. Bottles sterilised. Load of baby laundry in.'

'You're a good dad.'

I smiled gratefully, banishing my previous thoughts, and wandered to the kitchen to make a fruit tea. The group had behaved as though they were students in a psychotherapy lecture at uni, trying to please the professor. Not trying too hard, I hoped. I wanted the whole exercise to feel genuine, although I'd never run any self-help groups at the clinic. They'd all been so well behaved, except for the odd snide comment from the usual suspects. These people who'd been through so much, but knew there'd be no final diagnosis this time, no referral to a psychiatrist for the dishing out of pills, no conferring with my superiors. It was an entirely voluntary exercise. I hadn't pointed it out to anyone at the clinic, or Harry, but although I'd never reveal any of my private life to my patients, this group therapy thing was undoubtedly for my benefit too.

16

DANIEL

Eight weeks ago

It was the first time in many months that Daniel felt something close to contentment. He'd had a good week. Emma brought home a glittering school report. Her English teacher wrote a note for him, delivered by Emma in a sealed envelope. Since they both suggested Emma should write about her feelings of sadness, anger and loss following her mother's death, Mrs Blatchford said her work in class was incredible. Her poetry, specifically, was something to be encouraged. Mrs Blatchford would be sure to let Daniel know of any warning signs in its content. Emma then had a sleepover at her friend's house, the first since the accident. And it was successful, according to both Emma and her friend's mother.

Jasper had enjoyed his cricket session at the nets at the sports centre. Daniel was flooded with alternate waves of pride and relief. Jasper subsequently beat him at every game of Connect Four they played on Saturday. Daniel hadn't let him win once. It was a genuine battle.

But the feeling didn't last. The sense of being completely in control, his life carefully organised. Monday night rolled around after a tough day at work and Daniel dragged himself reluctantly to the old school hall in Queen Street.

Everyone showed up to the group therapy. Rachel and Olive were a few minutes late and until they appeared, Daniel thought he might have put them off after the previous week with his ludicrous introduction, his attempt at humour. He was relieved when they stepped through the door. He imagined everyone's curiosity, like his own, was what drew them all back, overcoming any initial distaste they might have had for each other.

Olive and Rachel were chatting about something as they opened the door but their conversation broke off as they entered. He felt as though they already knew each other quite well, perhaps they were sharing a room at the refuge. Daniel didn't know the extent of Olive's problems, of anyone's problems yet, but that girl was obviously damaged. Her eyes darted about nervously. She was wearing a slightly less revealing outfit this week, but evidence of some pretty severe self-harming was still visible. Both her arms had a multitude of scars. She must have been the sensitive one Trudy referred to when she'd asked if he'd be willing to participate in this whole charade. How twisted were her grievances that caused that drunken brawl in the pub? How could a man do that much damage to his partner? Oh... wait.

It wasn't long before they were settled, and when no one spoke, Daniel volunteered to go first. Particularly while that last thought was pushing itself to the forefront of his mind.

'Until recently I wanted to join Sarah,' he said. 'I was fastidious about my plans, arranging for my children Emma and Jasper to stay with my mother. I told her I was going to see the opening night of a play in the West End. Instead, I stayed at home and prepared a list of things I needed to do before I killed myself.'

Instead of the expected drawn breaths, all he heard was Rachel tutting. She was wearing far too much eye make-up, emphasising her pale skin. Her looks would have been much improved by putting a smile on her face. Daniel expected her to make some comment about abandoning his children.

'Who uses the word fastidious?' she said instead, under her breath.

Perhaps that wasn't meant for his ears.

It was going against what Trudy expected of him. She'd wanted him to talk about the accident, the trauma, not voice his thoughts about his subsequent thoughts of suicide. That had been a secondary reaction. He seemed suddenly compelled to talk about them, something he'd never done before. Look at the mess that had got him into already.

After the accident, was what Daniel always clung to. To stop himself thinking of all the things he did wrong *before* the accident. Planning the suicide was the lesser of two evils to concentrate on. He was indeed fastidious – a word he'd likely never use again – about his preparations, proving his whole life still revolved around carefully executed plans of action.

'I figured Sarah's parents were far better equipped to take care of the children than me. Jasper and Emma are young. They'd forget me.'

'How could you leave them?' asked Rachel, her eyes round and sad.

There, she finally said it. Out in the open. Someone had to say it. *How can you possibly love your children that much if you were ready to leave them?*

His sister had said the same thing. Only she wasn't simply bewildered. She'd been incensed, furious, with him. She wanted to take them under her wing, wanted to be the one to provide Jasper and Emma with the wholesome family future they needed. But she couldn't do that. She couldn't simply upend the children's lives and take them halfway across the country. For obvious reasons. One of them being that Daniel pretty quickly changed his mind. Letting her know about the plan, though, was a big mistake. She'd told him he didn't deserve his own children. It was the last thing she ever said to him.

'I know it was an insane decision now. They've already lost their mother,' he said.

He wanted to eventually reconnect and regain the respect of his sister, although that now seemed like an impossible task. The event that had fragmented their family went on to blow it apart completely when he'd planned his suicide. He still worried some-one would tell his children. At some stage he knew they would at the very least ask why their aunt didn't speak to them anymore.

'I wouldn't ordinarily stop you talking about that part of your reaction, Daniel,' said Trudy. 'Because if it helps you focus, that's not a bad thing. But we shouldn't lose sight of the main purpose of this group therapy. It's about the trauma, how you've dealt with it subsequently. I realise your desire to take your life was a *reaction* to Sarah's loss, but it's a separate issue.' And as though she'd read his mind, she said, 'It's also important that you don't keep blaming yourself.'

Daniel thought it was a bit harsh of Trudy to say that in front of everyone, selfish, even. They were all here to talk. Surely it didn't matter which bit of their traumas they talked about.

He looked at Rachel, whose gaze sank to the floor in the centre of their circle. If he'd surmised correctly, her rape had resulted in a pregnancy. But there was no evidence she was a mother. One leather-clad leg was crossed over the other, a paisley-designed Doc Martin twitching rhythmically as she chewed on a black-varnished fingernail. Although she spoke with a coarse accent – not as bad as Olive's, mind – he wondered whether it was genuine, or if it was her way of protecting herself. She was way more erudite than Olive. An accent didn't mean a thing, although people might judge.

Daniel hadn't made any effort to hide his public-school accent. People had expectations when they heard a voice like his. But none of them had any idea about his station in life. Yes, he was a suc-cessful foreign exchange trader with an office halfway up an angled mirrored tower in Canary Wharf, but what they didn't know was Daniel had started there as the mail boy and worked his way up.

Never went to university. Never went to any college. Prep school was the first and last institution of any repute that he'd attended. He failed abysmally to adapt at boarding school, so he was pulled out midway through the first year and went to Hitchin Boys. Even there he'd had issues with his academic development.

But his parents stuck by him, even when his older sister received a first at Durham Uni. They were good people, his parents. Sarah had stuck with him through those years before he made his money. He realised now that whatever his own children chose to do with their lives, as long as their one remaining parent was there to support them through their decisions, it would help them do the best they could in life. God, to think he wouldn't have been there to give them that.

He suddenly felt the need to write everything down. He did that a lot for all kinds of problem-solving, at home and at work. Something he'd inherited from his mother. Order. It helped to set his mind straight. It started with a pros-and-cons list.

Once he'd written the suicide note and the final to-do list back then, the wheels were set in motion. His discipline would normally have made sure he saw it through. An unexpected interruption breaking that order was why he was still sitting there in that circle.

And as long as Trudy kept insisting the memories of the *accident* needed to be dragged back from the recesses of his mind, he wouldn't be allowed to forget that to all intents and purposes, the biggest trauma of all was that he'd killed two people.

17

OLIVE

Eight weeks ago

Olive didn't know what to think about swanky Daniel with his designer shirt who tried to break the ice with that tacky introduction the week before. But along with his poncey attitude, Olive had also clocked his expensive watch. The guy was loaded. He had major potential. Perhaps she could show him a trick or two, wind him round her little finger. A bonus catch. If he was willing to save a stupid bird in the road, he'd be unlikely to put a fist in Olive's face. She could imagine Trudy admonishing. *Hands off, Olive. That's not why we're here.* Despite the whole set-up looking like a supervised speed-dating exercise.

'Can I ask you about them?' Daniel asked, surprising Olive when he pointed to the scars on her arm.

'Of course you can, darling,' said Olive, putting on some fake posh accent that made Daniel's mouth twist like a cat just shat in it.

'They're so... uniform. You've been so careful about placement.'

'When I started, I never thought they'd scar like that. So white.'

'They're almost... artful,' he said. 'A silver tattoo.'

Olive tipped her head to one side. She liked to think they were *artful* tattoos, but in reality each one was a trophy.

'How old are they? Do you still—?' he asked.

'Cut. It's called cutting. No, I don't do it anymore,' Olive lied.

The space on her thighs was now filled with the red-brown bumpy scabs that would eventually turn into these smooth spidery scars.

'What was it like? Did it hurt?'

'It's a searing pain. On the edge of being unbearable. Like nothing else. Takes you to a different place.'

What was his bloody obsession with this? She was sure he didn't even have any schoolboy tats on his body from stabbing himself with a compass and fountain pen ink to see whether he could make a mark. She had plenty of those as well. They were the ones she regretted. She'd improved the method since those early years. He likely thought his body was too perfect a canvas for that kind of behaviour. She wondered if she'd ever have the opportunity to check that theory.

Olive dug the nails of her right hand into her palm and conjured up the feeling of pain, although it wasn't as intense as the cutting. A scything sweetness at the first pierce of the skin, then a stinging sensation. She released her fist, and studied the purple crescent moons she'd made in her palm. Daniel's eyes widened and Olive felt a little thrill that she'd shocked him.

'Did that man hurt you *every* time you were together?' Alain asked.

Olive detected real concern in the foreigner's voice. His eyes flashed from hazel to green, as though one moment he was hiding dark thoughts and the next he'd rip out his heart for you.

'He was unpredictable,' she said. 'I never knew which direction it would come from, or when. If he'd had a bad day, it was my fault. If it was raining and he forgot his umbrella, it was my fault. If he couldn't get it up, it was my fault. The fist in my face or the hand at my throat always made him find his sex drive though.'

'Olive, please,' hissed Rachel, which made Olive raise her chin and continue, defiantly.

'And for some reason, that made *me* feel good. That I could make him feel good. I'm sure he's never hit his wife. She's too high and mighty. She'd have taken him to the cleaners in a messy divorce. His career couldn't handle that. Anyway, so yeah, it's a similar hurt.' She turned to Daniel. 'The cutting makes you take your mind off everything else except the pain. So you can forget about shit for a while. It's a kind of self-love.'

Olive glanced at Rachel when she said *love*. The person she would do anything for, the person she desperately wanted to make feel better.

When it was clear Olive was done, leaving them with that precise vision of her cutting, Trudy rounded things up and they stood to begin stacking those mega uncomfortable chairs.

Trudy approached Olive.

'You might want to think about lightening up your attitude,' she said quietly. 'There's no need to display so much aggression here. You really don't have to provoke these people, Olive. This is a safe place.'

Olive shrugged and turned to leave with Rachel.

'Do you feel better, getting that off your chest?' Rachel asked her as they exited the building. Olive couldn't read Rachel's tone. Was she being sarcastic? Did she expect an answer?

'You know I *do* feel better. Back on track,' said Olive, though she didn't embellish on which track she'd meant.

'Did you go to work today?' Rachel asked after they'd been walking a while.

Olive pulled her teeth over her lip. She'd had a job of sorts for the past couple of weeks with a farmer who sold his produce in a layby on the Bedford Road. She'd been in charge of the stall while he restocked his produce. Business had been good. Especially as it was melon season. But she couldn't resist dipping her hand in his cash tin. The farmer only had to do the maths. She might have been a little overgenerous with herself.

'I got fired last week. It was such a boring job anyway.'

'Oh, Olive. You know it's the only way things are going to get back to normal. You've got to hold on to a job. Get yourself out of the refuge. Hanging out with all these sad, beaten women isn't helping either of us.'

'Did you ask your boss about finding me a job at the bakery?' Olive asked.

'Yes, but he says there's nothing at the moment.'

She suspected Rachel might have been lying. Olive hadn't held a job down for more than a couple of weeks for the past three years. They walked along Queen Street together. Rachel was walking faster than usual and Olive had the feeling she was trying to shake her company.

'Do you think Trudy's looking okay?' Rachel asked suddenly, pausing in her stride to allow Olive to catch up.

'What, other than dropping the weight she stacked on last year and looking a bit tired, you mean? She probably has a bunch of new nutters just like us to *dismantle* at the clinic. Poor sods.'

'I hope nothing's going on at home. You know, awkward stuff in the marriage and all that. I thought she looked a bit frazzled tonight, that's all.'

You'd be frazzled too, thought Olive, *if you had to deal all day long with a bunch of losers like us.*

18

TRUDY

Present day

I come out of the bathroom with the back of my hand pressed to my lips. I can't stop the involuntary inward gasps like the reflexive sobbing of an inconsolable child. One breath after the other. My body is forcing me to haul in oxygen when all I want to do is wail. In turn my brain is triggering the release of endorphins, the release of tears trying to make me feel better. But all I want is Benny back. I want someone to put him in my arms, replace the part of my soul that has now been gone for almost two hours.

I've rinsed my mouth out with metallic-tasting water from the bathroom tap, but the nausea hasn't abated. A hollow gnawing cramps my stomach and I can't seem to swallow the bitterness of residual bile on my tongue. I want to fetch a mint from the kitchen but this will appear frivolous while my baby is missing. I visualise the Polos, sitting between the honey and the peppermill in the cupboard above the sink. I don't have the energy to explain that I need something to take the taste away. The taste of guilt.

Harry puts his hand on my shoulder. In his other hand, he's holding my phone. He's been calling contacts on my mobile who live close by. He took over after I became a bit hysterical on the first call to the farmer.

'You okay, Trude?'

I huff a sigh. Isn't it obvious I'm not okay? I clench my mouth, biting down hard on my pulled-in lips. Something about the way Harry asked the question. A tiny tone of exasperation makes me not want to look at him. Despite my earlier thought, I know he must be hurting too, but my emotions are now off the scale. I simply don't know what to do, where to look.

The front door is still open and I see my mother's dark blue Volvo pull into the curb behind the police car. I run down the path to her. She's having difficulty releasing her seat belt, agitation and worry preventing her from performing the simple task. Or maybe tears.

She opens the door, climbs out and clutches me.

'Oh, *mein Liebling*,' she says, her endearment reserved for Benny, not me. '*Wo ist er? Was ist passiert? Wieso?*'

For a moment I can't say anything. Seeing her has sparked a flood of tears and now my throat hurts with the burn of bile and the strain of muscles that are rarely used. Her emotion has made her revert to her German mother tongue.

I look back at Harry over her shoulder. His eyes are red. This physical display of sorrow is contagious. The previous look of what I interpreted as accusation is gone. For the moment.

I have begun shakily to explain to my mother what happened when I see a couple of people standing in the lane, hands over their mouths. It's the woman who lives at the end, a few hundred yards away with her grown-up daughter. They'll have heard the sirens. Did they hear me screaming for Benny earlier as I ran down the lane? Why didn't they come out then? DS Flatman walks towards them and I steer my mother towards the house, away from the curiosity of the neighbours.

My mother is much more upset than I expected. I can't imagine why I thought she would be offering comfort food. It's her grandson she wants to see returned home as much as we do. No one will be hungry tonight.

Approaching the house, I see Harry on his own mobile this time.

'She fell asleep…'

I hear the words as I step onto the creaky floorboard by the door and Harry turns away, heads into the living room. He must be talking to his parents. I visualise his mother, her aging incomprehension perhaps not quite as sympathetic as my own mother's. My stomach twists.

She fell asleep.

That tone again. The one that reconfirms that whatever happened, this is all my fault.

19

RACHEL

Eight weeks ago

The refuge service manager came to see her during the week. Rachel had managed to hold her job at the bakery for eight months now, and they'd been discussing the best way forward to secure a guarantee for a small flat rental she'd seen near the station.

They'd already let Rachel stay longer than normal for the volunteer work she was doing, mostly helping rape victims who were admitted to the refuge. Her employment at the bakery meant she was back most days by two in the afternoon and could look after the infants while their mothers went down to the job centre to look for work. Many of the jobs had childcare facilities, but mums had to have childcare to get to the interviews in the first place.

Rachel allowed herself to get a little excited, trying to quash the feeling that it might all eventually be refused by someone in authority. She didn't mention anything to Olive as they walked to their Monday meeting, because she didn't want anything to burst this little bubble of hope.

But dragging up old memories soon did that anyway. She was irritated that Trudy asked her to start as soon as they'd settled into their chairs.

'You might think getting raped was the worst thing that happened to me,' she said. 'I got over the humiliation pretty quickly. Had to, otherwise I'd have been branded most likely a liar, but definitely a slapper. It was the fallout that eventually got me.'

'Why didn't you ever report it?' asked Daniel.

Rachel already had this guy pegged for following all the rules. She expected Trudy to say Daniel should let her speak and ask questions later, but she didn't. Rachel frowned.

'What would you have done? Life revolved around the most popular guy in year twelve. Everyone would have abandoned me, probably wouldn't even have believed me. At the time it sounded insane, right? My main fear, after hearing all these stories of young girls *asking for it* was that no one would have trusted I was telling the truth. We were all friends, used to spend summers at their place because they had a massive swimming pool. I didn't want to be the bad seed. Didn't want to be the one who broke up the gang, although it fizzled out anyway afterwards. Not that it matters now. I ended up doing much worse.' She took a deep breath. 'The shit that goes through your mind when you're not sure what to do. I always wished I'd had more control over that. But it's too late now.'

'I hope you're not going to tell us what I think you did?' said Daniel.

Rachel had an irrational desire to shock. She hadn't planned to go into too much detail, but suddenly felt almost obliged to.

'The clichéd hot bath. When I first dipped my foot in, the temperature was so hot, my brain didn't compute. Have you ever done that? The water stung my ankle so much, it felt like it was stuck in an ice cube. But it gave me a bizarre kind of high. Cold. Hot. Hot.'

Olive was gazing down at her pale wrist and Rachel knew the neat white spider lines spoke about the same intense pain that induces a strange kind of high. Self-harming wasn't something Rachel had ever been into, except that one time. But she understood what the cutting might do for Olive.

'You laugh when you hear people talk about it. A Victorian solution that generally doesn't work.' Rachel paused, pressing both her temples with her fingers. 'There are many ways I could have been stopped. I almost dropped the bottle. It wasn't gin, it was cheap vodka, easier to take. It banged on the sink and could have slipped from my grasp. If it had broken, it might not have saved me, but the noise might have made my mum come up and ask what I was doing. She was listening to *The Archers* downstairs in the kitchen.'

Rachel sighed, placed her hand on her belly.

'I stayed there in that water, my body as pink as a Barbie dress, blood thumping in my head. A little voice shouting *murderer* in my head.'

Rachel still heard that voice from time to time. Usually in a bad dream.

'Why would you do that? There's nothing as precious as life,' said Daniel.

Here we go; a flipping pro-lifer.

Trudy put her hand up to silence Daniel. Rachel wanted to say 'That's rich, coming from you!'

Instead she glared at him. *I know!* she wanted to shout. No one had the right to tell her she'd made the wrong decision. Even if she *did* make the wrong decision. There was truth in Daniel's words. The little thing she murdered. She'd studied every baby she saw in the street since, and wondered what hers would have looked like.

Daniel was probably a born-again something. A religious nut, following God's rules, or the people who created his God's rules, right on the redemption trail. He sounded just like her dad.

He should have taken back the words 'I don't know what I'd do without my children' last week. The cheek of it, after he admitted he wanted to take his own life! Where would that have left those kids? He was always on about Emma this, and Jasper that. You'd think they were a fucking ground-breaking anthropologist and a rocket scientist. At six and eight, for Christ's sake! Who would have looked after them when he was gone? He couldn't have loved them that much if he was prepared to leave them behind forever.

What right did he have to admonish her for her actions when he'd been quite prepared to take a life, even if it was his own? What a fucking hypocrite. Worse than her dad, actually.

Conflict battled hot and cold inside her like that bath moment. *Simmer.* Daniel might have thought he was to blame for the death of two grown-ups, but at least he didn't murder his babies.

Rachel stood abruptly and knocked her chair over backwards. Trudy had told her this would happen. Said she was probably the one who was still the most vulnerable.

Trudy was half out of her seat, but Rachel held up her hand to stop her from following. She ripped her jacket off the hook by the door and stumbled into the hallway, clutching her open bag to stop her stuff spilling everywhere. There was a twinge of regret when she thought of Trudy imagining all the good work of their private sessions had just been undone. No, this anger was something she could latch on to. Stupid posh twat.

Instead of leaving the building, Rachel made her way to the toilets. She chose the middle cubicle and sat down, both hands clutching her knees. She closed her eyes, breathed deeply and her heartbeat slowed. She studied the black and white tiles on the floor, a chip in the corner of one revealing some ancient pink plaster underneath.

As she calmed down, she felt sheepish. Daniel hadn't been aiming his comments at her. He was simply reinforcing his own decisions and the result of a series of random chances. Daniel could stuff his pro-life views up where the light didn't shine. He was probably like a reformed smoker. Oh-so righteously going the wrong way once he realised he'd made a terrible mistake by planning to take his life.

Oh God. She felt like a fool now, and sat there until the heat of humiliation had cooled on her face.

Long after she'd finished peeing, she made the decision to simply go back to the refuge. She didn't want to return to the hall this evening. She didn't particularly want to return to the hall at all. Bunch of losers. Including messed-up Olive. She certainly didn't want to have to walk back to the refuge with her.

She was about to get up and slide the lock open when the outside door squeaked and someone came into the cloakroom. She wanted to wait until they'd gone before coming out. There was a clink of metal against the sink, probably a handbag buckle, and the noise of rummaging. Then silence. Then the tick-tick-tick of a fingernail on a mobile phone screen. She couldn't work out who it might be. She didn't think it was Olive; she'd bitten her nails to the quick and hardly ever carried a bag, preferring to stuff her pockets with anything she needed. It must have been Trudy. After a while the tap ran, water gushed and splashed. Silence. The sound of a towel being torn from the dispenser and the soft patting of paper against a face. Then a deep sigh.

Rachel glanced at her watch. She wanted to catch Tesco Metro before it closed. She needed teabags and milk for the refuge kitchen. Whoever it was, was still there, but she decided to come out.

It was Trudy, who about jumped a mile in the air when Rachel flicked the lock and opened the door.

'Jesus, Rachel, you scared the hell out of me. Are you okay? I thought you'd gone home.' She paused. 'I thought you were going to sock Daniel in there.'

Rachel smiled cynically as their eyes met in the mirror, and then shrugged.

'I've had enough of that shit. Next he'll be telling me I'm a cock-tease.'

Trudy put her hand on Rachel's arm and gave it a squeeze.

'Look, Rachel, I know it's not ethical, but we're officially no longer patient-client. I'm going to give you my mobile number in case you ever need to talk outside office hours. Here.'

She reached for her bag, took out a wallet and flicked it open. As her finger and thumb pulled a card out of one of the slots, the leather slipped on her other hand, still damp from the sink. The wallet fell and skittered across the floor towards Rachel's feet.

Rachel bent down to pick it up. A photo had spilled from one of the compartments. A photo of a baby. Rachel could tell it was a boy. He was extremely cute, had Trudy's eyes. She swallowed as realisation hit her.

She has a kid!

It was like a betrayal. She'd told Trudy a ton of stuff about herself, and all this time Rachel had known nothing about her therapist's own private life. Rachel had assumed she was single. It made her feel a little queasy. She glanced at Trudy's hand, something she'd never done until now. She hadn't noticed the ring before, a thin band of rose gold. Rachel's gaze tracked back to the photo.

'I meant to tell you, but it weirdly slipped my mind,' said Trudy. 'I hadn't seen you for months before the group sessions. It feels a bit ridiculous now.'

The photo trembled a little in Rachel's hand.

'Benny,' said Trudy, and then as though she could read Rachel's mind, 'Almost three months.'

There was an awkward pause, before Rachel passed the photo back to Trudy.

'Rachel, it's okay. I'm not like your dad. I get you. It doesn't change anything.'

And for the first time since her miscarriage, Rachel recognised the deep grief within her, and broke down and cried.

20

DANIEL

Eight weeks ago

Daniel was a good five hundred yards down the road when a gust of wind curled its fingers under his collar and he realised he'd forgotten his jacket. It was cooler that afternoon, and he hoped summer wasn't over yet. He'd helped put the chairs away after the session so tried to visualise where he might have left it, irritated with himself to have lost control over something as simple as an article of his clothing.

He looked at his watch. He was almost level with the NCP car park where his BMW was parked. Should he go back? He calculated whether his mother would worry if he was a few minutes late. A phone call home might only make matters worse if she was having trouble putting the children to bed. She wasn't quite so rigid about sticking to plans like he was, so he decided to go back and get his jacket.

He felt bad about Rachel storming out. He was shocked that she'd terminated her pregnancy. But his reaction must have made her feel as though he was preaching to her. He remembered the group's accusing eyes on him. Thinking how the hell could he ever consider abandoning his kids by taking his life? He was a total hypocrite in that respect.

When he arrived at the porch to the building, he was relieved to find the door was still unlocked. Most of the hall was in darkness but there was a light shining through from the cloakrooms. Daniel saw his jacket lying on the stage next to the stack of chairs. As he walked over to pick it up, he heard the sound of sobbing coming from the ladies' toilet. Then he heard Trudy's voice, comforting. Then Rachel's voice, wracked with emotion, barely able to get out her words between involuntary sobs that sounded a little like Emma after a tantrum.

'I'm – so – sorry! I – just – wish – I'd – known.'

Daniel bit his lip. Was she talking about him? It was his words that had made her storm out of the hall earlier on. But they'd been words of anger, not wretched sadness like this. Perhaps he should go to them, try to make things right with Rachel. Tell her he knew what he said was stupid in front of someone with her history. He felt he needed to appease his own guilt.

'It was just a shock. I'm sorry. Knowing you have a baby. You're so lucky. He's lovely. I'm sorry.'

Each of these phrases was stuttered out with Rachel's sobbing breath, and he felt a squeeze in his chest. Forget her foul mouth (though not as foul as Olive's) and her gothic looks, her *attitude*. What she'd been through, it simply wasn't fair for one person to suffer that much without some kind of – what would Trudy call it? – closure. Yes, some kind of closure.

But with this new knowledge, that both of them had only now learned that Trudy had a baby, and that this outpouring of emotion that Daniel interpreted as Rachel longing for a baby, he might have made matters worse if he went in there now. Trudy was far more capable of handling it than he would have been. It didn't stop him biting his lip to hear Rachel's deep-rooted sadness.

He tucked the jacket over his arm and crept across the wooden floor as quietly as possible, knowing a creak of a floorboard would give him away. He made it to the door without a sound, closed it behind him and hurried back to his car.

He'd never before even been curious as to whether Trudy had a family. She'd helped him through his thoughts of suicide with such compassion and understanding. Never once did he get the same negative vibes from her as he got from the other women in the group therapy. Or his sister.

Trudy seemed a little frayed at the moment, though. He knew how tiring motherhood could be. This child was probably her first. He smiled. Sarah had become pregnant so quickly. It was earlier than planned, really, as he hadn't yet started bringing in the annual bonuses that would award them the financial comfort of subsequent years. Emma was conceived alarmingly fast after Jasper was born. Sarah had said he should sell his sperm to a fertility clinic. They were always enterprising with their little money-earning side projects, knowing it would help set them up for the future. 'Don't laugh,' she'd said, 'I'm bloody serious!' In the end it had helped them finance a few extra groceries at Waitrose.

He was looking forward to his regular goodnight hugs with his children, looking forward to watching them sleep for a bit, knowing he would do everything in his power to keep them safe. He was slowly learning not to project his idiosyncrasies onto them.

As his thoughts flashed back to Rachel, he wished he could bring his own children up in a world that was fairer than the one she'd grown up in. Although nothing ever seemed fair. Perhaps if Rachel's abuser was brought to account, she could put closure on that part of her damage and she could find a way to repair the other loss. Justice should always prevail.

21

TRUDY

Eight weeks ago

I offered to drop Rachel off at the refuge on my way home. She was silent in the car, apart from the occasional residual sniff.

Was I really in a good enough place to make this project work? It must have appeared odd that I didn't have the chance to tell Rachel about Benny, not even dropping her an email after he was born. Not that any psychology patients needed to know the private lives of their therapists, but she was bound to find out at some stage, Hitchin being the small town it was. Rachel's reaction suggested she almost felt worse about terminating her pregnancy than she did about the rape that caused it. Why hadn't she brought this up in our individual sessions? It sent spikes of shame through me for not having picked this up.

I wished I'd admonished Daniel more forcefully for his attitude. It was completely unexpected for him to say something so thoughtless, given his own history. I hadn't wanted to reprimand him in front of the others. I simply wanted him to keep quiet for Rachel's sake. Could this have been another crack in Daniel's psyche that hadn't been considered? Had motherhood blunted my instincts?

When we reached the refuge, I scanned the street, stopped the car outside and kept the engine running.

'I'm okay,' said Rachel. 'I'm sorry I went to pieces like that.'

'It was a stupid omission on my part, Rach. *I'm* sorry,' I said.

Rachel climbed out. I waited as she walked up the path and knocked on the door. I recognised this small courtesy; it was late to be ringing the bell. I kept my eye on her back until she was let in by the service manager.

It still enraged me that Rachel's parents didn't support her after the miscarriage, that they kicked her out on the street when she'd told them about the rape. And her father a vicar! How spiritually supportive was that? Rachel seemed to have come to terms with that particular family fallout. But after tonight I realised what'd been eating at Rachel; a baby was missing from her life. It was something I – we – hadn't uncovered before.

And the fact that her abuser was still at large and might even still have been living in the same town made me shudder.

I pulled into the driveway of our cottage in Whitwell, noting how dirty the lane had become after the last heavy summer rains. A combination of farm traffic and the Mimram stream spontaneously flooding its banks back in spring. An inattentive council had led to several months' worth of muck covering the tarmac.

It was a metaphor for what was going on in my head. Too much confusing domestic muck. It was time to sort out the issues that were preoccupying me. I didn't seem to be doing the motherhood thing right. I felt worse each day, through lack of sleep and not wanting to face the regular routine, but mostly from the remorse experienced when I wished Benny would just please, for one moment, please stop crying. And then there was the sex. It had begun to verge on some kind of phobia. I was unable to even talk to my own husband about it.

Harry had eaten dinner when I came through the door.

'Hi, babe, how did it go?' he asked from the couch in the living room. He checked his watch. 'Did you go later than usual?'

He picked up the remote and turned off the TV. I wished he'd left it on, turned the volume low instead. Then I'd know he'd only expect a cursory report before going back to watch whatever had been on. I was so exhausted, and Rachel was still playing on my mind. All I could think about was crawling into bed, but now I had to satisfy Harry's curiosity.

'Remember Rachel Headley?'

'The one you thought might have a great future once she's back on track?'

I nodded. 'I don't think her need for individual therapy is over.'

'But I thought the benefit of this study was that none of these people are your patients anymore?' He followed me into the hall while I kicked off my shoes and hung up my bag.

'It's true, the clinical relationship isn't the same as before. But I'm worried I made a mistake in the dynamics of the group. Rachel didn't know I was pregnant when she was my patient, but she saw a picture of Benny in my wallet tonight, and it provoked a strong emotional reaction.' I bit my lip, knowing I shouldn't be discussing this with Harry, but continued anyway. 'I'm wondering if she should still be in the group with unresolved issues about her pregnancy and botched abortion. It sounds selfish, but I don't want secondary issues to fog the PTSD study.'

'Don't you think she'd be more upset now if you suddenly excluded her from the group? You *chose* her, after all,' he said.

'I could explain to her, but you're probably right. Especially as the other girl from the refuge, Olive, is also there. I wouldn't want Rachel to feel she's wrong for the group. She seemed to have become so strong. She trusts me. I feel terrible that discovering we have Benny has upset her so much.'

Harry put his arms around me.

'It's probably not as bad as you imagine. Perhaps have a quiet word with her before the next session to make sure she's still okay with the group?'

'Thank you for being my voice of reason,' I said, leaning into his chest. 'God, I'm exhausted.'

'Do you want something to eat?' he asked.

'No, it's okay. I had a snack beforehand. I'm not hungry. But I'd kill for a glass of wine.'

'I'll join you,' he said, going to the kitchen to fetch two glasses of red from a bottle we'd opened the day before.

I went to the living room, the sofa beckoning.

'Benny's asleep. Went down okay tonight,' he called from the kitchen.

He was in a jovial mood and I didn't want to ruin it by complaining about his raised voice. *Please don't wake the baby.* I wanted to drink my glass of wine and crawl into bed. I lowered myself to the sofa. Harry came through, passed the wine and sat next to me.

'So, tell me about the general feeling in the group. Is it a useful exercise?'

'Oh, I really haven't got the energy to do an analysis right now. When I'm less exhausted tomorrow.'

'No worries. Relax.'

I was glad he didn't bristle at my sudden lack of enthusiasm to talk, that I'd effectively given him the brush-off. We clinked glasses and I took a large sip of wine. Harry would have had a hard day at work as usual, and simply wanted to spend time with me. I let him hold my hand. The wine was going straight to my head. Instead of making me feel good, it accentuated my exhaustion.

Harry traced his finger lightly up and down the inside of my arm. The place we always joked was my most unusual erogenous zone. *This sexy inner elbow,* he used to say, making me laugh. All it did now was irritate me. I knew what that meant. Sex. I wanted to snatch my arm away, but I let him do it. As I turned towards him and forcing a smile, too late, he saw my fleeting frown, read the falseness behind my attempt at an affectionate gaze.

I didn't want this. I wanted to wait many more weeks, perhaps months, until the vision of Benny pushing his way out of where Harry would be pushing his way in had faded from both our memories. I didn't imagine Harry had the same recollection; it felt too disgusting to voice, as though if it hadn't occurred to him, then I'd be planting something in his head neither of us would want to think about. A combination of the pain, the tearing, the endless hours of backache, front-ache, womb-ache, blood, bodily fluids, the feeling that I was being slowly ripped apart for seventeen hours. How did anyone ever think about giving birth a second, a third, or even a fourth time?

It had taken a great deal of stress and angst to conceive our beautiful son Benny. In the end, choosing a donor from the clinic was like picking a flavour of gelato from the ice cream parlour. But because of that, I needed to show Harry I loved him more than ever for all his emotional support. But there was a difference between love and lust. Not only did I worry about how it would feel inside, I worried I hadn't healed enough, and I actually worried about getting pregnant, despite how medical science might say it was impossible, with Harry's zero sperm count.

But Harry wasn't feeling any of these things, although he'd been lovingly patient. Making a snap decision, to try to blot out the gory visions rushing through my mind and to ease the urgency of his desire, I unzipped his trousers and went down on him right there on the sofa. I did it before I changed my mind, and before he could insist we went to the bedroom where he would want to finish things off properly, inside me.

I vaguely hoped the effect of giving him pleasure would somehow ignite a desire in my own body as it would have done pre-birth. I did still want to give him pleasure. That was something ingrained from the deep-seated love I felt for him. And he surely deserved some attention after being out of the equation for so long. But all I could think about in my exhaustion was to get this over with as soon as possible, to be able to crawl into bed and simply snuggle in his arms.

22

TRUDY

Present day

Ushering my mother into the kitchen, it means I don't have to look at Harry on his mobile. I feel his eyes on my back, and concentrate on the spice rack on the kitchen wall to avoid seeing any accusation in his eyes.

My mother opens the fridge and scans the shelves from top to bottom. She opens the veggie drawer, a gesture that would on a normal day have me rolling my eyes and gently admonishing her for being controlling and nosy.

'I should have brought something with me. We need to keep your energy up in case... Oh *mein Gott*. I still cannot believe it! Benny, Benjamin, *mein Schatz*.'

With her hands full of onions and peppers and a packet of smoked bacon, she wipes her eyes on her sleeve near her shoulder. I know what she's planning. Soup. She's aware it will be the only thing I'll be capable of eating. I couldn't possibly take anything solid. I can't even think of food right now. Except maybe that Polo I've been visualising. There's still a metallic taste in my mouth.

Leaning against the kitchen unit where the saucepans are kept, DS Flatman glances at my mother fussing by the sink and takes a new notepad out of his pocket. What is he, made of notebooks? He sees me looking from the one on the table to the one in his hand.

'Jot names down if you think of anyone we might need to question, however insignificant it might seem to you.'

I nod numbly.

'Could you tell me a bit more about the people in your group therapy?' he continues.

After hearing my mother speaking German, perhaps DS Flatman thinks she won't understand what we're talking about. It feels inappropriate to talk about my patients, unethical to share so publicly. But share I must if it's going to help the police look for Benny.

'As I said, they used to be registered patients.'

'And why did you choose this group if they're no longer your patients?'

'When a funding opportunity came up for me to write this research paper for the therapists' association, I approached these ones from my patient database to ask if they'd help. It'd be too damaging to include patients still receiving treatment for PTSD flashbacks. Too many uncertain debilitating memories. I wouldn't expect current patients to be anywhere near ready to share their experiences with others.'

My mother slaps a knife onto the wooden chopping board next to the sink and turns on the tap to wash the veg, humming quietly to herself. I recognise an old German lullaby and press my lips together.

'Did these patients know each other before?' asks DS Flatman.

I take a deep breath, try to control my voice, the lullaby making my chest ache.

'Only Rachel Headley and Olive Stanton. They've been living in the same women's refuge.'

'How long have these sessions been going?'

'About four months.'

'And how does the group interact with each other?'

The knife *chop-chop-chops* the onions and peppers on the board.

'They were a little awkward in each other's company at first,' I say. 'I expected that. But they've settled and seem comfortable now.'

'So, is it like AA, or a drug dependency group?'

'A little. But the traumas they've experienced are very different from each other.' I don't want to say too much about them as individuals, patient confidentiality still at the forefront of my mind. 'I get them to talk about the smallest of memories,' I continue. 'As though extracting their visions. Talking about them in front of the others softens the impact. And the other members can compare their own experiences in small segments, like film clips. I call this dismantling. The group situation means they look at their own issues from a different perspective. I encourage them to ask questions about each other's experiences.'

'How does it work with both men and women in the group?' he asks as my mother shoos him out of the way to get to a saucepan from the cupboard behind him.

'One of my additional aims was to get the two young women from the refuge used to having men around. They're going to be moving on soon, integrating back into normal society. The two men, Daniel Lockyear and Alain Favre, are perfect for these two to interact with, both nonaggressive. Everyone was assessed beforehand. Each of them agreed – there seemed to be a hundred forms. The clinic asked them all to sign agreements and liability waivers.'

For a moment I've forgotten why we are here, and then the back of my throat constricts with a renewed threat of hot tears.

'Look, I don't think it would be any of them. They have no idea where I live.' I sob, a staccato intake of breath. 'I feel like I need to be out there looking. You need to be out there.'

'A team is coming, Mrs Greenwood. We're working on a strategy. We have to ascertain all possibilities. If it isn't anybody in your group, then we'll be able to eliminate them from our investigation.'

23

ALAIN

Seven weeks ago

'Where did you live before you came to England?' asked Rachel.

The two of them were setting out the chairs in a circle from a stack Alain had brought over from beside the stage. He almost hadn't come this week. The solicitor appointed to him through the fire investigation had called him with some new evidence from the structural expert. The beam under the badly-renovated hearth might have been compromised for many years prior to the fire that destroyed Alain and Annie's flat. That surely meant he was relieved of any liability?

But he had to wait until the case was officially closed. These things took so long. If he could have done, he'd have already left. When Trudy had asked him if he'd like to participate in the group therapy, he'd felt it might be best for his image and reputation. If he wasn't eventually charged with arson, the police would hopefully let him go home.

'I come from a small ski resort called Leysin to the east of Lac Léman in Switzerland,' he said.

He pointed to the chest of his sweatshirt displaying an image of parallel serpentine ski tracks leading down from the two mountains above the village, the Tour d'Aï and the Tour de Mayen.

'I adore the mountains,' said Rachel. 'I'd love to go to the Alps one day.'

Their chairs scraped across the wooden floor.

'Leysin is not well known for the skiers with more money. It's not like Verbier or Gstaad. But it's my home. Was my home. Some decent snow in winter and a few busy bars.'

They sat next to each other. Alain knew he hadn't been very sociable and he recognised she was wary about being around men, so was pleased she chose to sit there. It was already their third session, but he hadn't made much effort to 'integrate' as Trudy called it. He knew he'd been labelled the introvert of the group.

It wasn't the first time he wished he wasn't here, but of course he was humouring Trudy. After humouring the investigation team.

'I don't need to ask if you ski then. Are you a ski teacher?' asked Rachel.

Alain shook his head.

'I worked as a ski technician in one of the rental stores.'

'My dad took us skiing once to Glenshee in Scotland. My little sister broke her leg on the second day and my mum was worried we'd all end up in hospital, so she didn't let the rest of us ski for the entire week.'

'Seems a bit unfair on everyone else.'

'She was overprotective, back then.' She huffed. '*That* didn't last. But I was always a little pissed off at her for that. It's one of those things I wished I'd learned. Skiing, and maybe playing the piano.'

Alain immediately gets a flashback to Annie playing music for him. Although now he thinks about it, perhaps Annie was simply playing for herself.

Rachel pursed her lips and Alain couldn't imagine what was going through her head. He'd rather be back amongst his mountains than sitting here in this dusty old room.

'I miss the Alps,' he said.

The door opened and Daniel came in. Trudy walked through from the kitchen where she'd gone to fetch a glass of water earlier.

'Not many hills around here. I'm not surprised,' said Rachel.

Alain noted how Rachel seemed to shrink as Daniel came to the circle, as though she somehow felt threatened by men in numbers. Or perhaps she just wasn't clicking with Daniel. Alain was pleased she'd spoken to him. She definitely reminded him of his sister.

They both watched as Daniel brushed imaginary dust from his thighs and sat down, pulling up his chinos to avoid creasing them.

'The biggest hill in this town is the one I used to climb to get to my flat,' said Alain. 'It goes past the girls' school. There are some woods on the school grounds. I sometimes close my eyes and imagine the birds are the same ones who sing in my forest back home. Then I open them and the first thing I usually see is a group of *jeunes* smoking spliffs on the bench.'

Rachel laughed, and as though on cue, Olive crashed through the door, tripping on the step and righting herself as the door slammed against the wall.

'Don't they smoke weed in Switzerland?'

'Well, yes...'

'Why don't you go home, if you miss it so much?' asked Rachel, her eyes tracking back to Alain from Olive.

'I'm not allowed to leave until they close the case on the fire investigation.'

Until then Trudy was the only one who knew this. If the case went against him, he might have to serve a jail sentence.

'The case? They suspect you were to blame? Or was it the insurance? Let me tell you, I've had my fill with that bunch of wankers. The only thing they ensure is that they're able to fill their bank accounts and never give any payouts.'

Rachel sounded bitter, and Alain wondered what kind of claim she'd ever had that wasn't honoured.

'I meant to ask what happened to your girlfriend,' said Olive as she plonked herself down in the chair next to Alain and shouldered in on the conversation.

Alain needed to stay as close to the truth as possible. Trudy's positive report to the police could be his ticket out of there.

'I don't know where Annie is now – my girlfriend... my *ex*-girlfriend. I went to Benslow last week and they told me she does not teach there anymore. I could not believe it. This was the dream job, the thing we came here for. The perfect mix of teaching during the day and playing in chamber concerts on some weekends. I understand she dumped me, but why did she dump her job as well? It does not make sense.'

'Sounds like one of those Agatha thingummy mysteries,' said Olive.

'I thought I knew her well, for two years! And I do not know anything about her logic for decisions.'

'I hear you,' said Olive. 'Lovers who make dumb decisions.'

In what possible world could Olive compare his relationship to Annie with the way she'd been treated by her abusive lover?

Everyone was listening now, so he curbed his anger, took a breath and smiled.

'So, back to why we are here, I guess. I have been terrified of fire since I can remember.' He replaced the word *fascinated* with *terrified*. 'When I was a kid, a friend and I were playing in a farmer's barn up on the summer *pâturage*. We were about eight or nine years old. Neither of us knew how it happened, but suddenly the hay started smoking in the barn and then it flamed. So quickly, fire was rushing through the old wooden structure. The barn had a living area for the summer cow-herder – a small kitchen and a bed – but the herder was up on the Alp at the time, so no one got hurt. We were between the fire and the barn door. We took off our shirts and threw them over the burning hay, but it was too late. We had to get out before the whole place burned.'

'How frightening!' said Rachel. 'Were you hurt?'

'No, we were lucky to escape.'

What he didn't reveal was the feeling of immense power he'd felt that day. That from one tiny spark this great fireball could be created, an energy so immense it was as though, for one moment, he and Pierre had the power of God. Or the power of the devil. But for Alain, it was a divine thing. And it was the beginning of it all.

'Didn't the cops suspect you of starting it?' Olive asked, ruining his inner feeling of euphoria.

'No,' he lied. 'They investigated, but it must have been a spark from the wood-burner in the kitchen. The old chimney passed up through the *grenier* – the hay loft. Anyway, that is the fear I have carried with me. So this fear made the fire in our flat a trauma to me...'

He trailed off. Trudy looked quietly concerned, but when she saw he was okay, nodded with a smile.

Rachel was sitting opposite him. He thought of all she had gone through. Far more terrible than his own experiences. She wasn't like Olive who visibly damaged herself. Olive wanted everyone to share in her pain, as though by doing that it took away from her own madness, lessened the effect on her. No, there was something about Rachel. She was like a kindred spirit. He could relate to her. He thought they'd be close if they were friends. He almost felt protective. Like brother and sister. If his own sister had grown to adulthood, he thought she would have been like Rachel. Arty and creative. A good heart. And again he felt outrage for what she'd been through.

24

RACHEL

Seven weeks ago

Rachel was getting a bit tired of babysitting Olive. She was worried Olive might do or say the wrong thing in her company and would completely lose the plot. Even walking through town to come to the meeting, there was this expectation, as if something was going to spontaneously combust in front of them.

It didn't feel possible that a whole week had gone by. Olive had started to behave oddly. Rachel was aware that she was Olive's only friend. Not even a friend, really, but the only person Olive seemed able to engage with. Rachel didn't quite know how to extract herself from this bizarre relationship that was expected of her. She'd been willing to help, but Olive had begun self-harming again.

She wanted to tell Trudy, but knew that would be disloyal to Olive and there'd be repercussions. Living in that miserable halfway house was so depressing. It would have been nice to have a break from everyone there on the nights the group met, from Olive in particular.

But here they were again, stuck in this circle that she sometimes felt was suffocating her. Before they'd even heard the welcome greeting from Trudy that always officially signalled the beginning of the session, if there was actually an official beginning, Daniel suddenly leaned forward in his chair.

'Rachel, I have to ask, because things weren't clear to me last time, and I hope you don't take it the wrong way, but I think we're all assuming you... lost your baby. That the gin – sorry, vodka – and the hot bath thing worked?'

'Daniel, I think we're going to move on from that today,' Trudy said.

'It's okay, Trudy,' said Rachel and held her chin up.

'Actually, it didn't. At first. You want the gory details?'

Both men actually looked too shocked to answer. Rachel saw Trudy shift with discomfort on her chair. She obviously didn't want Rachel to throw another hissy fit.

'It wasn't until the day after. I felt sick in maths class, thought it was a hangover from too much alcohol, and went to the loo. It slipped into the toilet bowl like a piece of liver.'

'Eww,' said Daniel, with an emphasis on the 'w' at the end.

Rachel felt strangely pleased to shock him, but felt disloyal to the tiny thing she'd miscarried, not even the size of an orange. Calling the baby 'it' felt like such an insult. But her irritation at Daniel stifled the melancholy.

'I only had enough coins for two sanitary pads. Had to use a load of paper towels. On the school bus coming home there was blood all over the back seat. My best friend Sally thought I was having a heavy period. She lent me her jacket to tie round my waist, but by the time I got home I'd lost enough blood to make me look like a ghost. My mum had to take me to A&E. But when she and my dad found out what happened, they just left me there.'

'He should still be held accountable, the boy who did that to you. Was there any chance his actions could have been misinterpreted? I mean, perhaps he didn't really know what he was doing? Drunk at a party and all that.'

What the fuck?

'Daniel, this isn't what—' said Trudy, before Olive, who'd overheard, butted in.

'How can you possibly forgive rape? At any age. Whether it's a boy or a man? Fuck's sake,' she said.

For once, Rachel agreed with Olive. Trudy looked pointedly at Rachel, asking with her eyes if she was okay with all this. Rachel gave an imperceptible nod. During this exchange between the women, they'd all somehow pushed their seats further out of the circle. Putting distance between them and the men. Rachel took a breath and boldly slid her chair forwards a little. As though she wasn't feeling too claustrophobic (she was), as though this didn't bother her as much as they thought (it did).

'I've just realised I didn't make myself clear,' she said, her anger loosening her long-held tongue. 'You think it was the birthday boy, Tim, I was talking about. The person who raped me. Well it wasn't him. It was his dad. The one who paid for the party. Rich and famous, he is. Heads up some charity, has saved the football club from bankruptcy, invested a ton of cash in renovating the swimming centre and he's now running for a second term on the town council. Imagine the scenario. *Schoolgirl from vicarage claims local philanthropist raped her outside The Three Moorhens after a rowdy eighteenth birthday party.* Of course they'd fucking believe my claim. *Not.* I imagine him and his political cronies, sniggering behind their hands, saying they always thought I was the type of girl to seek financial advantage from a moment of passion.'

Rachel stared at Daniel. Did he even realise what he'd said before? Rachel swallowed her anger and her eyes rested on Trudy, who was looking down into her lap, one hand pressed over her open mouth.

Rachel realised the dam had broken; she'd said too much. The others in the room probably didn't have a clue. They hadn't spent their entire lives in that bucolic corner of Hertfordshire. But *shit*. This might not have been such a great result.

Trudy knew.

25

TRUDY

Six weeks ago

I dropped Benny off with my mother and drove to the clinic on Tuesday to type up my notes in the quiet of my office.

Walking through the door, I felt a moment of blissful peace. The venetian blind was pulled down and tilted. Thin strips of sunlight shone against the poster of the Grand Canyon on the opposite wall. The Boston fern on my bookshelf had been faithfully watered by the office cleaners in my absence, but the leaves were pale due to their lack of full light. I tilted the blind open a little more.

I stared at my couch and felt its pull. Perhaps I could steal a few minutes' sleep. I laughed to myself with the vision of someone coming in and finding me there.

Papers and letters lay in the in-tray on my desk. I'd look at them later. I pulled my notes and laptop out of my bag and spread everything out – another reason to have come here rather than working from home where every surface was covered with the mess of parenthood and would probably end up getting stained with blobs of puréed food.

As I opened my notes and saw Rachel's name, it all came rushing back. I should have talked to her immediately after last week's meeting. I was sure she hadn't meant me to figure out the identity of her rapist. She hadn't said his name out loud, but her furious diatribe had allowed me to put the pieces of the puzzle together. The football club saviour comment had confirmed it was

Councilman Kenneth Harper, a man who'd done quite a bit for various institutions and charities. He had a fair amount of support in the community. Supporting charities, quite the philanthropist, no matter the origin of his wealth. I couldn't believe it. But no wonder she'd wanted to keep his name under wraps. I made a mental note to take Rachel aside the following Monday.

I began typing up my notes, starting with Rachel, trying not to let thoughts of Kenneth Harper cloud the general issues of her rape. Rachel was an intelligent girl and although there were unresolved issues with her parents – I didn't even want to start on that in the context of her trauma – I was sure Rachel had the inner strength to muddle through. But what would I have done if I were in her shoes? Knowing that my rapist was out there leading a normal life in a socio-economic world that was way beyond anything I could currently aspire to? A messy trial with counter-accusations and an unsatisfactory conclusion might only have made things worse.

Recalling Rachel's snowflake analogy, I wrote a few notes about visualisation and flash memory scrutiny, thinking I might prepare this as a separate section of my paper, and then moved on to Olive.

The first thing I saw was the large asterisk and the note I'd marked by Olive's name to organise a prescription for some additional individual therapy sessions. I hadn't seen any physical evidence, but I was pretty sure Olive was still self-harming, and had perhaps migrated to her lower body where one couldn't see it. The way she touched her thigh sometimes, avoided crossing her legs. Otherwise, the way she so casually described her ex-lover's abuse with a good dose of sarcasm indicated that the more times she told her story, the less mental impact it seemed to have, which in itself was a good thing. But she seemed to relish recounting the violence. I typed a note to highlight this. And the self-harming meant she still had a lack of confidence and self-image issues.

Alain was still an enigma to me. We originally connected after his hospital stay when he couldn't remember what had happened in the fire. I thought, like Daniel, that rather than relive the event, a type of memory loss had set in to soften the horror of being caught in the fire. He was gentle and quiet, but there was something I couldn't seem to grasp, a kind of simmering frustration that things weren't working out for him. I typed a paragraph about how the brain enforced amnesia as a coping mechanism, and possible solutions for easing the reveal of the memory without causing a shock. He hadn't seemed to replace his passion for skiing with any other kind of sport while he was in the UK, and I noted that he should think about using physical activity as a way of increasing positive hormone production. We hadn't addressed that issue previously because he was still recovering from second-degree burns and smoke inhalation.

I leaned over to my bookshelf and picked out a book, found a chapter on the brain's capacity to trigger the production of serotonin and referenced it in my notes.

Daniel had veered away from his trauma at the last session and preferred to talk about his suicidal thoughts, which surprised me. I assumed he'd be too ashamed about this secondary reaction to admit it to the others. But some people would often say anything in the company of strangers. I was curious about the fantasies he'd created for himself after the accident, to try to keep his wife alive in his mind. These visions hadn't yet materialised back when we'd had our one-to-one sessions, mainly because it took him so long to remember and accept the unravelling of events. I made a note to monitor this.

After the morning's work, satisfied I already had a good portion of material for the different trauma sections of my report for the BACP association, I went to the clinic's little kitchen to make myself a cup of tea. I waved to the receptionist who was typing something on her computer with headphones on.

I returned to my office and sat at my desk. As I was sipping my tea, I studied a photo of Benny in a wooden frame. He was wearing a knitted red hat, head thrown back, laughing, his eyes scrunched in joy, with a little milk pooled on his tongue. One of my favourite happy shots.

I rubbed my eyes.

I wished I had someone else to talk to about my own issues other than Harry. He was so busy with his current projects at work, voicing my concerns about motherhood would simply have loaded him with extra worries he couldn't really be expected to deal with. It was enough that he made it home every Monday evening for me to run my group therapy.

I touched the photo of Benny with three fingers, like a girl guide's promise. Such a precious baby. A lot of hard work, sacrifices and determination had made him. I should have appreciated him more because of that. But I was exhausted. I still had nightmares about the birth, flashbacks about when it all started to go wrong. A horrendously long labour, planned with no medication, and the horror of when it became completely unbearable, being told it was too late for an epidural. When Benny's head wouldn't engage, he got stuck in the birth canal. They couldn't do a caesarean at that late stage and I thought we were both going to die. When Benny's heartrate began to falter, they had to go in with the forceps and ventouse to get him out. I had torn badly. I thought it was never going to end.

In the sanctuary of my office, I put my hands over my face, and the realisation came to me that I should probably be analysing my own trauma. PTSD. The irony. A practitioner was often her own worst patient. Perhaps I should have made an appointment with one of the other psychotherapists at the clinic.

Sometimes I felt like I was drowning. There was nothing I could do about the way Benny's colicky tummy made him feel, but his constant crying was setting me on edge. As I let the atmosphere of my own psychologist's consultation room sweep over me, I even wondered if I was regretting the decision to become a mother.

I picked up Benny's photo, hugged it to my chest and imagined what I might say to a patient on the other side of my desk, perhaps lying on the couch. Every mother might ask themselves whether they were too young, too old, too ill-equipped. And every mother's first child meant they were doing parenthood for the very first time. All the baby books in the world couldn't truly prepare you for that experience. And afterwards, each baby behaved differently, reacted differently. So mothers would always be asking themselves if they were doing things right. It was natural to ask these questions. Not even my own mother would have had the same experience as me.

Closing my eyes, I lectured myself with the voice of reason that I was a perfectly normal human being, a wonderful, caring mother and that everything was going to be all right. I loved Benny and tried to remind myself that each phase of his life would come and go quickly, that I should enjoy his childhood. But I couldn't stop the irrational alternating feelings of panic and total lethargy.

I didn't want to resort to medication unless I was truly fraught. But I recognised the things I'd said to many of my patients with issues resulting from depression. I tried not to dwell on the fact that I hadn't had a good night's sleep for almost four months.

After having a quiet cry and giving myself a good talking to, I felt a little better. I looked at the papers in my in-tray and glanced at my watch. I should have gone through them quickly in case anything needed urgent attention. Patient re-referrals or bills to approve for accounts.

There was a letter from one of the NHS charities about increasing the funding from a benefactor for my case study. This gave me a lift. This was what was keeping me linked to my professional world. Also that I was contributing to the household, albeit with a minimal part-time stipend. Now I was getting financial recognition, pride sparked. And I wouldn't have to fund the group therapy sessions myself for the sake of the report now that their individual sessions were no longer covered by the NHS.

The letter asked reasonably for an update every couple of months on the progress of methods, which made me relieved that I was periodically typing up my reports and findings. Apparently, the benefactor wanted to become involved himself. He saw how my methods could be useful for the treatment of a wider group of patients working in the public sector: soldiers returning from combat, police personnel witnessing terror attacks and other atrocities. The letter talked of setting up additional funding for an ad campaign. This was getting exciting. It meant my work would get a wider audience.

And in the next paragraph, the charity named this generous benefactor with whom I was to have contact. I squinted in disbelief. My stomach did a flip, bile rose and I eyed the wastepaper bin next to my desk.

Kenneth Harper, MBE.

26

TRUDY

Present day

The doorbell rings and my mother and I jump. I run down the hallway. Harry gets there before me and opens the door. A short woman with longish brown hair folded casually into a double ponytail is standing on the doorstep. She's wearing a jacket, a skirt and a pair of tights that looks far too hot for a day like this. A weekend day like this. But this is no ordinary Saturday.

'Sal, how's it?' asks DS Flatman behind me in what sounds like an uncharacteristic greeting to my ears. 'Mr and Mrs Greenwood, this is Sally Johnson, your family liaison officer. She'll stay with you for the evening. She can help you through any issues.'

He already makes it sound as though Benny will never be found. It's only been a couple of hours. My throat closes again, but this time there are no more tears. Instead I take a shaky breath.

'You can call us Trudy and Harry, please. The way you're referring to us as Mr and Mrs makes the whole thing sound so... impersonal.'

Harry has finished his call and raises his eyebrows. He shows the FLO – 'Sal' – into the living room. My mother takes orders for tea. She'll be searching for biscuits in the cupboard. We have some stale Jaffa cakes somewhere. I bustle past her to the kitchen and take the opportunity to finally pop one of those mints into my mouth to take away the taste of grief.

DS Flatman and his assistant prepare to leave and promise to be in touch if they hear any news. Sally 'Sal' Johnson scans the photos in the hallway, makes all the appropriate noises about Benny's good looks. This just makes me feel worse.

I begin pacing in front of the window.

'Have you had a case like this before?' I ask Sal.

'Not a baby, but two child cases, one toddler and an adolescent,' she says.

'And were they returned to their parents?'

Sal clears her throat. 'Probably best not to compare yours with other cases.'

What the hell does that mean? Did they only find dead bodies? Oh God. Why not say at the beginning that it's best not to ask at all about other cases? Is everyone a monster?

I wonder if it's the same FLO who was assigned to Daniel to go and visit the site of his accident. I always thought at the time it was crazy to have taken his kids. There could have been an adverse reaction they wouldn't have wanted to witness. So unprofessional. Maybe I should say something to my police friend Suzy who's been my liaison at the clinic since I started working there.

Instead I claim I've had too much tea, glance at my mother making yet another round in the kitchen, and go to the upstairs bathroom. I sit on the closed toilet seat sucking my mint, head on my arms crossed on my thighs, one ear listening out for the phone or the doorbell.

The bloody FLO. She could have at least lied. No harm in that. White lies are there to protect the victims. Doesn't Sal realise that psychotherapists are all evasive with the truth?

27

DANIEL

Six weeks ago

There was a pub called the Half Moon about a hundred yards down the road from the old school house near the mini-roundabout. As Daniel glanced in its direction, the light flickered on over the sign outside in the approaching dusk. Trudy was running late that Monday, and they were all waiting for her outside the old school building. Daniel made a spontaneous decision, most unlike him.

'Does anyone fancy going for a drink after tonight's session?' He nodded towards the pub. 'The first round is on me.'

This suggestion surprised even him. Perhaps he was craving the adult company of anyone other than ambitious work colleagues or his mother. He couldn't claim the members of this group were really his friends, because since Sarah's death, there had been so few friends of any kind.

He had no idea what it was like in the pub; he'd never been. He would usually check somewhere first to make sure it wasn't a filthy hovel. But that part of town didn't seem to be the type of place where the residents would frequent a hovel. He simply figured it was easier for everyone to meet close by, with all the different directions they had to head off to afterwards.

Rachel quietly snorted as though suppressing a laugh, but then must have realised he was being serious and nodded. He was surprised she was the first to agree. Alain said, 'Why not?' Olive shrugged, muttered, 'cool,' under her breath. So they had a date.

He wasn't sure why this made him feel pleased with himself. They were such a sorry bunch. Was it because he wanted to be liked again by adults?

'Do you think it's a good idea though?' Rachel asked.

Daniel tipped his head in query.

'Shouldn't we invite Trudy?' she said.

'Should we even tell her?' asked Olive. 'It's not really her business, is it?'

Daniel shrugged.

'I think it's okay to meet,' said Alain. 'But don't tell her. Then she will not have to make that decision if she thinks it is not appropriate for *her*. It is not against the rules, *n'est-ce pas?*'

'Good point,' said Daniel, wondering not for the first time what made Alain tick.

He unlocked his phone.

'Inviting someone else?' whispered Olive.

'Texting my mother to say I'll be late. She's babysitting my children.' He was irritated for having to justify anything to Olive, but still wanted to qualify his actions.

'Well done for being spontaneous,' she said.

Daniel detected no sarcasm in Olive's eyes.

'I'd have preferred to have given her more notice.'

Now Olive rolled her eyes. He knew his mother would be pleased, though, because it would be the first time he'd done anything social unattached to his business since the accident.

'You're a planner, hey? Must have shocked yourself tonight,' she said.

Daniel smiled and once his mother had texted back 'Of course!' he put his phone back in his pocket. He couldn't imagine Olive planning anything.

Where was Trudy? She should have been there by now. Olive put her hands in her pockets and blew air through her lips in a silent whistle. Rachel was leaning against the brick wall of the schoolhouse smoking a cigarette. He wanted to tell her it would kill her, but kept his mouth shut. Enough of the advisories for one evening.

'If you're such a planner,' continued Olive. 'How do you manage all those constantly changing figures? I've seen *Trading Places*. That kind of work environment would give me a heart attack.'

'The foreign exchange market isn't as unpredictable as everyone thinks,' he replied. 'A trader just has to be on the ball. It's a case of studying all the scenarios. Little signs in the world's economic shifts. The inkling of a movement in the share market of huge global conglomerates. The mapping of political changes in unstable economies. The passing of legislation in the world's leading governments. Every action has an equal and opposite reaction.'

Olive's eyes had already glazed over, but Rachel moved closer to listen. He'd never excelled at science in school, but the one thing he'd learned from Newton was that forces came in pairs. Even monetary forces. And he'd been exceptionally adept at predicting them. Hence his success at that desk in Canary Wharf.

'It's a shame I can't choose when to embrace this meticulous detailing.' He was addressing an empty space now that Olive seemed to have lost interest. 'It has spilled over into my private life. Or maybe it has always been there and I adapted it to make a living. But I'd like to be able to leave that precision on my desk in the office when I come home at night and not let things like untidy toy boxes or crumbs in the bread bin drive my obsession for perfection.'

'You should be saving this revelation for the meeting,' said Rachel as she ground her cigarette butt on the pavement with the toe of her boot, then picked it up and threw it into a drain at the curb.

Daniel found this endearing, somehow. Clearing up the rubbish. He realised his little obsessions had become worse since Sarah's death, as though the accident had shifted something on his personal axis. Perhaps he'd learn something from each of these people's resolve. After all, that was why they were all here, to share experiences in the hope that they could learn from each other and – how did Trudy put it on that first evening? – not slip back into those old habits that triggered the memories of the trauma. It would have been easier to renounce physical habits. It was the mental reactive habits that were harder to control.

Trudy finally showed up, fumbling with her keys. He sensed stress wafting off her in waves and was glad no one said anything to her about the pub. When Trudy unlocked the door, they all filed into the hall.

Alain was on chair monitoring again – the organised Swiss – and Daniel's mind was taken back to the classroom tasks he might have performed if he'd been a student here when it was still a school a century ago. Blackboard duty perhaps. Everyone wanted to be blackboard monitor when he was in primary school. An inherent desire to erase the tedious workings of teachers at the end of every lesson with that wooden felted rubber.

As they took their seats, Daniel stared down at his feet, and noticed the leather bow on his left shoe had fallen to the side. He leaned forward, and was about to place it back into the centre on the tongue, when his fingers hovered over the shoe. He lifted his hand away without touching the lace. It remained skewed to the side, and although he felt it burning into the top of his foot, he forced himself not to look down at it again. A victorious defiance.

Trudy started the session by reiterating some of her old recommendations in the one-to-one sessions for deep-breathing and visualisation. Daniel recalled the yoga and meditation classes he signed up for in parallel with Trudy's therapy. They'd helped him look at things in a different way, to a certain extent. The yoga teacher misinterpreted his needs, though. She thought he'd had burn-out. Anxiety issues. It was hard to explain to her what went on in his brain when he saw a pile of contracts on a fellow-worker's desk that weren't all stacked together with their sides straight, no pages askew, no stapled corners sticking out. They had to be as neat and correct as the figures that were typed within their profit and loss columns.

That seemed to sum up what he'd been searching for since the accident.

Restoring order to chaos.

28

RACHEL

Six weeks ago

Rachel knew Trudy would want to talk to her after the group session this evening. But Trudy had arrived late, and by the time the session was over, Rachel managed to avoid being alone with her. Not that she *couldn't* talk about Kenneth Cock Harper, but now she'd decided she wanted to join the others, the pull of the pub was too strong. When Trudy tried to catch her eye, Rachel stated clearly to no one in particular that she had to leave promptly after the group therapy session because she had a job at the refuge.

'But what about—'

'A task, Olive!' said Rachel, looking pointedly at Olive.

'Duh. Yeah. Of course,' said Olive, making a zipping motion across her lips.

Rachel rolled her eyes. There was never going to be a good time to talk about Kenneth Cock Harper. Not until he was out of the picture. She wasn't sure, though, when she'd ever be ready. It was one thing to relive the horror of her rape, but quite another to identify the perpetrator of the deed to others. It would only mean trouble in the long run.

Trudy's mind must have been reeling. It would have been a lightbulb moment for her, after all that time guessing the identity. In their initial therapy sessions, she'd promised never to report Rachel's rape without her permission – that would have been un-ethical – but she'd always wanted to set things right, to see justice served. Perhaps now she'd understand how impossible a task that would be, given who the man was and the influence he had on their community. Stupid to have given away so many clues. After Daniel's assumption that it was a case of misplaced affections from a fellow student, she'd been too irritated, and couldn't keep her mouth shut.

The others had been oblivious. They probably had no idea what went on in the real world anyway. Olive would have blurted his name out right there and then if Rachel had told her at the beginning. She'd only ever mentioned his name to one other person for that very reason.

That person was Martha. She was a new girl at the refuge, arrived a couple of weeks ago. For the first week she didn't make eye contact with anyone. Rachel had started calling her Mouse because she was small and shy. Martha didn't take offence. They'd laughed together about the new nickname. Rachel was the only one who was allowed to call her that.

Mouse wasn't very tall. Pale and fragile, she looked about twelve but was almost nineteen. Her pale blonde hair was like a child's and was in a constant state of static, flying about her pixie face. Her eyes were pale too, the bleached blue of a summer sky. Rachel had seen something in those eyes as soon as she'd been able to look into them. Martha had been raped too.

Rachel had been happy for this friendship to germinate. The girl looked as though she could do with a little sympathy. She was damaged, but wasn't crazy like Olive. There was an underlying strength, and Rachel knew she wouldn't want any of her pity. She shared her own story to convince Mouse she wasn't alone, and in the short time they'd known each other, they'd probably helped one another more than any psychotherapy sessions.

But Rachel wasn't sure how worried she should be about Mouse. Because although Olive was hard to decipher at the best of times, she seemed to have become more and more attached to

Rachel. Knowing Olive's spikiness, she hoped jealousy wouldn't raise its ugly head.

Alain was the last to share this evening, but he seemed to have run out of things to say. Rachel felt they'd all probably had enough of him embellishing the fire at his flat. He kept repeating the same thing, and what should have been a terrifying story had become quite mundane after a couple of weeks reiterating the events. It was as though he was filling in time, trying to find something to recount, for the sake of being in the group. He spoke admirable English, so she didn't think it was that. But something didn't ring true. Rachel no longer felt any vibes of his panic. Vibes of trauma.

Olive suddenly leaned in.

'I don't feel his terror,' she whispered in a conspiratorial tone to Rachel, keeping her eyes on Alain. 'Can you detect any fear at all?'

Rachel shook her head, surprised that Olive had picked up on this too. Olive was rubbing her thigh absently. Of all of them, she should have understood the most about fear. Never knowing when your lover was going to explode.

'It's nice that Daniel's invited us all to go to the pub afterwards,' she whispered to Olive, as the session wound up. 'But remember not to mention it in front of Trudy.'

'Nice for you, maybe,' Olive replied with a wink, the point of her tongue peeking out between her teeth as she gave a lewd smile.

'Jesus, Olive, I don't fancy him. What are you like?'

'So, you going afterwards as well?' she asked. 'To the pub? Or is that job waiting for you back at the refuge?'

Rachel sighed. 'That was to put Trudy off the pub thing.'

'Sure you don't want to run home to your new friend?' asked Olive.

Rachel swallowed and clenched her jaw. She wasn't going to provoke Olive by saying anything else.

'That was a great session!' Trudy called out, giving Rachel the excuse to turn away from Olive. 'I really feel like some of you are getting down to the heart of your issues by opening up about your experiences. I hope you can see how you have each been able to cope with your trauma. It's great to be sharing your methods of control. We'll be talking about how we can build on that in future sessions. New ideas. New approaches.'

When Trudy pulled the door closed and locked it at the end of the session, they all stood around for a bit, unsure what to do. They hadn't formed a plan. But they needn't have worried. Trudy seemed preoccupied. Would she be hurt she hadn't been invited to the pub? It was likely not professional for a therapist to go drinking with her patients, but she'd already emphasised these weren't typical therapy situations.

'See you next week,' said Rachel, waving over her shoulder, making as though to move along the path she always took. She was glad Trudy didn't feel obliged to drive her back to the refuge like she'd done last week after losing her bottle.

'My car's that way,' said Alain, veering almost comically away from the direction Trudy was taking.

Was it now obvious they'd planned something together? It felt childishly conspiratorial. Once Trudy had rounded the corner to cross the market square, presumably to where her car was parked, Alain doubled back and came back to the group walking slowly towards the pub.

'I felt bad deceiving Trudy, but she looks completely stressed out. Not herself,' said Rachel as she turned to catch up with them. 'I hope her baby's okay.'

'You know about her baby?' asked Daniel.

Rachel wondered how *he* knew about the baby. Had Trudy told everyone except Rachel about her baby? How weird was that?

'Yeah. Found out last week. Was a bit miffed she hadn't said anything about her precious little Benny before. Felt a bit daft finding out on the spur of the moment. It's not like I need protecting from everyone's little babies or anything.'

Rachel glanced over her shoulder, to make sure Trudy had really gone.

'I don't think she intentionally kept it from you,' said Daniel, feeling the need to defend Trudy. 'I remember something from one of my one-to-one sessions with her. I think she might have had a hard time getting pregnant in the first place.'

Rachel bit her lip. Why the heck had Trudy told Daniel *that*? Perhaps it had slipped out while Daniel was talking about his kids. Why did Rachel suddenly feel like Trudy might even have been *hiding* the fact that she had a baby, even though they hadn't seen each other before this project for months?

'Yeah. She told me about that last week. She stopped individual therapy with me more than a year ago. Apparently, endless rounds of fertility treatment made her nervous about telling people she was pregnant – can't blame her. She'd had so many miscarriages and didn't want to say anything until she was sure, even to her family. And then we hadn't seen each other. I had no idea, so it was a bit of a shock, given my own circumstances...'

Daniel stopped as his mobile phone rang, gave Rachel an apologetic smile, and moved to the side of the pavement to take a call. He waved the others past and they walked into the pub without him. As Rachel stood for a moment in the bar getting her bearings, she glanced through the window to where Daniel was talking animatedly to someone on his phone outside. Strange to instigate this pub outing and then not rally the troops.

'What can I get you?' Rachel asked Alain as they drifted towards the bar.

She felt strangely empowered to ask. Trudy had been right. Rachel didn't feel intimidated by either of these men. Probably because they were carrying equally as much baggage as her.

'I'll have a beer, thanks,' said Alain, pointing to one of the taps with the flicker of a smile.

Rachel ordered a gin and tonic and watched the barmaid pour a pint of Twitchell. It felt liberating to be doing something so normal. A couple of drinks down the pub with friends. Well, perhaps not friends yet, more like acquaintances.

29

OLIVE

Six weeks ago

O live had been on the point of going back to the refuge after the session, but changed her mind to stick around and go to the pub with the others. She didn't have any money and she shouldn't have been drinking – it was one of the conditions for her to be allowed to move on from the hostel – but she was sure she could sneak a pint of soda water into someone's first round without feeling bad about not being able to pay.

Rachel would likely be keeping an eye on her anyway – making sure she didn't order anything alcoholic or get out of line. Truth be told, it was Rachel who needed to be watched. So Trudy had a sprog. Blimey, who knew? Well maybe Olive did know, but had forgotten. She didn't always listen.

Anyway, there was no reason a young woman couldn't have a family *and* a career. But Trudy didn't strike Olive as the mothering type. And the way Rachel had mentioned Trudy's baby on the way into the pub, Olive detected the pang of something in Rachel's voice she couldn't put her finger on. Why was she suddenly interested in Trudy's baby? Oh! Was she regretting having got rid of her own?

They had a connection, Olive and Rachel. It wasn't just because they were both living at the refuge. They'd each been served several shit sandwiches in life. Olive smirked when she remembered saying this to Rachel, who'd told Olive she should nevertheless be careful how much extra mustard she chose to put in hers.

The difference between them was that Rachel didn't ask for any of her grief. Olive wanted to help her to feel normal, feel accepted, get to the core of what she really wanted. Rachel was the only one Olive allowed to go anywhere near her at the refuge. It was Rachel who often took the razor blade from Olive when she caught her in the act. They helped each other.

She thought about the last time she'd cut, and placed her palm against the skirt resting on the inside of her thigh. She couldn't wear jeans at the moment because she'd gone a bit deep, and the scabs kept rubbing off.

She was surprised Daniel had suggested going to the pub. Perhaps he wasn't as straight and poncey as Olive first thought. As they were about to go in, he'd stopped outside on the pavement talking secretively to someone on his phone. Olive narrowed her eyes as he'd waved everyone past. Was he trying to get out of shouting the round? He'd cupped his hand around the phone as she passed. Had she heard right? Had he said 'Mummy' to whoever he was speaking to? Blimey. She was constantly changing her mind about him. Perhaps not shaggable, then. So she'd had to ask, and he really had been talking to his mum. Not shaggable at all.

Olive sidled up to Rachel in the pub who was standing near Mr Swiss at the bar. There weren't many customers in, probably because it was the beginning of the week. Rachel sighed deeply as Olive approached. She chose to believe the sigh was her own sorrow and not because Olive was there.

'You okay? This lot opening some old wounds?' she asked, glancing at Daniel through the window.

'Yeah. People certainly have some weird predisposed ideas about teenage pregnancies,' said Rachel absently.

When Rachel pulled her purse out of her bag, Olive hovered behind her.

'Can you get me a pint of soda water, Rach?' she whispered.

Rachel frowned and ordered a gin and tonic, a beer for Mr Swiss and a soda water. Olive picked up her drink and drifted over to the tables by the window. She glanced at Alain on the way past, and slurped her soda water, making her snort. Not making a good impression if she thought she had a chance. He was probably too *foreign* for her anyway, but he was a bit of eye candy. A bit of alright. Not prim and proper like Daniel. Full head of shiny, dark hair, olive skin, or perhaps an old tan, sexy eyes.

She sat on a stool and waited for them to come over from the bar. Rachel turned around, eyed a table on the other side of the pub. Olive patted the stool next to her. Rachel took a deep breath, changed direction and put her drink on the table and sat next to Olive. As Alain followed behind, Olive patted the stool on her other side.

But Alain walked around the table and sat next to Rachel. Olive's spike of jealousy soon turned to concern. Rachel had gone quiet and must have been feeling nervous about sitting next to a guy. Olive was determined to try to protect her from Alain. They were all in very close proximity, and danger signals were flashing in Olive's mind. This was all happening too fast. In the guise of protecting Rachel from being close to a man she didn't know, she was desperate to get Alain to engage with her.

'What's your real story, Alain?' asked Olive, her voice coming out a little more accusatory than she'd intended. 'What's the trauma you're really dealing with?'

Alain looked nonplussed. Rachel's comment earlier meant Olive wasn't the only one who didn't believe he was "traumatised" by the fire in his flat.

'Olive, why are you being so rude suddenly?' Rachel hissed in her ear, surprising Olive with her defensive tone.

'I... it was fire,' said Alain.

Definitely lying. Took one to know one.

'The heat—'

'Olive, we're not in therapy now. Can we talk about something else?' said Rachel.

Olive shrugged. She didn't really care. Just wanted to catch him out. Still, she enjoying listening to him talk, about anything really. She could get on with that accent all night, despite the secrets she was sure he was hiding. Although that might be because he was Swiss. Weren't they all supposed to be born with constipated personalities? Reserved? They were probably all hiding something. Nazi gold in their wardrobes, drug-lord numbered bank accounts. It seemed a little odd that he was in group therapy if he wasn't willing to share what was really going on in there.

She leaned into Rachel and tried not to notice that she moved imperceptibly away. Olive didn't want to lose her. Especially not to a suspicious tosser like this foreigner. It was time to work out what she could do to bring her back. Get her away from that waif at the refuge. She wasn't about to play happy families with someone else in the mix. Olive needed a plan that would make her indispensable to Rachel.

30

RACHEL

Six weeks ago

'Do you think they'll let you go home soon?' Rachel asked Alain. 'You seem pretty keen. I'd rather be in the Alps than here, so I don't blame you for wanting to get out of here.'

'There are reasons I am not able to just now,' he replied. 'But I do not want to talk about them.'

Lots of secrets. They were all holding them. But Alain was keeping his cards very close to his chest.

'Fair enough,' she said, shrugging.

'And you? Where will you make your home when you leave the hostel? Will you stay local?'

Olive was stuck to Rachel's side like a barnacle. She didn't want to talk about what she would do when she left the refuge. She didn't want Olive to know her plans at all. Olive bent over to examine some fresh marks on the inside of her elbow, pretending not to listen.

'I hope to find a place of my own soon.'

Her feelings towards Alain were conflicting. She recognised a lingering claustrophobia. Maybe it was because he was being so secretive. Maybe it was simply a man thing. One of the goals of this whole group therapy was to assist Rachel and Olive in their integration back into a world where men were present. It wasn't like they *all* ended up reminding her of her rapist. Some of them reminded her of her father. But that was another story.

As she weighed up and pushed back her anxiety, enjoying the fact that she was having a semi-normal conversation with Alain, it was Olive she secretly wished would leave her alone. Alain was good-looking, a little mysterious. But it wasn't about sexual attraction. If she could put a finger on what she was feeling, she'd say it was... fraternal.

Alain had been twisting the paper wrapper from a stick of gum into a loop, over and over. He reached into his pocket and pulled out a Bic lighter, placed the wrapper on his beer mat and set the end alight.

'Hey, that's dangerous. You shouldn't do that in here,' said Olive.

Rachel raised her eyebrows. Since when did Olive worry about what was and wasn't appropriate anywhere? But Rachel could see the risk. She searched for an ashtray and remembered smoking wasn't allowed in pubs anymore. It had been a while since she was in one.

'That's going to stink,' she said. 'You'll draw attention from the barman. Are you trying to get us all kicked out?'

Alain's gaze pulled back from whatever dreamland he'd been in and he crushed the flame onto the beer mat with the bottom of his glass. It left a black sooty smudge on the Greene King logo.

'That's a cool tattoo,' he said, ignoring his little extinguished bonfire and pointing to Rachel's wrist.

It was as though he never flicked that lighter. Rachel turned her arm to show the seven intertwined roses in various stages of bloom.

'Thanks. Got it done last year. It'll be the first and last, though. Not doing that again. Bloody painful. Especially this bit here.' She pointed to the delicate area on the inside of her wrist where the stalks of the roses joined a rope-like design. Two blue veins crossed at the base of the tattoo under her white skin.

'Don't suppose your girlfriend would have any problems with getting one done. If she could stay still for long enough,' Alain said with his voice lowered.

'She's not my girlfriend,' said Rachel.

Olive was making puffing noises through her lips, eyes darting around the bar, scanning a handful of new arrivals, no longer listening to them.

'*Ah oui*, girlfriend means something different here. I should have said "friend".'

'She has enough of her own self-made tattoos.' Rachel paused. 'I don't know why I got one, really. To go with my image, perhaps.'

'The need to express your inner self, or to try to be someone else.'

Was that meant to be a question? Rachel bit her lip and rubbed her palm up and down her arm over the image of the flowers. A symbol for her own development, with a smattering of thorns to remind her of the pain along the way.

'Were you into all this before?' asked Alain, leaning back and sweeping a hand from her head to her feet. 'The make-up, the leather, the hair?'

'Not really. Fashion and all that. We weren't allowed to *express* ourselves when I was younger. It's the one good thing about wearing a uniform at school. Everyone's the same. But no, I didn't go goth until I left.'

She pulled a strand of jet-black hair across her face.

'But this has become another uniform,' said Alain.

Rachel didn't reply and hid her smile in her glass as she sipped her gin. She surprised herself by admitting he had an attractive accent. The gin sliced a satisfying chill down her throat and sent a shard of lightness to her brain. She sat back. Breathed deeply. She was having a proper conversation with a man.

'Rach, shall we get going?' interrupted Olive.

Rachel shook her head.

'Here, go and get a couple of packets of crisps.' Rachel handed Olive a tenner.

'What is it like at the refuge? Do they have a lot of rules there too?' asked Alain once Olive was out of earshot.

Rachel huffed cynically, which answered his question. For the first time in weeks, she'd rather have been sitting here than heading back to the safety of the refuge, a place she'd definitely had enough of.

'How long have you been there, and why so long?' continued Alain.

'It's hard for someone who's already homeless to find somewhere to live. Kind of *Catch 22*.'

'Were you not living with your parents when... it happened?'

'My dad's a total tosser. He kicked me out, told me I was a slut, refused to believe getting pregnant, getting *raped*, wasn't my fault.'

Alain raised his eyebrows.

'After a few days sleeping in the back of the parking area off West Alley, I called the refuge number I found on a poster glued to the wall in the Arcade public toilets. I can't tell you how grateful I am that they took me in. But it's definitely time to move on. There's a load of damaged women there, and some of them might not be fixable,' she said, staring at Olive's back at the bar. 'Once I've saved up enough money from the job I'm doing at the bakery, I'm getting a place of my own. They've kept me on at the refuge because I'm doing voluntary work, but I've got to get out of there.'

Her salary would be going into her bank account that week, and the irony struck her that she could probably even have afforded to keep her baby. She swallowed. It was too late for that, but there was still time to set right the regrets she'd been hiding deep in her soul.

She was determined to get her own back on the world, take back what she deserved, what should always have been hers.

31

TRUDY

Present day

I want to be on my own, but as soon as anyone in the house clears their throat or sighs, or their clothes rustle in motion, or whispers are exchanged, or quiet conversations are heard, I want to be near them. I want to know what they're thinking, to know whether there's any news of Benny, who has now been missing for more than four hours. The longest four hours of my life.

As soon as anyone moves, I want to follow them, hear what's being said on the other end of phones, even if it's nothing to do with us. I want to be told what the chances are of finding Benny in the next few minutes, half hour, before nightfall. As soon as I sit down I want to stand up. When I stand up, I want to walk around, but feel shaky and really wish I could stay sitting down. I might topple over with the weight of all this anxiety.

The wash of emotions has sapped any energy. I feel sick. My heart races, my chest feels tight and hot. I imagine this is what a physically broken heart feels like. I'm suppressing my tears because if I cry I might not hear a car arriving, a knock at the door, or a phone call to say they've found Benny.

There's a flurry of activity as the FLO takes a call from DS Flatman. Hope rises and then is dashed when Sally Johnson explains that – should it be necessary – a press conference has been arranged for the following day.

In the end, though, I'm so exhausted that to avoid the worried looks from everyone else in the house about my state of mind, I go upstairs. I sway for a moment in the doorway of Benny's room, ears straining to pick up his little voice, a gurgle, a giggle, even a plaintive wail.

I lie down on my bed in the foetal position, knees tucked up to my chest, hair plastered across my hot, damp forehead, blood pounding at my temples.

I feel like I will never be able to sleep again.

32

ALAIN

Six weeks ago

The pub was suddenly hot, suffocating. As Alain drained his beer he saw the charred paper stuck to the bottom of his glass. He put the glass with its lukewarm dregs on the mat and pushed it away from him. He needed something cold to put out the fire in his throat.

It was hard to know what the rules were about buying drinks in this situation. The only person who could probably afford an entire round for everybody was the other man, Daniel. And he'd offered, but was kept back by some phone call before they came in. Alain had been one of the first through the door, so had intended to buy a drink for himself and let the others sort out who was going to buy theirs. Then Rachel offered.

He was happy to have avoided a ten-minute discussion on who would get the next round. It was always the same – the overpolite way the English had of apologising for everything and appearing to be doing the right thing. They were terrified of breaking the etiquette of social or political correctness. Everyone was either in a state of indecision or making outrageous excuses. No matter how sterile or mechanical people thought the Swiss were, the rules were perfectly clear. But he was at least happy his ambivalence had scored him a seat next to Rachel.

'Did you know, students don't wear uniforms to school in Switzerland,' he said.

Rachel laughed. The sound was music to him. He was beginning to enjoy her company. And she seemed to be relaxing.

'That's decidedly un-Swiss of them, don't you think? Don't you have rules and uniforms for everything over there?' she asked.

'It's true. I only just realised that. It could be why everybody wants to secretly be a *gendarme*.' He laughed. 'I don't want to start an argument about what does or doesn't constitute a uniform outside schools or prisons.'

'But you were criticising my choice of clothes before, *n'est-ce pas?* The black.'

He raised his eyebrows at her use of French. Her accent had led him to believe she wasn't very educated. He was becoming more intrigued by her.

'That was never my intention. Can I get you another drink?' he asked, wanting to find out, but not asking, whether she spoke more than a smattering of French.

Rachel pouted as though considering breaking a rule. Perhaps she wasn't supposed to be drinking while she was living at the refuge.

'Okay, same again, please. G and T. You can put all the tonic in, you know, to avoid carrying the bottle.'

Alain didn't ask Olive if she wanted another drink. She was still nervously sipping her pint of what might have been lemonade, and eating crisps annoyingly loudly. He wished she would leave him and Rachel alone. At the bar he ordered a bottle of Corona and a gin and tonic. The barman didn't have any lime. When Alain half-heartedly complained, he was offered a limp slice of lemon from a small dish the barman had used to dress the gin and tonic. Alain shook his head and headed back to the table, to *la Ténébreuse* as he now thought of her – the Dark One.

He placed the drinks on the table. She smiled and lifted the glass.

'Changed to bottled beer,' he said as he clinked his Corona against her glass. 'I don't know how you people can drink warm beer from the tap. That draught ale is disgusting. No class.'

'I agree,' Rachel said. 'Don't let anyone try and convince you it's tradition and that's the way real ale should be drunk.'

Alain felt a wall had been gently breached. He couldn't work out why he was intrigued by Rachel, but the emotion was bordering on protective.

'By the way, I have a tattoo as well,' he said, lifting the sleeve of his tee-shirt to show a narrow armband of skin ink with a swirling design of waves and flames.

Rachel lifted a hand, and her black-nailed index finger hovered. She traced the pattern in the air, just above his skin. He was sure she wanted to touch it. He wanted her to touch it. His bicep flexed involuntarily.

'It... beautiful,' she said.

'Based on a Polynesian design. I got it on a trip to New Zealand about five years ago.

'New Zealand...' she said dreamily. 'Somewhere I'd love to go too. Nature and wilderness and hardly any people. What were you doing there?'

'I was working as a technician for the Swiss ski team.'

'Oh, that sounds like a great job. The travel, the excitement.'

'I was dismissed,' he said, bursting any illusion.

'Oh! What happened?'

'There was an incident in the tech room with some ski wax equipment overheating. Listen,' he said, changing the subject abruptly. 'I think it would help you if the man who did that to you – you know, the snowflake guy – it must be better for everyone if you reveal his identity to the police. I cannot believe he is allowed to be free.'

Rachel frowned.

Had he offended her by suddenly coming out with that?

'The thing is, I don't think I could cope with long, drawn-out court sessions,' she said. 'All the questions, all the reverse accusations, all the money thrown at a case, so in the end it's only my own reputation that's sullied. I couldn't stand it. I would still come out the loser. I have no idea how I would react, what I would do, in those circumstances.'

Rachel's eyes flickered briefly to Daniel as he came back from the bar with his own drink, and Alain followed her gaze. Was she talking about Daniel's kind of not coping? Taking her life? Surely not. She seemed so full of life. Something in her might be damaged, but like a sapling beaten in a storm, she would find a way to bloom again.

Olive was sitting so close, he imagined Rachel could feel her breath on her neck. She was staring past Alain with a frown at Daniel. Alain felt dangerous vibes coming off Olive in a way that generated no sympathy. After what Rachel had said about wanting to get away from the refuge, he imagined Olive was like a stone around her neck.

'If we were living in my home town, I'd show you how to ski,' he said.

'That sounds cool. I'm almost ready to move out of the refuge, but it's a bit beyond my means to think of emigrating to the Alps right now.' Rachel smiled and it made her face light up, her dark eyes sparkled. He was suddenly reminded of Annie and experienced a stab of remorse.

'Why on earth did you end up coming to Hitchin?' asked Rachel.

'Annie was offered a dream job at Benslow. She could teach piano and also perform in their regular chamber concerts. There was nothing like that in Switzerland. I guess the beauty of the Alps wasn't enough to keep her there. We moved into a flat just off the Cambridge Road. From our one-bedroom attic flat the view from the back window was the railway track full of rubbish. A little different from the granite peaks of the Alps.'

Daniel and Olive turned to listen to their conversation. Alain had been quite happy keeping the chat between him and Rachel.

'So why don't you try and earn some money, at least to get a ticket, to go back?' asked Daniel.

'I... can't just yet. But soon, I hope...'

Alain fingered the lighter in his pocket, counted to ten in his head. The smooth plastic and the wheel on the flint brought him a sense of calm as he zipped his thumb over it, the flame spout pressed against his thigh so it couldn't ignite. It was like a talisman, keeping him grounded.

'I miss the mountains,' he continued. 'I miss my friends. I miss the thrill of the slope. At the time being with Annie was all that mattered. I didn't start to miss that other stuff until she'd gone. She was very persuasive in getting me to come with her to England. She told me there was some bright future here for me. I gave up so much, was stupid to think I'd be happy here, working in the bike shop on Walsworth Road. This world is so different from the one I came from.'

He pulled his tee-shirt away from his neck, watched Rachel's eyes go to his collar bone. She blinked and looked away. Alain did the same.

'It's too warm in here,' Alain said to no one in particular, thinking he might make an escape.

'It's so cold in this country,' Daniel said. 'How can you possibly be hot, even in summer?'

'I'm always hot now, since the fire. *Mais oui.* You remind me that England's not a great place to live in winter. The sky sits just above your head, grey and oppressive, hiding the deep blue up there somewhere.'

Alain thought of the warmth of the Swiss chalets in winter and how cold it was when he'd arrived here, even though it was late spring. This was a country where no one wanted to turn up the heating because they didn't want to waste five of their extra pennies to keep warm.

'Yeah, well, we all wish we could live in the Alps,' said Rachel a little sarcastically.

'I think it was a mistake Annie made. Thinking she could bring a ski bum into this.' Alain swept his hand to indicate the world beyond the pub. 'Sometimes it's not good to follow something for love. You're right, it is a good place to live, the Alps. I do want to go home.'

It wasn't about the money. It was about the authorities.

Putting a match to his and Annie's splintered life had seemed so cathartic at the time. He couldn't have stopped himself. But he might have jeopardised everything else this time.

33

DANIEL

Six weeks ago

When Daniel finally joined the other three at the table, they made space for him. He started out chatting a little about his job, allowing them to think he'd had an important work call instead of the conversation he'd had with his mother about where to find Emma's favourite velveteen rabbit. He'd stayed on the phone with her until it had been located down the side of a cushion on the sofa.

What to talk about? Experience had taught him there was only so much anyone wanted to hear about foreign exchange trading, unless they were a foreign exchange trader. Olive was the first one to drift into the half-focus of boredom.

Daniel had missed female company, but not like Sarah. His entire office was staffed with men. It could be a brutally bullying environment in the foreign exchange industry and the world of banking. Conversations with his mother had been limited to his household supplies and the timetables of his children. And his sister still refused to talk to him. He felt saddest about that. They'd been so close as children. He'd missed female conversation.

So when Rachel asked, 'Tell me about your family,' he immediately felt like opening up, giving information to these virtual strangers he wouldn't normally have shared.

'Do you have pictures of your kids?' she asked.

Daniel hesitated, then pulled out his phone, and their heads leaned in together slightly as he swiped through a handful of photos. He tilted the phone so both Olive and Alain could see as well.

'They look happy. See how Emma is gazing at you. Loves her dad,' said Rachel. 'Do your parents get to see much of them? Do you have siblings? Sorry, I'm nosy.'

'My mother's been incredibly helpful. She looks after them a lot, although we're not sure how much longer she's going to be capable. I don't think it's a case of the occasional bout of forgetfulness anymore.'

'Signs of dementia? Alzheimer's is a cruel illness.'

Daniel tipped his head. He felt a little guilty having said that about his mother. Alzheimer's. It certainly wasn't that far yet.

'And your dad?' Rachel asked.

'Dad's still around, spends his days mostly playing golf. He was a hard-working man all his life and my mother always worried he'd be both bored and boring once he retired. Everyone's happy he loves his golf. I have a sister, but we haven't spoken to each other for the past few months. She lives in the Lake District with her husband. They can't have children. She was furious when she found out I'd planned to take my life. Said Jasper and Emma didn't deserve me after that.'

Daniel probably didn't need to remind them that's what they'd all thought when he'd first mentioned it.

'My little sister Ruth and I used to be so close,' said Rachel. 'Until my parents cut me out of their lives. I'd scoot back to her in an instant if I thought something was wrong, though. I'd still do anything for her.'

'I completely understand why my sister is disgusted with me. I just wish we could all move on from it,' he said.

'You have to make it right, Daniel. We have no choice with family. The connection is important; she's got the same blood running through her veins as you.' Rachel paused, and Daniel dwelled briefly on the irony of them both being ostracized by members of their families.

'I lost my sister,' said Alain. 'Cancer.'

'Oh God, I'm sorry. Here we are banging on about losing our sisters.'

'It's okay. But I think you should make an effort to reconnect with yours. Before it's too late.'

Daniel swallowed.

'Is there anything your sister really wants?' Alain asked Rachel. 'Maybe there's something you can help her achieve?'

'Talking to you like this makes me realise I should simply pick up the phone and at least talk to Ruth. There's no way she would be a hundred percent okay with my parents banishing me from the home.'

'Sometimes you have to do something big, make a sacrifice, to keep hold of those close to you. You only get one shot. My cells were no match for my sister's bone marrow, to try and cure her blood cancer.'

'You're right, Alain. I'm really sorry. There's so much more at stake with siblings than friends and lovers somehow. Is there anything you could do for your sister that would help?' Rachel asked Daniel.

'Well the thing she wants most of all is a baby. But I guess that will pass with age. I'm sure it will right itself in the end. One day soon.'

Rachel drew in a breath. Daniel bit his lip; he'd spoken before he'd even thought about the consequences of that statement.

'Oh God, that was thoughtless of me. I'm so sorry,' he said.

Rachel placed the back of her hand against her chest, fingers curled outwards, as though scooping out a hollowness there.

'Please, don't worry. I don't think anything can shock me after the weirdness of the past couple of weeks. Months. Years. I'm a grown-up now. Time to move on.' Rachel paused. 'What decision do you regret most in your life, Daniel? Apart from swerving around that bird in the road, of course,' she said.

'Probably telling my family that I'd intended to take my life.'

Daniel sipped his Bloody Mary. He'd only managed to grab a soggy sausage roll at King's Cross and hoped the tomato juice would help soak up the alcohol. He was determined to stick to one drink. He hadn't ended up buying the first round for everyone; they were probably thinking he was a fraud.

'It was stupid in retrospect,' he continued. 'If I'd kept quiet, torn up the note, perhaps phoned in sick and gone back to bed to sleep it off, things would have been very different. I'm lucky my mother still talks to me; I guess that's what parents do, love their children unconditionally. But I feel like I've lost my sister's friendship and respect for ever.'

Rachel bit her lip, perhaps thinking about Alain's sister. Daniel watched her take a sip of her drink, a pensive look on her face.

'What was that pivotal moment then, the one that made you change your mind?' Her voice lowered until, 'What happened?' came out in barely a whisper.

'I have the postman to thank that I'm still here,' Daniel said. 'An invitation to a birthday party from one of Jasper's school pals. I was coming down the stairs, remember the moment so clearly. It clattered through the letter box with the other bills and junk mail. I had my hand on the newel post, almost ignored it. But this handwritten yellow envelope was sticking out from the pile. I was curious, couldn't leave it unopened. Jasper had been invited to a cricket afternoon.'

Daniel leaned forward on his stool smiling to himself, only now realising Jasper hadn't berated him for opening his mail.

'Do you know anything about cricket?' he asked.

'A little. Not really,' said Rachel, with an uncertainty that made it sound like she was expected to know all the rules.

Alain rolled his eyes and shook his head.

'We'd been practising his spin bowling up to the end of last summer, and I knew I couldn't let him go to that party without first perfecting the swerve ball I'd seen him deliver several times in the back garden. I suddenly wanted more than anything to make sure his opponent's wicket would be the first one to fall. So despite my precise list and my obsessively charted plans, I never actually made it to the viaduct that day.'

Rachel put a hand to her mouth, her eyes round. Although this dark-haired, mascara-eyed goth looked nothing like her, he was suddenly reminded of Sarah. He swallowed the tightness in his throat with the dregs of his Bloody Mary.

'Whoa. I thought you were planning to take pills or something. You were going to *jump*?' Olive hadn't spoken for a while, but she was fully committed to any drama. 'I remember a boy in my teens who jumped off a train bridge in Stevenage,' she said. 'When they told us, all I could think was, what was he thinking before he walked to the bridge and jumped? I mean, he'd made that decision, but had to go through all these motions before he actually carried it out. That takes some flipping guts.'

'He might have made a list. At least, made one in his head.'

Rachel frowned at Daniel. 'A list?'

'My mother was always making lists when I was a boy. We all thought she had a problem with her memory. Shopping lists, laundry lists, lists for which medication to take on which day. I think there's now a list to remind her which list to look at.'

Rachel laughed. Daniel thought about his gentle, patient mother, grateful for her support. He smiled, remembering her call right before they'd gone into the pub. His obsessively organised mind had gone through an orderly list of the places Emma's rabbit might be.

'So it seemed natural for me to make a list,' he continued. 'There's a satisfaction, ticking off tasks you've completed. It removes the unpredictability, sets the goals in concrete. Each item on this list, though, had to be struck off in exactly the right order. Like the instructions for a piece of IKEA flat pack furniture. It could be inherited, if I think of my mother.'

They'd finished their drinks and were preparing to leave, putting away phones, pulling on jackets and sweaters.

'Look at us! Putting the world to rights in the pub. It makes our efforts in the therapy group seem so constipated,' said Rachel.

'Perhaps because it's for the study she is doing,' said Alain. 'I don't really want anything I say to be written in a report.'

'Trudy's been good to me,' said Rachel. 'I don't think she would misuse anything we say. Although she doesn't seem quite herself, which would make it hard to talk in that place. She seems a bit stressed out at the minute.'

'I saw her in town with her baby last weekend when my daughter Emma and I were shopping for a new pair of shoes. I was on the verge of going over to say hello but she seemed so harassed.' Daniel had caught a glimpse. The baby had reminded him of Jasper when he was an infant. 'From where we stood, we could hear the baby screaming in the stroller. I didn't say anything to Emma in the end, despite knowing she'd love to have seen the little thing. In the end, we walked away to avoid contact. I hate to hear babies crying. He seems quite old to be so distressed.' Daniel cleared his throat. He hadn't expected to talk so much about his children, wasn't sure he'd wanted to share that much information with these relative strangers. 'Well, I must be off. Early start,' he said, though it would be no earlier than usual.

He had a sudden desire to check on the children. As they left the pub, he felt good about having instigated the get-together. It might not happen again, but perhaps it had released something in each of them. Made it easier for them at the next meeting.

When Daniel arrived home, he hugged his mother and sent her on her way.

'You can always ask me to babysit for any event, Daniel. It doesn't just have to be for a drink after the session. You should start going out more. I'm only down the lane. It'd do you good to have a social outing every now and then. The children... they know you're allowed to go out. They're too young to understand what you're going through.'

'I know, thanks. I might take you up on that soon. We're all so lucky to have you.'

'Oh... you,' she said, and ruffled Daniel's hair. 'By the way I started a new shopping list. You only have a pint of milk left in the fridge. I'm not sure that'll be enough for the children's breakfast cereal, so go easy on the cappuccino in the morning.'

'Thanks so much. See you tomorrow.'

After his mother had gone, he went up to check on them. First Jasper, who was lying on his stomach, one leg hanging out of the side of the bed. He'd taken his pyjamas off again. His grandmother always made sure he wore them while he brushed his teeth and said goodnight to her. But Daniel knew that as soon as the bedroom door was closed, Jasper took them off and stuffed them down the side of his bed. Daniel understood something about waking up in the middle of the night feeling the weight of the world on your chest and wanting to rip anything away that threatened to suffocate you. He kissed the top of his son's head.

Then he went in to Emma. In contrast she was tucked tightly under her unicorn duvet with the cover pulled up under her chin. Her nightie-clad arms were crossed over her chest, the velveteen rabbit squeezed into her elbow, her fists tucked into her neck. The corpse pose. One of the positions he'd learned on his yoga courses. This one resembled a sava-shove-something-or-other, a position of intense relaxation. He kissed her on her forehead and turned out the bedside light. The nightlight in the corner came on automatically, the LED glow going through the colours of the rainbow as he left the room.

As he stood in the hallway, Daniel's heart swelled. They'd had no idea of his plans that day back then, but he vowed he'd never consider leaving them again.

He went back downstairs, crossed the restored Victorian tiles of the hallway, stepping only on the black ones on the balls of his socked feet, and headed to the drinks globe that Sarah had bought him for his fortieth in the main living room. He poured himself a balloon glass of armagnac and carried it to the kitchen. He put the glass on the island and pressed the button on the ice machine, imagining his father shouting 'sacrilege!' It spat out several cubes at once, directly into his hand. The pressure at which they shot out of the dispenser could have broken the delicate snifter. One cube missed his palm and skittered across the kitchen floor. He stared at it and in defiance left it, knowing his socked foot would probably step in the puddle later.

He sat on one of the swivel bar stools at the kitchen island and pulled open a drawer to his left. He took out the well-handled list. He hadn't looked at it for a few weeks. He unfolded it and smoothed it onto the polished granite surface.

He was once again transported back to that morning.

He'd woken up late. Hadn't set the alarm. Checked the clock with a sigh, knowing on any other day he would be at work by then. On a normal morning, he would have driven past the entrance to the Roman baths, under the A1 flyover, into Sherrardswood School where he would drop Jasper and Emma for preschool breakfast club and then driven past the Digswell viaduct to Welwyn North station. He would have taken the 7:18 into London, rumbling out over the top of that viaduct. Depending on the state of the tube and the DLR, he would be at his shiny desk in his gleaming office on Canary Wharf by 8:30am.

But not that day. It had been well beyond 8:30am by the time he woke that morning. He'd felt strangely calm, knowing everything had been put in place. His mother would have driven the kids to school from where they were staying with her. She was the one who would have suffered the fallout.

He smoothed the list with his hand and made himself read it again. It was like a penance. But also a grateful ritual now that he was still here. And it felt good telling the others about it in the pub earlier in the evening, even if he wasn't sure it would have conjured any sympathy.

Sleep late ✓
Shower ✓
Dress – best suit ✓
Put kids' laundry away ✓
Collect post ✓
Kettle on ✓
A good strong brew ✓
Skim the morning paper ✓
Weetabix ✓
Open the mail
Leave instructions for outstanding bills
Wash the dishes
Make the bed
Brush teeth
Lock the door
Key under pot
Walk to Digswell Viaduct
Jump

34

TRUDY

Four weeks ago

T he sun was shining through a crack in the curtains when I awoke. A slice of bright yellow dazzled off the duvet. The promise of a summer's day. For just a moment, I was carefree, rested, content. I felt positive about the progress the group was making and was looking forward to writing up my notes. I'd ideally like to have gone to the clinic, to have access to my main computer and my files.

And then I remembered Benny and my mood plummeted. He was now my prime responsibility. Although I'd be receiving a stipend for the study I was doing, I was still only on part-time maternity leave, and possible publication of the paper was still months away. Benny should have been my priority.

I turned my head from the window. Harry's side of the bed was empty. I luxuriated in this blissful moment of silence. He'd already left for work and Benny was still sleeping. But as though that thought somehow had an opposing kinetic connection to my son's brain, a series of little choking sobs emanated from his room. My stomach clenched at the idea of dragging myself from the comfort. I wanted to stay in that moment, in that ray of sunshine, listening to the pigeons cooing in the trees in the garden.

But the sun was reminding me there'd been positive moments. Between feeding and the subsequent crying, I had slept relatively well for at least three solid hours the previous night. I'd taken to going out for a walk before bedtime. It helped to clear my head.

Benny was usually still asleep when I arrived home, which meant Harry often was too. Slipping quietly between the cool sheets on my side of the bed and then tucking myself into Harry's back and drifting off to sleep was a small luxury. He always whispered a sleepy 'goodnight' or reached round to pat my hip. As long as he was still doing these little gestures, it was clear he didn't mind, and I often whispered a quiet 'I love you' to emphasise my gratitude. Everything could almost be classed as normal when Benny wasn't crying.

Then I was up sometimes three or four times in the night to attend to Benny. His incessant wailing was starting to blend into a tinnitus in my head. It wasn't that I was becoming indifferent to it exactly, it was just becoming the norm. I'd run out of energy to be anxious.

I stretched my legs and threw back the duvet, ready to face my baby. I called my mum while Benny was feeding, and she agreed to look after him while I popped into work at Pinehill to organise my notes. She lived in the next village en route to the clinic.

Benny had already started fussing again when I put him in the baby seat in the back of the car. I hoped he'd go back to sleep so at least my mother could have half an hour of calm with him. The cows were being led back to the field from the farm after milking, which meant we were stationary in the car for several minutes. I drummed the steering wheel with my fingers. Benny inevitably started to cry without the soporific movement of the car.

'Please, please, Benny. Not now. We want Oma to enjoy this so she can look after you more often.'

My knuckles squeezed the steering wheel. My mind was full of hoping Benny would sleep or at least calm down. As I rounded the corner before heading up Parsonage Lane to my parents' house, a huge brown bird swooped across my line of vision. It flew close enough to the windscreen for me to make out its hooked beak and a mean yellow eye. It brought to mind Daniel's Sarah and all my senses returned to the road instead of thinking about how to quieten Benny. That had been a near miss. It must have been a sign.

After repeating, 'I'm sorry, Benny, I'm sorry, Benny,' under my breath, I started singing a lullaby, my throat cramping and my voice croaky with unshed tears.

The narrow lane opened up to the village of Preston and my parents' cottage came into view. I parked on the driveway and carried the car seat into the hallway when my mother opened the door. Benny gave her a big smile.

'*Hallo, mein Schatz*,' she said.

He smiled back, and shook his arms up and down, delighted to see her. Why did I ever doubt my gorgeous boy?

'Are you okay, *Liebling*? You look tired,' said Mutti, touching my cheek.

'He's still crying a lot. Do you think I should take him back to the paediatrician? The doctor said he would grow out of it, but it seems to me his discomfort isn't getting any better. And it's happening during the day now too.'

'Some babies just cry a lot. I've forgotten now, but I think you were also a bit *anstrengend*.' She used the German word for fussy; it carried heavier weight, more like *stressful*.

I knew how that felt.

'Perhaps these digestion problems are inherited,' Mutti continued. 'It will go away, I promise. Colic is horrible, but doesn't last forever, and if the doctor says it's normal... well, don't go bothering him.'

Driving to the clinic, I thought about talking to one of my colleagues about the issues I'd been having about Benny. As I parked the car, I put it from my mind as there were only a couple of hours to get my work done, and right now that was the thing that was keeping me sane.

In the end, it was a good day. I successfully typed up everyone's notes at the clinic and managed to read through a couple of cases similar to Olive's. We still hadn't got to the core of that girl's problems; there were issues to deal with her destructive self-image. I made a note to contact the refuge and recommend further sessions with her.

Back at home, by the time Harry came in from work I'd managed to tidy up and prepare a decent home-cooked meal from scratch. Benny kicked and giggled in the baby bouncer on the floor while we both successfully ate and finished our meals. He fed well after dinner, some from me, some from the bottle, and dropped off to sleep. I calculated there'd be a couple of hours before he woke with the first of the night's cramps, but I didn't feel like going to bed, so Harry and I sat together on the couch and watched television.

I wasn't paying attention, knowing when *Look East* had finished we'd switch to a David Attenborough programme we'd promised to watch together on playback.

'Wait, Trude, isn't that the council bloke who approved the funding for your project?'

I glanced at the screen, but the face faded before I had a chance to focus. The image was replaced by a reporter standing in front of a large country house set in a beautiful garden with a pristine lawn. A fire engine and a police car were parked in the driveway, and a wisp of smoke curled up from the roof tiles on one corner. A maroon-coloured Bentley was parked in front of the house, its number plate fuzzed out, which meant the news report was not live but had probably been on a loop since earlier in the day.

'Turn it up!' I said.

As we listened to the reporter, my mouth hung open and my breath stuck in my throat.

'*Kenneth Harper MBE, North Herts council member and philanthropist, was found burned in his bed in the early hours of this morning at his five-million-pound home in Gosmore, on the outskirts of Hitchin. Mr Harper, a long-standing member of the council, was renowned for his generous financial donations to keep the local football club from bankruptcy. He was also the main investor in the renovations to the swimming centre.*

'*The fire appears to have started on the upper floor of the family home where the master bedroom is located. By the time rescue services could access the room, Mr Harper could not be resuscitated. It is not yet known how the fire started. It has been suggested an electrical fault may be to blame.*

'*Mr Harper's wife returned this morning from where she was spending a long weekend with a friend at Champneys Spa. Apart from telling journalists her husband was not a smoker, she has not been available for comment. Mr Harper also leaves behind two sons, Timothy and James, who are returning from their respective universities to be with their mother today.*'

'Bloody hell!' I gasped.

The reporter went on to talk in more detail about the many benevolent gestures the councilman had undertaken. The football club, the swimming centre, the school projects, the charities.

'What a horrible way to die,' said Harry.

I recalled the utter horror when I discovered he was Rachel's rapist. It made my heart race with anger that I'd voted for that monster in the last council elections. Everyone considered he was a saint. To think I'd admired him for what he'd done for our community. Keeping the town alive with his golden funds. Getting everyone to admire him for his altruism and generosity. The excitement I felt having been chosen to lead this study for the NHS charity. And now knowing he'd been contributing to something that he was the cause of in the first place. He'd been effectively paying my salary. Until now.

So I had to curb the *'Bastard deserves it for what he did'* and pressed my lips together. There was something karmic about this.

Had Rachel seen the news? She'd once told me that she didn't watch much TV, was more of a reader. But she might have seen an article in a newspaper. This would certainly make front page of *The Comet* the next day.

This couldn't wait until the next group session. I checked my watch. It was way too late now to be calling the refuge. I'd have to go in the morning. It was important to know if Rachel was okay.

35

Present day

The aroma of garden flowers and freshly-mown hay is now a distant memory. It's been replaced with the artificial smell of fake leather and the moulded plastic of the interior of a vehicle, and something slightly unpleasant, stale urine perhaps. Although Benny hasn't been fussing, they check their watch. It's well beyond the time to feed and change the baby.

Until now Benny seems to have been content in a state of half-sleep, eyes occasionally widening at passing street signs and bright shop front signage. But knowing this baby is a difficult one, who knows how long the peace will last? Important to keep him calm for the journey at least.

When they climb out of the vehicle, a cool evening breeze ruffles Benny's fine hair, and his forehead wrinkles. He seems to become more alert and studies his surroundings in the fading light. The person holding the baby carrier doesn't linger on this otherwise endearing expression, must not allow any emotion to divert attention from the task.

Benny's body tenses as he is lifted from the carrier. He has to be held firm to avoid him squirming out of their hold. They press the shell of the baby's ear against their chest, hoping he'll pick up a heartbeat, enough to comfort him, perhaps with the instinctual memory of the constant concert that kept him calm and content within the amniotic fluid of his prenatal home.

Benny hums in delight when the teat of a bottle is worked between his lips. He drinks hungrily, stopping only briefly at the beginning. They figure the baby is registering the bottle's cooler than normal contents. Ultimately, he's hungry enough to refrain from complaint. After the baby has finished most of the bottle, they lay him down on a weather-beaten wooden park bench covered in a fleece blanket and take off his soiled nappy.

Benny's eyes open in brief surprise as a chill breeze puckers the skin around his exposed midriff. They put on a clean nappy, fasten tapes, tear them off, loosen them a little, and refasten them.

Benny's body is folded and forced back into the baby carrier, his limbs fed through loops, straps placed over his head. Benny arches his back with a frustrated grunt.

'No, no, no, young man, you just keep calm,' says a voice, and the fight momentarily ceases. Benny is pushed back into the seat with the palm of a hand, and gives up the struggling completely when the click-clack of the belt mechanism echoes against the fence at their side.

The door of the vehicle closes, and the muffled sounds in the restricted environment makes Benny look around him. Different smells this time, some familiar, some new. Baby lotion, some kind of cleaning fluid with ammonia, a sweetness from a cheap air freshener that might trigger a future longing on his infant tongue. The engine of the vehicle rumbles into life and the gentle vibration of movement sends Benny back into slumber.

Thank Christ for that, they think.

36

OLIVE

Three weeks ago

O live had done something bad. She crept back into the refuge, making sure she didn't disturb the service manager sitting in the communal lounge who appeared to be taking a nap. Olive had told her earlier that she wasn't going out today. She didn't want the manager to have cause to ask her any questions.

She sneaked upstairs to her room. She closed the door quietly and put her chair against it, tucking the back under the door handle. Even if it didn't stop anyone bursting in, the confusion would give her a little extra time to hide her stuff.

She sat on the bed and pulled out the packet of safety razor blades she'd shoplifted from Lloyds Pharmacy on Bancroft, turned the box over and over in her palm. She had intended to get Stanley blades from Brookers, but thought she'd look less suspicious in a chemist's rather than the building supply shop.

It was a while since she'd nicked anything, and she'd forgotten the satisfaction of not getting caught. She now wished she'd pocketed some chocolate too. She could have swiped some of that diabetic stuff on the shelf behind her in the chemist's.

She started to tremble with the anticipation. It was the same feeling she used to get hearing the tick-tick of the vodka bottle top splitting from its seal as she unscrewed the cap and took her first swig.

She took off her sweat pants, folded them and placed them on the end of the bed. Taking a tissue from the box on her bedside table, she flattened the square of soft paper next to her on the blanket. She took out a blade from the packet in the box and placed it on the tissue. Her thighs were pale and a little blotchy. She took a deep breath and her body calmed, relishing what was to come. This was her secret world, the place where she could let the negativity out. The pain was like a sweet song, an outpouring of anything bad that festered in her soul. It was like her new best friend.

It seemed that Trudy never really understood the reason why Olive kept going back to *him*, when he would inevitably beat her again. She didn't understand that they were the perfect fit, at least for a while. He couldn't beat his own wife. If he did that, she would undoubtedly leave him. There was a familiar need in him, too. This release. This addiction. A sweet, satisfying violence. It wasn't the memory of his fists on her cheek that kept her away. In the end it was the hurtful words. Yes, the pain was always a release. It was still a release. And this type of pain was better because she was in control.

She no longer cut her arms. She was now cutting the soft area on her inner thigh. So far only the left leg. Those six or seven lines were now faint white threads like the ones on her arms. She hadn't felt the need for a couple of weeks. But now her canvas was crying out for new strokes.

She was proud of the care she took to keep the lines parallel on her arms. It was a work of art. The skill was especially noticeable on her right arm, seeing as she had to use her left hand. People could be cruel, asking her what she'd done to ruin her body. It wasn't ruined. It was enhanced. Why hadn't they shown such anger when *he* decorated her face with purple and yellow and red? They'd only ever shown disgust.

She had control over this. Over herself. Over her body. These scars were more beautiful than any tattoo she'd ever seen. Even Rachel's. All that black. The poison of the ink. It wasn't pure.

She'd never dreamed when she'd started that these scars would turn out to be so white, so pure.

As the blade sliced a fraction of a millimetre into her skin, she thought of Rachel. Tried to mentally channel some love and positivity. Olive was worried she was hiding something. She'd certainly become withdrawn since her new friendship with that skinny bitch arrived.

She was a clever one, that Rachel. Although she talked like she came from the gutter, like Olive, she actually had a head on her shoulders. There was a bunch of certificates in a drawer in her room that Olive had seen, although Rachel didn't know she'd been through her stuff. One was for a prize in science, one was a merit in something called visual literacy. Rachel wouldn't have got great marks in English for the kind of stuff that came out of her mouth now, but Olive was sure that was all part of a tough mask to give the impression that she was doing all right.

Rachel needed something. It wasn't retribution, and it wasn't justice. She was pining for something she could no longer have. And that Martha girl wasn't going to get it for her.

As for herself, Olive. Well, she hadn't got a fucking clue. It had been a few weeks since she lost her fifth job in as many months and wasn't quite sure what was left for her to do. At least she had this.

Olive ran the blade laterally along the inside of her thigh, trying to maintain the exact same depth, singing along the sensory receptors in her skin. A clear fluid rose first, the plasma, and where she'd gone a little deeper, the first tiny crimson swell of blood. She raised the blade when she'd cut a three-inch line. She wiped the blade on the tissue and was about to start a second one when she heard Rachel's name being called from the hallway downstairs.

Footfalls along the corridor outside her door caused the handle to clunk against the back of the chair. Olive wrapped the blade in the tissue, shoved it into the drawer beside her bed and quickly pulled on her jeans, sucking in her breath when the denim rubbed against the wound on her thigh.

She moved the chair and opened the door a crack. She recognised Trudy's voice. Their exchange was whispered, although there was a low urgency in Trudy's voice. Olive moved quietly to the top of the bannister, leant over, tucked her hair behind her ear, strained to listen.

Fuck.

They were talking about *him*.

37

RACHEL

Three weeks ago

Rachel vaguely heard the front door buzzer on Friday morning while she was sitting on Mouse's bed, listening to a playlist with her on Spotify through a pair of shared headphones. She recognised Trudy's voice in the hallway with her free ear. She must have been there to talk to Mouse.

It was how Rachel first met Trudy. The service managers made sure all the women who came to the refuge had a psychological assessment, even if they didn't need individual counselling. And Rachel had already assured Mouse that Trudy would be the perfect person to talk to.

But it was soon apparent that Trudy wasn't here to see Mouse. She was here to see her. The woman who let her in called up the stairs to her from the hallway, and Rachel frowned. She wondered if it was about her breakdown in the ladies' loo a couple of weeks back at the group meeting. Perhaps Trudy would suggest resuming their one-on-ones. Rachel didn't want that. It would feel like going backwards. She wanted to stop dragging out all the memories and laying them bare on the floorboards. She was ready to move on now.

And then she recalled the article in the news. Trudy might be here to talk to her about Kenneth Cock Harper.

She walked down the stairs reluctantly, but flashed a friendly smile.

'Hi, Trudy. How's it going?' she asked, indicating the way to the kitchen, knowing Trudy would follow her.

'Did you see the news?' Trudy asked.

'I saw the paper,' Rachel said carefully. 'Tea? Coffee? I'm afraid we only have instant.'

She wasn't sure she was ready to make eye contact with Trudy just yet. She hadn't expected her to show up for that. She'd expected she would pull her to one side after the next group session the following week. Rachel hadn't had time to process how she felt or what she should have said about the news.

'I'll have tea. Builder's, with a splash of milk if you have any,' Trudy replied.

Rachel reached into the cupboard for two cups. She picked two teabags from the caddy on the counter and the top snapped closed.

'I need to talk to you about Kenneth Harper,' said Trudy.

Rachel wanted to ask "Who?" but knew Trudy wasn't that stupid. 'What about him?' she asked instead.

'You know, I know,' continued Trudy. 'I worked it out. He's the one.'

Rachel pressed her lips together. She was stupid to have given it away.

'I wanted to make sure you were okay. How do you feel now that he's dead?' Trudy asked.

Rachel swallowed. She still wasn't sure, except that she'd recently been thinking of a far stronger profanity than 'cock' for his fantasy middle name. Another C-word.

'It was an accident, wasn't it?' Rachel asked, looking at her for the first time.

Trudy raised her eyebrows.

'They haven't confirmed it. But I can't imagine it's anything different. They said they hadn't ruled out an electrical fault of some kind.'

'I don't know how I feel, Trudy. There's certainly something karmic about it.'

Rachel didn't tell her that she'd read the article more than once. That his wife said he didn't smoke. That when she closed her eyes and recalled the scene outside the pub all those years ago, she could smell beer and something meaty on his breath. And nicotine on his fingers. Trudy touched her arm.

'Listen, Rachel, I know you didn't want to go to the police with the identity of your rapist, and I understand now. I understand your reluctance. But once you've accepted he's gone, you should think about it.'

'Why? Why now?'

Rachel's heartbeat spiked. Surely justice had been done. Trudy knew she didn't want her whole sorry history dragged out and exposed, even if there was no court case. She thought this was actually quite intrusive. Should she ask her to leave now?

'I'm worried there might be others out there. Victims who might still need help.'

Rachel shrugged, didn't trust herself to speak at that point. She guessed anger was better than fear. At least she didn't need to fear *him* again.

'There may be girls just like you. Girls who feared the same outcome you did. Disbelief from a population who would rather roll in the riches of that man's generosity. Girls who've never had the chance to talk with a psychotherapist about what happened to them. They should have that opportunity now. Given the chance to voice their grievances, their anxiety, their trauma. You're strong, I believe you would be strong enough for this. If the police are informed, then maybe they can make a sensitive appeal. Since I guessed, I've wondered whether others might need help. But now the perpetrator is out of the way, perhaps these girls or women won't feel so intimidated about coming forward for help.'

Rachel shrugged again.

'Are you going to be all right? I'm sorry. Have I overstepped the mark?'

'No, I'll be fine. I just haven't really had a chance to absorb it all. I know I should be... relieved. But what's done is done. It can't be undone. If there's anyone else, maybe they would only think that too. Let it go. I just want to move on.'

'I know, Rachel. I'm so sorry. I guess I felt strongly about this. Knowing what I know. Would you be okay if I went to a police colleague of mine and at least asked her about the possibilities, the protocol in this situation? I won't mention your name.'

'I guess...'

Trudy patted her arm. At odds with the words she had just spoken, it wasn't the first time in the past few weeks Rachel had the strangest feeling that Trudy was the more anxious of the two of them. Why would she be so insistent on wanting to expose him now?

38

OLIVE

Three weeks ago

O f all the unbelievable coincidences, Olive would never in a million years have put two and two together and figured it was Ken who raped Rachel back when she was seventeen. That fucking bastard! In the years between he must have developed his habit of beating his lovers to get his kicks. Rachel had never mentioned she was subjected to any physical abuse aside from the actual sex.

Olive remembered the night she first met Ken in a pub in Luton. They'd shagged in the corridor beyond the door to the men's loos, behind a stack of old beer barrels. She'd been about to say no. Truth be told, one of her mates had bought her a Bacardi and coke, a rare generosity, and she didn't want the drink to go flat. But they'd ended up making it a quickie. Ken had seemed surprised she was so consenting, but they were both gagging for it. It was as though he'd expected her to be an unwilling participant. Perhaps that was it. He hadn't started the violence until she'd invited him back to her grotty flat for the first time the following week and by then she'd been reeled in. He'd wanted her to refuse him. He'd actually said to her, 'Tell me you don't want me.' Now she understood.

Shit. Poor Rachel. She wondered whether there were others. And if it hadn't been for Olive, how many others there might have been.

When Rachel showed Trudy out of the refuge, she turned to come up the stairs. Rachel appeared to concentrate on each step as she slowly ascended, preoccupied. She didn't seem to see or hear Olive sneak back to her room. Olive turned quickly and watched her through the crack in her door. She held the door firm, hoping Rachel would knock, ask if she'd got time, needing someone to talk to. Olive would tell her, then. They'd have something in common, a grievance to share. Like warm bread from the oven, this thing would comfort them. Would bring them even closer together.

But Rachel didn't stop at Olive's door. She walked down the hallway and Olive had to open the crack a little wider to see where she was going. Rachel stopped outside the skinny bitch's door.

Rachel held the door frame on each side with her hands as though the house would collapse if she let go. She leaned her forehead against the door of the girl's room.

Bile rose in Olive's throat. She swallowed and swallowed again so she didn't have to run down the hallway past Rachel to the toilet.

'Mouse, are you there? Can I talk to you?' Rachel asked softly. *Mouse?*

As the door opened and the ghostly girl let Rachel into her room, Olive's determination kicked in. She had to do something to earn Rachel's love and respect. It was time to show Rachel that *she* was the one who could save her. Olive was the one who would make everything right, would still do anything to help Rachel, to make her better. Olive could give her what she wanted deep down inside. Olive had no idea why Rachel had suddenly teamed up with the new girl, but it wouldn't matter after this. Their shared history.

Ken Harper might be dead. He might no longer have been a threat in either of their lives. But someone needed to know what he'd done. The type of man he was. He couldn't get away with simply fucking *dying*.

Olive pulled on her shoes and jacket. A tiny dark stain had seeped through the bleached denim on her thigh. She needed to be careful later when she was peeling off her jeans. Ripping a scab could ruin the subtle art of forming a scar.

Olive tiptoed down the stairs and out of the door. It was a fair distance into the town centre, so she picked up her pace, knowing Brookers might close soon. She had a fiver in her pocket from cashing a bribe with one of the girls who'd tried to sneak in drunk. An assurance of silence.

She walked from Oughton across Butts Close, where she'd once honoured its name with a gypsy from the annual fair. She continued down the hill into town, through the Arcade, past the charity shops, the offy and the Corn Exchange.

She pushed open the door of Brookers. It had a little old-fashioned bell that rang above the wooden frame. Not many customers today. There was a rumour it would close soon due to lack of business. The massive B&Q was sucking away its customers. She was aware the shop manager in his grey shop overalls would be sitting behind the desk in his little office, looking up occasionally through a one-way mirror. If someone needed help or wanted to pay for something, they would go to the front desk and he'd miraculously appear from behind the silvered window. She knew she was being observed. She wandered down the car maintenance aisle. Picked a smelly pine-tree shaped freshener with her left hand and sniffed it. Put it back. Chose another. At the same time her right hand reached for an aerosol can with a white plastic lid matching the colour of the paint inside and she slipped it into the deep pocket of her jacket while she sniffed another sunshine-shaped, lemon-smelling freshener, nodded to herself and took it to the counter.

She paid for the car freshener, 95p, and left the store, turned along Bucklersbury and began the two-mile walk to Gosmore.

To Kenneth Harper's fucking country mansion.

39

TRUDY

Present day

The faces in front of me double and merge like a multiple ocean swell. The police conference room is hot and bright. As we wait for the news appeal to begin, a high-pitched ringing in my ears warns me I might pass out. Benny has officially been missing for almost twenty-four hours.

A monotonous murmur of voices accompanies the sound of shifting bodies and the soft clack of extra lighting equipment being moved into the room. Why so many people? And on a Sunday? In the centre on a tripod is a large camera, its deep black eye ready to capture my tortured expression and words.

I sway on my feet and my calves push the chair backwards. It honks on the linoleum as I sit down heavily, my thighs digging into the rim of the hard seat. Every head turns towards me; reporters, journalists and police staff momentarily silenced by the sound. I've done the one thing I hadn't wanted to do until it became necessary – drawn attention to myself.

Harry sits down next to me, leans over, puts his hand on my knee.

'Are you okay, love?' His voice is fuzzy.

I swallow, but the pebble in my throat doesn't shift.

'I think I'm going to faint.'

'Trude, you need to be strong. Benny needs you to be strong.'

At the mention of my baby, the pebble grows bigger, pushing a wad of cold sorrow up the back of my head and filling my eyes with tears. I press my lips together, determined not to lose control.

I try to concentrate on the minutiae, the thing I'm always telling my patients to do. I think of DS Flatman recommending waterproof mascara. A tender, but peculiar piece of advice from such a burly man. That tube of mascara in my bag is the first thought I can grab, a line to a dubious mental lifeboat. I cling on to other things in the mush of my brain to avoid thinking about the crowd in the room. The hiss of the bottle as Harry pours me a glass of mineral water, the shape of the microphones, like two Liquorice Allsorts on the table in front of us. And I remember something clearly – the velvet muzzle of my favourite old grey mare at the farm on Saturday, her whiskers against Benny's fingers making him giggle with delight.

The last time I held my baby in my arms.

A rapid-fire click and whir of a camera draws me away from my guilt, bringing my focus back to the people in the room. How wretched will I look in print or on the screen? I recognise nobody, but as I look from one face to another, they morph into the members of my group therapy.

I think of what they've been through, those long-suffering former patients of mine. I recall the fragments of memories they've shared, fitting together like pieces of a puzzle to help them collectively address their individual issues. Each of them recognising and accepting the traumas they've experienced and moving on from them. Or not.

Sitting here, waiting to talk to the world about my baby, I remember writing the names of the group down in DS Flatman's notebook. They are now burning into my mind.

Rachel Headley

Olive Stanton

Daniel Lockyear

Alain Favre

Could any of them have been capable of abducting my baby?

40

ALAIN

Three weeks ago

Since the fire, Alain had been staying with a guy called Ron who he'd met when he and Annie first moved to Hertfordshire. Ron ran a recording studio, and had allowed Alain to sleep in his storage room at the back of the building. Annie had originally hoped Ron would record some pieces she'd written, but Ron said he didn't do classical on principle. He thought he'd be some big shot record producer one day and wanted to stick with the weird and terrible synthesised music he was a fan of. He and Alain had hit it off when they talked about the winter runs in Leysin where Ron had been on a ski week.

It was Friday morning and Alain was woken by the sound of banging on the roll-up door out front and voices. Ron opened the door of the storeroom where Alain sat up in his sleeping bag on a camping mattress in the corner.

'Al, mate, afraid you've got company,' said Ron as Alain rubbed the sleep from his eyes.

'Afraid?' asked Alain, confused.

He looked at his watch. He'd slept late. He cleared dusty phlegm from his throat.

'Cops,' hissed Ron. 'I don't want them poking their noses around here – get them out of here, mate.'

Alain's heart thumped. He thought he'd get a letter by post from the solicitors dealing with the fire inquiry at the flat. He didn't think they'd come here in person. Before he could grab a tee-shirt, two of them wandered through to the storeroom. They glanced at his makeshift bed. Their eyes scanned the room and Alain's sleeping corner, the mess of magazines, album covers, old *NME* newspapers and an array of fast-food packaging.

'Morning. Mr Favre?'

Alain nodded.

'We'd like to ask you a few questions,' said the male cop.

Alain shook his head, confused. He ran his palm down his chest, realised it was bare. Good job he had his jeans on. He caught the female cop looking at his tattoo.

'Are you arresting me?' They didn't seem to be treating him as though he was a criminal, but he remained guarded. 'What is this about? Why do you need my answers?'

When he saw the cop clench his jaw and impatience spark in his eyes, he held up his hand. 'Okay, okay. Look, I have no idea what's going on. Is this about the fire? In my flat?'

The two cops looked at each other.

'Best we talk in the car, Mr Favre, more private,' said the man.

'Let me grab a tee-shirt,' he said, as he took the first one from a pile of clothes on a box in the corner.

He combed his hair with his fingers and tucked his tee-shirt into his jeans as he walked through the studio. Ron was sitting at a mixing board with one side of his headphones hanging off his ear. He was pretending to twist buttons, eyes downcast, but kept darting looks in the cops' direction.

After taking a piss in the toilet, Alain climbed into the back of the car while the female cop held the door open for him and then sat beside him when he'd shuffled over.

'There was a fire last night. Suspected arson. We're speaking to everyone on our records who's been nicked, or suspected of arson.'

'But the fire in my flat. It wasn't arson.' Alain's voice took on a pleading tone.

'This is an elimination process, if you like, for another case. Look, we'll do a quick interview with you, on tape at the station, ask a few questions, then type up a statement for you to sign.'

Alain remembered the police station from having to give a statement after the flat fire. He didn't want to go back, had a bad feeling about that building, but figured he'd better comply. He had nothing better to do that day anyway, and he might get a cup of coffee out of them while he was there.

As they drove off, he wondered if he should call Trudy, although he wasn't sure what she could say to help.

They pulled up to the ugly seventies concrete and black glass block on College Road. Alain followed them into the building. For a relatively small town, there seemed to be an unusual amount of activity around the front desk. Before he registered what was happening, the barrel of a camera lens was thrust in front of him and fired a series of shots with a frantic whirring and clicking. He brought up his arm in automatic self-defence and realised a second afterwards that it looked as though he was trying to hide something.

'Enough of that, Bishop,' shouted the cop who'd driven him here. 'This is not an arrest!' He turned away and muttered, 'Bloody reporters.'

Alarm bells began to ring in Alain's mind.

'This way, Monsieur Favre,' said the female cop.

Alain smiled at her for using the French form of address. The cop blushed under his stare and he hoped this would register in his favour. He was taken to a room that said 'Interview 2' on the door, and nervousness made his heart thump.

The female cop left the room, and he realised his one police ally might have fled the scene never to return. Instead the uniformed cop and a man in a regular suit sat on the other side of the table. Alain took the spare chair on his side.

The suit rose slightly, pushing the tails of his jacket out from his seat so they didn't crease. It was cool in the room and Alain wished he'd brought a sweatshirt. The uniformed cop, his driver, flicked the button on a recorder at the end of the table, and Alain was reminded of a chess competition he'd once entered at school. He had the compulsion to reach out and smack the button on the little machine with his palm. Instead he put his hands on his thighs and squeezed.

'How long have you been in this country?' the suit asked.

'Not quite a year. Maybe... ten months.'

'Your English is very good.'

'I lived in a ski resort before. Lots of British tourists.'

'Ah yes. Leysin, wasn't it?'

'Yes.' Alain was surprised. Where was this going?

'Our Swiss friends have been most cooperative.'

Alain frowned, the suit continued.

'You have lived there all your life, grew up there.'

At first Alain raised his eyebrows, momentarily thinking they were about to discuss his skiing skills.

'Your country has a very thorough data retention system. The *gendarmerie* in your town was able to supply us immediately with some information – open connections in their criminal records where your name is still attached as a witness in a barn fire when you were a child.'

If Alain felt cold before, he now felt ice in his spine.

'And when we delve a little deeper, you might be interested to know that your name has a question mark beside at least two further cases of arson in the past ten years.'

The suit opened a manila file in front of him and slid a photo across the table. It was a photo of a well-dressed man standing behind a microphone on a podium, salt and pepper hair cut short at the sides but long enough on top to cover any evidence of baldness.

He reminded Alain of his father. He thought how disappointed his father would be with him now.

'Do you know this man?' the suit asked gruffly.

'No... I... I've never seen him before in my life,' said Alain.

The policeman sniffed and let air whistle out of his nose as though resigning himself to a long session in the interview room.

Alain frowned.

'I guess you're going to tell me who he is,' he said.

'His name is Kenneth Harper, MBE, Mr Favre. Would you like me to tell you about him?'

Alain shrugged. The suit sniffed.

'Mr Harper was a member of the town council, a generous financial donor in the fields of sport and education, supporting several charities. And last weekend he burned to death in his bed at his home in Gosmore.'

Alain paused. *'Merde,'* he muttered to himself.

41

TRUDY

Three weeks ago

Benny had been grizzling all afternoon. It was late for a nap, but I needed a moment without the noise and fuss so I put him down to sleep. I was about to collapse onto the sofa with a cup of tea when the doorbell rang. When I answered, I had to rack my brains. Did I phone Suzy, and then forget about making the call?

I'd known DS Suzanne Dawson as a friend since uni and in a professional capacity since I started working with some of the women at the refuge. Following cases of domestic abuse after admission, or petty crimes of some of the residents, I was often the choice of counsellor for these women. Through these cases, Suzy and I had struck up a working friendship. I'd been asked more than once to give evidence on the witness stand. I opened the door wider to welcome them in.

'Hi, Trude, how's it going?' asked Suzy.

I was a little wary. Suzy's manner was relaxed, but this couldn't be a social call, and not because she was in uniform. She'd normally have called or texted first. And she was accompanied by a young DC who looked decidedly more awkward than Suzy about disturbing my afternoon.

I immediately thought something had happened to Harry. Since the terrorist incident on Westminster Bridge earlier that year I tried not to let my imagination run wild about how random commuters could be the next victim of a madman. This only added to my worry. Every time Harry left for his journey to the city, I had to repeat my own mantra to myself, the one I'd told all my patients at some time or another. *Do not worry about things you cannot control.*

'I wanted to have a word with you about the Swiss guy we've been questioning at the station,' said Suzy as we walked through to the living room. 'Benny sleeping?'

I nodded, frowning.

'You've arrested Alain Favre?'

'Not arrested, exactly. He's been released, but has been told to stay around. We still don't have a satisfactory conclusion about the fire at his flat. Contrary to the misinformation on factionary TV shows, investigations of this kind can take weeks. SOCO's findings have been outsourced to several different labs. Collating the information is not a speedy process. But because of his possible... involvement, or history, should I say, he's now become a suspect in the Kenneth Harper case.'

'But why? He can't possibly have a link to that man.' I couldn't avoid saying 'that man' with a tone of distaste, and Suzy narrowed her eyes.

'We didn't know you were still in contact with Favre,' said Suzy. 'But the secretary at the clinic told us about your group therapy project with your former PTSD patients. So I thought I'd come and chat to you in a less... official capacity. I know he was referred to your clinic, partly on our recommendation, when he was discharged from hospital after his flat fire. Our inquiries have turned up an interesting history for Favre. I understand you can't reveal details about his PTSD, but it would help us if we knew whether he has displayed any other psychologically related conditions.' Suzy paused. 'Whether we have a firebug on our hands.'

I drew in my breath. 'A pyromaniac! What? I just can't see that...' I wondered, not for the first time, if I'd missed something.

'It was only a hunch, hardly a lead,' said Suzy. 'Everyone was so sure the flat fire was an accident. But there are very few coincidences in life. Besides this, there is a vague connection, Trudy. Kenneth Harper was indirectly a benefactor of the charity funding your project. I assume you've heard about his death.'

I swallowed, remembering when that particular bomb had dropped into the in-box on my desk. I thought about my mantra to combat the fear of a terrorist attack, and how coincidences only serve to increase anxiety.

'But why would Alain have a grudge against Harper when the group has been set up to help my ex-patients?'

'That's what we're hoping you'll clarify for us. So we can sniff somewhere else instead.'

I felt suddenly protective of Alain. I'd never fully understood his various issues and had often questioned whether trauma was ever really amongst them. When I first met him, I hadn't ruled out the possibility of psychosis, but I'd changed my tune since then. I mean, I invited him to be part of the group therapy. I must have been sure, right?

'Have you found any evidence that might put him in Gosmore that night?' I asked.

'We're still checking his alibis. He's staying in the storage room of some colleague's recording studio on the industrial estate. That's not legal in itself, and there's something dodgy about their set-up, but we're not quibbling his living situation right now. We're trying to work out a possible involvement in an arson attack. To be honest, we don't know what we're looking for. It's only his history that led us here.'

'Crikey. Well, honestly, I really don't think he's capable of doing something so horrific. I never thought he was responsible for the fire in his flat, either.' I put my hand to the back of my neck. 'There's something you should know about Kenneth Harper, though. Underneath that squeaky-clean reputation of his, is a dark history.'

Suzy and her colleague looked at each other with unreadable expressions. I felt out of my depth, was suddenly unsure about saying anything. Rachel didn't want the exposure. She didn't want to have her name plastered all over the paper, or to be brought in to be rigorously questioned, or stand before a judge, even for a posthumous case.

But I'd have to elaborate now. I'd already said too much, and I wanted the truth out. Rather than exposing Rachel, I used my patient confidentiality card.

'I've been treating a rape victim for PTSD. I'd prefer at this stage not to reveal her identity. She hadn't told me who her aggressor was when we started sessions, but I recently discovered the identity of the person who attacked her...'

'Let me guess... Kenneth Harper, MBE.'

I sighed and nodded. Suzy didn't seem surprised. Everyone else seemed to think the man was a saint. So why not Suzy? It was my turn to narrow my eyes.

'Well, that answers something else that we hadn't made a connection with until now,' said Suzy.

The pit of my stomach clenched.

'Last night someone spray-painted the word RAPIST on the side of Kenneth Harper's Bentley. It was still parked in his driveway in front of the house. No one had thought to put the car in the garage. Mrs Harper called us this morning, understandably upset. There's an investigation team there now. Trudy, if you have any idea who could have done this, you must let us know.'

I chewed my lip. Would Rachel have done such a thing? Perhaps she wasn't the only one, as I had feared. Perhaps it was one of his other victims?

'I find it bizarre that this vandalism with this allegation has been made *after* Harper's death,' continued Suzy. 'We realise the investigation might reveal that the fire at his family home was an accident. But if someone was responsible for his death, spray-painting this graffiti seems like not only a senseless act, but risky for the vandal. Horse, stable door, so to speak.'

This brought to mind the revelations that came out about Jimmy Savile after he'd died. Many of the victims had still been experiencing nightmares and a messed-up perception of life for many years after their sexual abuser's death. If I said too much, I'd be putting Rachel's confidentiality at risk. The girl had been through enough.

'With your suspicion of Alain Favre, do you think I should stop the group therapy sessions?' I asked Suzy.

My own instinct said yes, but I'd been getting so much great material for my paper, a selfish part of me didn't want to stop seeing them.

'Got any more suspects in there? We might have to arrest the lot of you,' Suzy said jokingly, then continued more seriously. 'I see no reason to stop at this stage. At least we know where to find you all if we need to.'

'I really don't know who could have done this,' I said.

Suzy's brash comment had nevertheless put a seed of doubt in my mind.

'I can't imagine it's the same girl,' I continued. 'It just doesn't feel right. I want to speak to the patient concerned before I give any more information about the sexual assault. I promise if there's anything you should know, I'll contact you, Suzy.'

'Thanks, Trude. Quite the drama recently in our sleepy little corner of North Herts. Who'd have thought?' Suzy walked along the hallway towards the front door. 'Cute little fella,' she said as she passed photos of Benny framed on the wall. 'Are you enjoying being a new mum?'

'Oh, you know, took me a while to recover from the seventeen-hour labour and forceps birth with no pain relief, to nurturing three months of chronic colic, and now the blighter is teething. Don't have kids, Suzy. They're more trouble than they're worth.'

Suzy laughed, and I joined in.

It was meant to be a joke. But more often than not recently, I'd found myself yearning for the days before the upheaval of motherhood.

42

TRUDY

Present day

Maybe I could have delivered our plea better. They said I should be the one to speak. The public will be more sympathetic towards the mother, they said. It didn't take long, the usual 'please return my baby' after pictures of Benny were flashed on the screen behind Harry and me.

My attention is drawn to a hand waving in the front of the crowd, behind the television camera.

'Mrs Greenwood, do you see...?' begins the reporter.

'No questions, thank you!' says DS Flatman standing behind me.

'... a correlation with the Madeleine McCann case almost twenty years ago?'

What did that man say? Maddie McCann? Jesus. My vision is blurred with tears, and I feel one spill onto my cheek.

'No... I... not at all,' I stutter.

Harry leans over to me, his hand on my knee.

'Ignore the man, Trude. Don't dignify his question with an answer. Look at me! Look at me, Trudy.'

I remember how the McCanns came under suspicion at some point during the investigation into Maddie's disappearance. Such a notorious case, still being discussed in the press. Do these awful people think we have done something with Benny? My baby! He must be so frightened. Cold. Hungry. Alone. *Oh God*. I turn to

Harry, holding his gaze, my eyes now pleading with him to get me out of here.

I fight off visions of doom in my mind.

43

RACHEL

Two weeks ago

Trudy took Rachel aside after the latest meeting and asked if she could meet her in town somewhere the next day. Rachel had a good idea what it was about. Harper. She probably wanted to ask whether she'd had any more thoughts about going to the police. But it would also be a good opportunity to mention to Trudy that Olive was in desperate need of more therapy.

They quietly agreed to meet at Rose Buds in the Arcade the following morning. Rachel didn't want Olive to find out. Trudy seemed to understand, probably didn't want the rest of the group to find out either. This was overstepping the boundaries of 'therapy'.

When they left the old school building and the others had gone their separate ways, Olive turned to Rachel.

'Did you hear about the local councilman who died in that fire?' Olive asked.

Rachel sucked in a breath. They hadn't seen each other for a couple of days what with Rachel's work and spending more time with Mouse. Why would Olive ask this now? She'd never been interested in the local news before, never wanted to talk about the world at large. Did she suspect Rachel of something?

Rachel shrugged.

'Yeah. Something to liven up the *Hitchin Comet* headliner,' she said.

Once upon a time, Rachel would have spilled the beans, discussed the whole thing with Olive, seeking sympathy and laughing about Kenneth Cock Harper's comeuppance. But not now. She feared the weird behaviour Olive had been displaying recently was an increasing sign of instability.

She'd begun leaving Rachel little gifts. Small things. A pen. A sweet. A keyring. Rachel was pretty sure they'd all been stolen from somewhere. They didn't always look new. Olive's behaviour most days was psychopathic. She seemed happy to believe she'd been saved from some kind of trauma. But she also seemed to be constantly looking for the next thrill. And the next thrill was something really bad. Something that no normal human being would consider a thrill at all. Olive actually enjoyed people treating her terribly, beating her, telling her she was a slag. She'd already admitted to Rachel she missed it. Apart from that, Olive constantly asked Rachel for her opinion, kept grabbing her arm. It was giving Rachel a headache. The girl was skittish and Rachel wondered on top of everything else whether she'd been taking drugs.

She'd be glad to have the opportunity to mention something to Trudy the next day. Rachel didn't want to be involved in Olive's journey any more.

When they arrived at the refuge, instead of hanging around for a pre-bedtime hot drink, Rachel made the excuse she was tired and went straight to her room.

When she'd removed her make-up, put on her mismatched tartan pyjamas and brushed her teeth at the sink, there was a light tap at her door. She was lucky enough to have one of the single rooms, normally allocated to the mums with babies in their cribs.

'What's up, Mouse?' Rachel asked Martha affectionately as she let her in.

'I'm... I'm having a bad evening. And I'm cold. Can I just... I know it sounds weird. Can I just get warm with you? Under the covers.'

Rachel didn't even think twice, she climbed into bed, threw back the covers and let Mouse crawl in.

'No wonder you're cold, girl. You'll need to wear more than that at night when winter comes,' she told her, looking at her thin vest and white cotton undies. 'They turn off the heat at night.'

'Thank you,' whispered Martha.

She turned and they spooned together in Rachel's single bed. It felt like the most natural thing. Rachel took comfort from this unexpected intimacy. She couldn't remember the last time she'd touched anybody with affection, apart from Trudy, briefly. She wrapped her free arm over Mouse, who pressed herself into Rachel's torso. Rachel gently rubbed Mouse's arm and felt the prick of tears. Not of sadness, but of some seed of gratitude, knowing this comfort was two-way. It made her happy.

In the night, Rachel woke once with a strand of Mouse's hair across her mouth. It smelled of apple shampoo. Mouse turned in her sleep and her face fell against Rachel's neck. She could feel her warm breath against her throat, her soft lips lightly touching her skin. Rachel felt an overwhelming warmth of something deep in her belly that she could only think must have been a strong mothering instinct.

Her regret about that baby was stronger than ever.

44

ALAIN

Two weeks ago

'You are no stranger to the perils of house fires, Monsieur Favre. I know it's late, but we were hoping you could help ignite our investigation a little further, excuse the pun.'

Even though Alain hadn't understood the meaning of the word 'pun' he grasped the word 'ignite' and didn't think it was appropriate for this policewoman to be making jokes at such a time.

'What are you implying? That I had something to do with that man's death? It seems a little... random. "Oh look, Alain Favre was rescued from a fire so he must have something to do with another fire in the same town two months later." *Merde.*'

'Your flat here isn't the first fire you've had a connection to though, is it? We've been delving further into the unsolved mysteries of those fires in your home town in Switzerland. When so many coincidences add up, I'm afraid we don't have a choice. Put yourself in our shoes, Monsieur Favre.'

Alain realised now he should have insisted on the solicitor being present. Perhaps he should have called the one appointed for the investigation into his flat fire; she'd believed his story. He'd never had any experience of arrest, had no idea what it involved. Back in Switzerland, his name must have been permanently on some kind of juvenile record, even if they'd proved he had nothing to do with those fires. Perhaps there was a dubious connection as a witness. If he ever got out of there, he wouldn't be returning to this country. But now he wondered whether warning bells would be ringing back in his home town.

He wondered why they came back for him this afternoon. How much information did they have?

'Did you check out my alibi?' Alain said. He wasn't sure whether the Latin word was used in English too.

'Your *alleebee* is still taking a little time to confirm, Monsieur Favre,' said DS Dawson, mimicking his pronunciation. 'But we've had a new development in the Kenneth Harper case and would like to continue our questioning regardless of where you were on the night of the fire in Gosmore.'

'A new development?'

DS Dawson pushed a photograph across the table. It was a side view of one of those old-fashioned English cars the aristocracy drive. A Daimler or a Rolls-Royce perhaps. It was unclear from side on. The word RAPIST was sprayed across it, covering the front and back door.

'*Aïe*,' said Alain. 'I am guessing that was not shaving foam. Not able to wash.' And against all his best instincts, he laughed out loud. Big mistake.

'Look, I'm tired, Mr Favre.' She'd dropped the Monsieur. 'I think we should continue this conversation in the morning when I might have recovered my sense of humour. Let's see how cooperative you are after a night in the cell, shall we?'

'Hey, I didn't write that on the car, okay? You cannot do that, keep me here with no... *motif*!'

'Our metal-barred rooms with ensuite stainless steel bogs here on College Road are probably more comfortable than where you've been sleeping, Mr Favre. I could report your current living arrangements to the local authorities if you like. The storeroom on the industrial estate is clearly not meant for habitation.'

'But... Do you have the results of the investigation of the fire at my old flat? You cannot keep me here indefinitely.'

'We can keep you here for up to twenty-four hours if we wish. Are you trying to make up new rules?'

Alain could hear frustration in the DS's voice. She probably wanted to be home for an aperitif. He'd have done anything for a bottle of wine right now. But he gave up. Grabbing blindly at the idea that he had any rights wouldn't work here, when he didn't know what his rights actually were.

It wasn't quite as awful as he'd thought it was going to be. One of the guards, a young police officer, chatted to him when he brought what looked like a supermarket ready meal of pasta with some unidentifiable meat. The officer told him they'd continue the interview with him first thing in the morning after a designated rest period, as it was late. Despite the smell of urine and a strange ticking sound in the building, he managed to get a few hours' sleep on the hard bench bed.

In the morning, he was brought a weak cup of instant coffee, two slices of cold toast with something that could have been margarine and a sachet of jam. They didn't even have those little metal containers of *confiture*. Avoiding anything sharp for the prisoner.

In the interview room, DS Dawson sat at the table beside another recruit who looked even younger than Alain.

'You might be able to enlighten us about something else. We haven't been able to locate your girlfriend, Anne Winthorpe,' said DS Dawson.

'Ex-girlfriend,' he reminded her.

'Her parents didn't even know she'd returned to this country. Her contract at Benslow wasn't officially terminated. They're all as confused as we are, so we thought you could tell us her whereabouts. She will need to be questioned as well.'

So they'd discovered Annie was missing. During the night, Alain had thought there was an ulterior motive to all this. Her parents would have been concerned. He had to be careful how he approached this. One councilman had died, possibly murdered, and a bright young musician had gone missing. Did they think he made Annie disappear too? It wasn't looking good for him. Too many coincidences.

DS Dawson was back to calling him *Monsieur* Favre. She picked up a manila folder that had been sitting on the table in front of her, stood up and walked around the room. She tapped the edge of the file into her palm, going behind Alain, annoying him as he wanted to keep an eye on her. But he didn't want to strain his neck and turn his head in case that gave the impression he was somehow concerned. She stopped in front of him and placed the file on the table.

'We're still waiting for the final confirmation from forensic services on that one. In the meantime, where is Anne Winthorpe, Alain?'

It felt condescending somehow, to suddenly use his first name. It was as though she'd like to wrap this case up and charge him with all of North Hertfordshire's recent crimes. The expression on her face was sour, like she was about to tell him to go back where he came from and stop sponging on society in this country. He'd seen too much of that recently with all the Brexit shit going on.

'Is Ms Winthorpe likely to be alive when we find her?'

'*Quoi?* You think I killed my girlfriend? *Nom de Dieu.*'

Alain was scared now. Like they really were trying to pin many crimes on him. He wondered why they were being so hard on him, before those results about the fire in the flat had been made available. Police investigations couldn't be based on *coincidences*, surely? But it was more than that, these people seemed really angry.

'We found something else last night, in the storeroom where you've been sleeping illegally.'

Her voice was now vaguely disgusted. Alain imagined them finding the stub of a spliff, some items of laundry and the rubbish Ron had been leaving about the place. She opened the file and slid out a set of photos. They were all of children, some very young – babies – some toddlers.

'The SOCOs aren't letting us have access to the more incriminating photos just yet. We found them in that filthy space.'

Alain shook his head. This nightmare was getting bigger. He held up his hands, palms pushing the air between them.

'What sick thing is this now? I hope this is not what I think. Shouldn't you be talking to the guy who rents the studio? This is *nothing* to do with me. *Rien du tout.*'

'Don't worry, your colleague Ron is also helping us with our inquiries. I wanted to see your reaction. Ms Winthorpe isn't the only person in our missing persons files. It will take a while to find out who all these children might be. And whether these images have the appropriate permissions.'

'I do not know why you accuse me of doing something to Annie. For what reason? *She* left *me*. But I did not do anything to her. Maybe those photographs of the children are for the project Ron is doing with his music. I know nothing about them. I don't know who they are. Ron was giving me a favour, letting me sleep there. I did not have anywhere else to go! It sounds to me like I should get an *avocat*.'

The DS didn't say anything. Alain shook his head and looked down at his hands on the table. How was he going to get out of all this?

45

TRUDY

Two weeks ago

As I was getting ready to take Benny round to my parents, my mother called to say she was feeling ill. She had a sore throat and a headache, was sure it was just a cold but she worried Benny would pick it up from her.

Making Benny even more grouchy than normal was the last thing I wanted. It was short notice, but I sent Rachel a message to cancel our meeting in Hitchin, saying I couldn't get childcare.

Rachel texted back. She was already at the café, had taken the morning off work especially. She didn't have a problem if I brought the baby with me. This wasn't the best idea, but I figured Rachel already knew he existed. If she wasn't comfortable, she would have said so. If I cancelled our meeting, she would have taken the time off for nothing. I really needed to talk to her about Kenneth Harper and I wanted to do it in an informal setting. Making Rachel come to the clinic was too much like therapy, and going to the refuge was too public. It surely wouldn't hurt to bring Benny along, so I agreed to meet anyway.

I arrived at the café and Rachel waved to me from the corner, closing the book she'd been reading and slipping it into her bag. Benny was still too young to use a highchair, so I wedged the pushchair with the car seat clicked into to the frame next to me by the window. He was sleeping, but once his body had registered that we were stationary, he'd soon wake up. And then everyone would know we were there.

Rachel sat up and peered over the table, trying to get a look at Benny.

'I'll pick him up when he wakes, which will probably be soon,' I said.

We ordered cappuccinos from the waitress.

'I never consciously chose *not* to tell you about Benny, but we simply hadn't seen each other for so long and I was going through a pretty tough time. The reveal probably couldn't have happened at a worse time for you. But I'm glad it's out in the open. I'm so sorry, Rachel, it was a weird way to find out at our group meeting.'

'It's okay, Trudy. I was probably due for a good cry.' Rachel smiled.

I bit my lip. What I had yet to tell Rachel might still make her feel worse. Before the waitress had even delivered our coffees, Benny began to wake. I unstrapped him and lifted him out.

'Aw. Look at the little man,' said Rachel. 'He's so gorgeous. Oh, Trudy, well done you!'

Despite my exhaustion, I grinned. Any praise at this point was welcome. I had to grab at anything to help me believe it had all been worth it.

'It's a kind of healing for me, seeing Benny,' said Rachel. 'The baby thing, I mean. I shouldn't regret anything, not keeping it, especially because I hate that man for what he did to me. But Daniel's words made a strong impression. I keep dreaming about babies. Of course, I wake up in the morning and the horror of it all comes back in snippets.'

How educated Rachel sounded, despite what my father used to call a lower-class accent. Could it be that Rachel was losing her normal enunciation a little? Her aggression had certainly softened. She didn't have to lower her standards to be accepted into that other corner of society anymore. Perhaps it was time to return to her middle-class home-counties roots. The vicar's daughter.

'I'm living proof that it's usually quite difficult to get pregnant,' I said with a laugh bordering on cynicism. 'An embryo often only adheres the second or third time. Many women lose their first babies, and don't even know it. I suspect it happened with me more than once. That might also have been your case. A natural miscarriage.'

'Except I'll never be able to have children,' said Rachel, swallowing. 'Perhaps you weren't aware, but a D&C wasn't enough after the miscarriage. Something more than the stupid vodka and hot bath went wrong. I had to have a hysterectomy.'

I put my fingers to my lips. Maybe that explained the tears that day in the ladies' cloakroom after the group meeting.

'God, I'm sorry, Rach.'

'It's okay, Trudy. At the moment at least. My biological clock hasn't started winding down yet. Perhaps it's stopped altogether, physical restrictions and hormone supplements all considered. Maybe it's best for me anyway. In my head that clock stopped ticking that night outside The Three Moorhens.'

Benny squawked from my lap, stretched his legs and arched his back as though trying to fight his way off. I kissed the top of his head, now grateful that this pregnancy at least went to term.

'There's something you need to know, Rach. The police came to see me, and I think they might be on their way to see you, too.'

Rachel put her head on one side, picked up her cup to take a sip.

'About Harper? I thought you didn't tell them about me.'

'I didn't. But someone spray-painted the word RAPIST on the side of his Bentley parked in his driveway a couple of days ago.'

Rachel gave a little snort of laughter, and a bobble of cappuccino foam appeared on the end of her nose. I handed her a napkin from the holder on the table and she wiped it off. A grain of relief bloomed in my chest. Rachel's reaction meant it wasn't her.

'The thing is,' I continued as I lifted up Benny who was now fully awake, grabbing at my hair. 'They might push for an identity reveal.'

Rachel shook her head, a look of confusion on her face.

'Especially if they think that same person is the one who sprayed his car,' I continued. 'Or worse... burned his house.'

'Holy shit! Oh, sorry,' she said, looking at Benny. 'Do they suspect it was arson? They think someone actually *killed* him?'

'They haven't ruled it out, although it's being treated as an accident at the moment. But with the graffiti on his car, it changes their direction a bit. If they insist on my records, because we're entering the realm of a criminal investigation, they'll find you anyway. So I figure the best thing is for you to meet the police, before they come to you.'

'But why would they want your records? What investigation? Meet them?' Rachel asked.

I felt suddenly awkward.

'I told them one of my patients – but not who...' I said as Rachel's eyes widened. 'I did not give them your name. After they told me about Harper's car, I told them I know for a fact that the allegation is true. I wasn't thinking about the consequences. I know DS Suzanne Dawson who's part of the investigation into Harper. She's a tough cookie, but a good person at heart. I wouldn't let her get to you without your permission. She told me I can be present if that person is questioned.'

'Oh God, Trudy, I don't know. Shit.'

'You don't even have to go to the station. We can do it at the refuge, or in my office at the clinic. It's better to agree to be questioned rather than brought in for questioning, if you see what I mean.'

Or put under arrest, I thought.

'Okay... Let's do it in your office. Not at the refuge. I wish you'd told me first.'

'I know. My mistake. My post-baby brain isn't always doing things the right way around these days.'

'There's something I wanted to mention to you too,' said Rachel. 'About Olive. She seems to be going off the rails again and I'm worried. I'm pretty sure she's been cutting again. I saw a tissue in the bin the other day in our bathroom. It had blood on it. Not monthly blood. Little dots of it. As though someone had dabbed at a wound. I once caught her cutting on her thigh, so you'll see no evidence on her arms. Please, she needs help. She's beginning to worry me. There's no predicting what she might do.'

'Of course I'll talk to her. I'll speak to the service managers first, and try and get her on her own at the refuge. I've been worrying about her too.'

I picked another napkin from the holder on the table and wiped my mouth.

'I'll go and pay,' I said, getting up awkwardly with Benny wriggling in my arms.

'Can I hold him?' Rachel asked, and without hesitation I handed him over.

Benny studied Rachel's kohl-lined eyes. I got up and headed to the counter stacked with iced buns and cakes. I turned back as the woman rang our coffees up on the till and watched Benny reach for one of Rachel's dangly earrings. Rachel kissed him on the nose and he giggled as a lock of her hair tickled his cheek. I was glad he was well behaved for once. I studied Rachel's face, noting the softening around her mouth, the shine in her eye that could be longing, before the woman at the till called to me and handed me the change.

46

Present day

They hope to prevent any disturbance by anticipating the baby's hunger or changing needs. If Benny starts crying, they don't want him to work himself into a state that will be hard to calm. Perhaps it would be better for both of them if they change their mode of transport. Then Benny can get all the attention he deserves while he's awake. It's important to keep this baby a hundred percent content. Anything else would be off-putting while they're on the road.

They prepare another bottle with a flask of water and premeasured scoops of formula in a plastic container pulled from a backpack. The baby sits on their lap, hands clasped around the bottle, sucking hungrily and occasionally stopping to smile at the toys still in his line of vision on the handle above the baby carrier. For a moment he holds the bottle by himself. They smile, wondering if Benny just learned to do this. Cute kid.

When Benny's finished the bottle, they place a towel over their shoulder, lift the baby and tap his back until a bubble of air escapes his tummy with a gutsy burp. They laugh. Benny laughs.

They put the baby back in the carrier and scroll through their phone to locate the nearest train station.

47

OLIVE

Two weeks ago

'We understand how upsetting it can be for you to be taken out of a familiar environment, so we're hoping you can clarify something for us here at the refuge.'

The service manager had let the policewoman in while Olive was grabbing some breakfast with Rachel in the kitchen. The cop was now standing in the doorway watching them. Her spotty side-kick who looked like he hadn't even left school was right behind her. Once it was clear they wanted to talk to Olive, Rachel turned, a piece of buttered toast in one hand.

'I'll be upstairs in my room if you need anything,' she said, flashing a look to Olive which said *don't say anything stupid.*

'Ah come on, Rach. Don't leave me on my own with them,' hissed Olive. 'Please stay.'

Olive suspected why they were there, but had suddenly lost her nerve. She wasn't sorry for what she'd done.

'They probably don't want me hanging around anyway,' said Rachel.

'It's okay. You can stay,' said the policewoman. 'You're a friend of Ms Stanton?'

Rachel shrugged.

'Yeah,' said Olive, looking pointedly at Rachel.

Rachel bit her lip, took a plate out of the cupboard and put her toast on it. She cut it diagonally in two with a knife. Olive wished she'd done that with hers. She bet it tasted better like that.

Olive pulled a teabag from the caddy and stuffed it into her mug, pushed down the switch on the kettle and sat down at the table, making the not so subtle point that the last thing she was going to do in that kitchen was make the cops a fucking cup of tea. Rachel leaned against the kitchen counter nibbling on her toast. Olive felt nervousness buzzing off her like a swarm of bees, and narrowed her eyes.

The woman, whose name tag said DS S Dawson, pulled a photo from her pocket, put it on the table and slid it towards Olive. It was a photo of Ken's Bentley, the bright white letters of the word RAPIST covering two dark maroon doors on the driver's side. Olive sucked in her cheeks. An electric thrill coursed down her spine. Rachel leaned forward to squint at the photo over Olive's shoulder and hissed through her teeth.

DS Dawson slid a second photo next to the one of the Bentley. It was the aerosol can Olive nicked in Brooker's. Olive swallowed and a quiet 'shit' slipped out of the side of her mouth. She looked at Rachel, whose eyebrows were raised.

'This can of spray paint was found in the bushes about half a mile down the lane from the Harper residence in Gosmore. We were able to lift a set of prints from the metal cylinder. A thumb and the outside of a palm. They match a set we have on our juvenile records for a handful of shoplifting misdemeanours. But that was a long time ago, and we'll need you to come with us. Judging from your expression, Ms Stanton, you recognise this object. As you're now an adult, we have to take a new set of prints. And we'll need to ask you some questions.'

Olive hadn't had to deal with this cop before. She was the first female DS she'd met. She pulled up her sleeves, placed her arms on the table with the backs of her hands against the surface so the scarred insides of her arms were on full display. *See if I care*, she was saying without words. The scars usually unsettled people the first time they saw them. She wanted them to know being questioned by the cops was not the worst thing that had ever happened to her.

She wished she'd been more careful. She was angry at herself. Then she was angry at Rachel. Why the fuck hadn't Rachel said anything to Olive about Ken Harper? She'd questioned her enough times about who raped her, but Rachel had never said anything. Kept it a secret. But then again, Olive never told anyone who her abusive lover was either. If Olive hadn't overheard Trudy and Rachel that day in the hallway, she'd never have known the identity of Rachel's rapist.

'Look, you don't need to bandy about any messy inkpads or a pair of handcuffs,' said Olive. 'I'll come quietly. I admit it. It was me who sprayed that. But truth be told, he deserved what he had coming to him.'

She wasn't sure she meant it. A part of her still needed him.

She glanced at Rachel, who'd stopped chewing and was staring with her eyes wide. Olive hadn't intended to get Rachel involved in this, and regretted not letting her take her toast to her room. But it complicated matters a bit. Because now it was obvious Olive had a history with Harper. And through her own stupidity, the police might now have suspected that Olive had a hand in his death.

'Then we'll have to take a statement. It's gone beyond a simple questioning; you need to come with us now.'

'It's true, though,' said Olive. 'He was a rapist, you know. Folk can be so unassuming. There are mean fuckers everywhere. It's got nothing to do with the way they all talk or how much money they've got.'

Olive would much rather have saved Rachel's reputation than Ken's, who wouldn't know shit now he was dead. As the assistant put the photos back in his pouch, DS Dawson narrowed her eyes. Rachel turned her back to the room. She was moving stuff around on the counter, rinsing her plate in the sink. Trying not to meet anyone's eye.

'As I'm sure you're aware, it's not the only thing that's happened at Kenneth Harper's residence over the past couple of weeks, is it, Olive?' said DS Dawson.

Ice sluiced through Olive. Why couldn't she keep her big gob shut? She remembered the time she'd found out who Ken was. How she'd gone to sit on the wall outside the gates at the end of his driveway, hidden from the massive house by a tall hedge. How she'd wished she could live in a mansion that big. How she was tempted several times to walk up and show his frigid wife her latest bruises; that her husband had been responsible for them. That he was the one who'd left her flawed.

'The refuge has saved us,' Olive suddenly said, meaning her and Rachel. 'Surrounded only by women. No threat. We feel safe. There are a bunch of arseholes out there. And some of them are allowed to get away with some really bad shit.'

She stared pointedly at the policewoman. Rachel had stopped moving, remained with her back to them, her hands on the edge of the sink. Olive couldn't stop herself.

'If you've never woken up in the middle of the night with your hand wrapped around your throat to protect it against an elbow, if you've never had to mop the blood away from your snatch when someone's forced themselves on you, then you won't know what I'm talking about.'

'Olive, please,' whispered Rachel. 'There's no need to be so bloody dramatic.'

Olive ignored her and looked at the policewoman. She could tell underneath that cool exterior she'd shocked DS Dawson. Rachel was the only other person in that room who knew that kind of fear.

As Olive pulled on a hoodie and prepared to leave with DS Dawson and her sidekick, she reflected how weird Rachel had been behaving over the past couple of weeks. Especially since she'd been spending time with that new girl. She'd been ignoring Olive more and more and Olive didn't like it. It was what drove her to write that word on Ken Harper's car. He had to be held accountable, and Rachel should have been grateful to her for outing him.

Olive was perfectly aware that under normal circumstances, Rachel might not be her 'friend.' But these were not normal circumstances. They were allies. Didn't Rachel know this?

The cops waited at the bottom of the stairs while Olive fetched her jacket. She thought about climbing out of the bathroom window and doing a runner, but there was really no point. She didn't have anywhere to go.

'If I don't make it to the meeting, tell Trudy for me, will you?' Olive said to Rachel as she came back down the stairs and left with the cops.

At the nick, they took a new set of Olive's fingerprints and confirm that they matched the ones on the can of paint.

'I know!' she said. 'Coulda told you that without all this faff.'

As she'd fully admitted to the damage to Ken's car, they issued her with a caution. She certainly couldn't afford to pay for the repair to the Bentley. But Mrs Harper didn't want to press charges, despite now knowing it was Olive who'd vandalised her late husband's car.

'Perhaps she also suspects her husband was a cheating bastard rapist,' said Olive.

'And how come you think he was, as you so eloquently put it, a cheating bastard rapist?' asked DS Dawson.

'Like sisters, ain't we? Mates. He done worse to her, before what he did to me.'

'Do you mean your friend Rachel at the refuge?'

'I'm not saying nothing.'

'And what about the fire at the Harpers' home, Olive? Do you know anything about that?'

Olive felt the blood drain from her face. She swallowed, had to think fast.

'Call the duty manager at the refuge,' she said. 'We was both at home. Water-tight alibi.'

They left her in the room with a young cop standing inside the door. It didn't take long before they were back. There was apparently some confusion as to who had been on duty in the refuge that night, but they told Olive she was free to go within the hour. She had her alibi.

'Don't you be taking a luxury cruise anywhere though, Ms Stanton,' said DS Dawson. 'We might want you to help us further with our inquiries at some stage.'

'Pfft,' said Olive, before slinging the strap of her bag over her shoulder.

As she left, she heard a familiar foreign voice through the open door of the interview room next to hers. Shit. It was the Swiss guy. *Poor bugger.*

There'd been a rumour at the refuge a few weeks ago about the fire that had swept through a couple of houses in the terrace up by the train track. It wasn't until she'd started the group therapy sessions that she'd realised that was where Alain had lived. For a moment she thought she should wait for him.

Just for a split second, she missed Ken. His need for her, the attention, his deep wallet, his inadvertent generosity. At least she'd never gone hungry.

But Olive didn't want to spend more than one extra second in the nick. Neither did she want to go back to the refuge before the meeting. She grabbed a Coke from Pret, paid for it at the counter and took it to a bench on Butts Close. She sat down, took her denim jacket away from where it had been folded over the crook of her arm and unwrapped the ham baguette she'd nicked in Pret.

As she ate, she watched a couple of mums pushing their children in buggies across the green. The fair used to come there. She used to ride the puke-inducing waltzer, hang around the candyfloss stall, fish for rubber ducks with magnets on rods to win a goldfish in a bag. She'd wanted to run away with the troupe when they began packing up to leave, especially after she'd shagged more than one of the travellers.

She wasn't the last to get to the meeting. Alain was missing. He must still have been with the police.

As she perched on her seat, Olive dug her nails into the soft skin on the inside of her wrist and pressed and pressed until she felt the sting of broken skin. Three tiny crescents of blood filled the imprint of her nails. She slid her sleeve down to her hand and was annoyed with herself that she'd blemished her canvas for the sake of a hit.

If Alain wasn't going to come back, Olive hoped Trudy would replace his slot in her little speed-dating experiment with another man.

48

DANIEL

Two weeks ago

He was the only man at tonight's group session, and felt a little self-conscious. Alain didn't show up. Daniel wondered whether the quiet Swiss chap had finally slipped back to the Alps. He hoped he'd found a way home, eyed the empty seat, and calculated whether it would be appropriate for him to do the same.

Trudy looked a little dishevelled.

'Sorry, I look a state,' she said. 'The result of three hours' sleep last night.'

'Oh no! Benny's colic's bad again?' Rachel whispered, and Daniel pretended he hadn't heard.

Trudy bit her lip and nodded.

'We'll wait a few more minutes for Alain,' she said.

'He's still at the nick,' said Olive. 'I heard him being interviewed there just now. Don't think he'll be coming. Looked like they were having a right old shindig down there.'

'Wow. Do they think he set the fire in his flat on purpose?' asked Rachel. 'I thought they proved it was an accident. Oh… no,' she said, as though something had just occurred to her.

Olive frowned.

'Yes, well, let's not make assumptions on why he's still being questioned,' said Trudy.

'Poor bastard. I guess once they pulled him in for questioning on the fire, everything started going wrong for him.' Olive paused.

'Fuck me! The fire thing! Do you think they might be questioning him about Ken Harper's death?'

'Olive,' said Trudy sternly. 'It could be something different, perhaps about where he's living at the moment. No one's supposed to be inhabiting those industrial units.'

'So the only suitable home for him is a holding cell at College Road Police Station? Pfft, I can tell you that's hardly a holiday camp, poor sod,' said Olive.

'Seems a bit harsh,' said Daniel. 'He's a decent bloke. If I'd known, I could have offered him my spare room.'

'That's very kind of you, Daniel,' said Trudy. 'Things haven't been going quite to plan for all of us recently.'

Daniel raised his eyebrows as Trudy directed a look at Olive. It must have been like having a recalcitrant teenager in her group therapy. He hoped Emma never adopted any of that girl's attitude.

'Truth be told, there's never smoke without fire,' mumbled Olive, chewing on a nail.

Daniel tutted, a little louder than he'd intended. Olive could be really quite obnoxious at times. He wasn't surprised she'd been on the receiving end of physical abuse in the past, although he'd *never* have said that out loud. Wait, had he really just thought that? She was enough to drive anyone crazy, the way she provoked people.

'God, Olive. Please stop,' said Rachel, who was sitting next to her.

'You know I was only trying to protect you,' Olive whined quietly.

When Olive said the word 'protect' Daniel heard only the word 'control' in his mind. The way she hung off Rachel, never leaving her side during those meetings. Rachel was obviously trying to distance herself from the mad girl. The feeling was clearly not reciprocated.

'I've recognised a weird jealousy since we've started these sessions,' said Daniel.

Olive widened her eyes and Daniel knew he'd hit the nail on the head. His comment might have been meant as a warning to her, but his dialogue wasn't going to be what she thought.

'I was jealous that the driver in the other car got to die at the same time as Sarah. I think that's another reason I've blocked out the day of the accident. Part of the thing that led to thoughts of taking my own life is this vision I had of them ascending to heaven together and spending eternity wondering why I would rather save the bird than my wife. Jealousy is a monster, can take over your emotions in a way no one expects.'

Olive's jaw was clenched and she scratched her left palm with the fingers of her right hand. He broke eye contact and looked at Trudy, who had the tiniest wrinkle of a smile on her mouth. He'd done a small part of her job for her, although he wasn't sure Olive would get the subtlety. He hoped Rachel would though, she didn't deserve someone like Olive holding her back.

'It was part of the letting go I needed to go through. Letting Sarah go so I could devote my time to Jasper and Emma. To be the best father I can, given that they now only have one parent to bring them up.'

He looked at each member sitting in the small circle. If nothing else had come from this whole exercise, he felt an affinity with these people, except maybe Olive the nutter. It was also helping him move forward, form decisions, make new plans.

49

RACHEL

Two weeks ago

For the first time Rachel was desperate to talk to Olive, and she wasn't around. The irony, given that most of the time Rachel was trying to shake her off. Olive had gone straight from the police station to the meeting tonight, and then Trudy had asked to talk to her afterwards, probably at the request of the police. It was clear the discussion might take some time, so Rachel didn't wait for her. Olive still wasn't back by the time Rachel had gone to bed.

They released Olive with a caution after she'd admitted her vandalism, so she was still able to turn up to the meeting. There was no way she would have been able to come up with any cash to pay fines or compensation. And honestly, who would have wanted to deal with that kind of messed-up madness in the holding cells? Rachel was sure they would have been happy to be rid of her. They were probably still trying to work out how to deal with her crime, and had likely engaged Trudy for some kind of assessment.

When the police had come to the refuge and were curious to know whether it was the only thing Olive had been doing at Kenneth Harper's house over the past few weeks, Rachel had wanted to step forward and say, *you mean the fire? Yes, it was me. I did it.* Because the beauty of that revenge would have been so sweet. But no one wanted to spend the next twenty years in prison, even if she might have had her time reduced for the definitive crime of passion with all the emotional trauma she'd been through. And there was the unaccountable deceit of claiming someone else's crime. She was still curious about who would have killed Kenneth Cock Harper.

The following morning, Rachel rose early for work. It was barely light as she left the refuge and she mourned the shortening of the days even though summer wasn't yet over. She felt as though she'd wasted the hot weather and wished she could take a break from the stifling atmosphere at the refuge.

Her boss asked to see her during her morning break, and her stomach dropped. Was she going to get fired? She couldn't think why. But she had a pleasant surprise when her boss said she'd had a letter from the landlords of the flat Rachel had had her eye on near Hitchin station, asking for a reference. Her boss was happy to give this, but in addition told Rachel that she was also willing to guarantee the rent deposit to give her a better chance of getting the place. At last! Something to look forward to.

Her shift finished mid-afternoon and she walked with a light step back to the refuge, wanting to share the news with Mouse who was the only person she could confide in.

But when she arrived, the service manager's glance slid towards the kitchen and Rachel saw a uniform and a suit of two visitors. DS Dawson and her assistant. Her stomach fluttered.

She walked in on tenterhooks, to see Olive sitting at the table scraping the bottom of a plastic caramel pudding container and making annoying sipping sounds off the teaspoon.

'At last, Rach. We've been waiting for you,' said Olive with an annoyingly admonishing tone.

'Hi, Rachel. Just need to have a quick word with you,' said DS Dawson.

Rachel frowned.

'Olive's artwork?' she asked, referring to the graffiti on Harper's car. 'What's that got to do with me?'

'We need to ask a few questions about the other issue. The fire that killed Kenneth Harper.'

She felt sick just hearing his name. So they thought it wasn't an accident. They couldn't have thought Olive was clever enough to do such a thing, especially if the initial investigation had led to uncertainty. Olive had messed up so obviously with the can of spray paint. Why chuck it in the bushes so close to his house? Any idiot could see it would have taken them all of five minutes to find the evidence. No, they'd figure Olive wasn't clever enough to have arranged his death by burning him in his own bed. Otherwise they would surely have arrested her for *that* by now.

Had Trudy told them something about her and Harper? Why would she have done that without talking to Rachel first? Perhaps, like Trudy, they'd worked it out for themselves. Should she ask if Trudy could be present, as her psychotherapist, even though she was no longer her patient? She was hardly going to be able to suddenly drop Benny and turn up.

A few women wandered in and out of the kitchen, curious about the presence of the cops. Two of them were now milling around in the hallway, seeing if they could catch any gossip. The assistant policeman herded the others out of the kitchen.

'Is there somewhere more discreet we can go?' DS Dawson asked Rachel.

'We can go outside,' she said, looking through the window at the clouds scudding across the sky. 'If it's warm enough.'

DS Dawson opened the back door and walked out to a paved courtyard where they often hung their washing to dry on fine days. Rachel had tried to grow tomatoes there, but kept forgetting to water them. Now it was late summer, the brown sticks with dead leaves and desiccated flowers were still lined up along the wooden fence at the back. They'd never had a chance to produce tomatoes.

Through the window, they watched DS Dawson go to the rear of the courtyard by the tomato plants, reporting something quietly into her radio.

'Is she reporting us for being veggie murder suspects?' Olive asked with a huff.

'Actually, the tomato is a fruit,' said the young police officer.

'Those sticks aren't producing anything, mate. You've got a great imagination.'

'Olive,' hissed Rachel, to stop her saying anything she might regret.

DS Dawson waved for Rachel to join her. Rachel walked outside, closing the kitchen door behind her. The DS looked like she'd just sniffed something bad in the courtyard.

'Are you a marijuana smoker?' she asked Rachel.

Rachel frowned. Through the window she saw Olive in the kitchen, talking to the young officer. He must be asking her the same question judging by the burst of cynical laughter she heard through the window.

'No,' said Rachel. 'Gave up smoking altogether last year. Cigarettes,' she qualified. 'I only have the occasional puff when I'm stressed. Purely nicotine.'

'Can you tell us what you were doing on the night of Friday July 14th?'

A pair of pigeons who'd been cooing quietly on the neighbouring roof flew off, their wings slapping like stiff taffeta. Rachel's heart spiked.

'I'm pretty sure I was here, at the refuge,' Rachel answered. 'Yes, I remember now.'

She remembered because it was the night before she read the news in *The Comet*. She was racking her brains to think who else had been there. That week's live-in service manager would have been in her room. They hardly ever saw her in the evenings unless there was an incident. She was pretty sure Olive had been there. Olive didn't have any money to go out and it wasn't a group therapy night. Rachel would have spent most of the evening in her room, as usual.

'I guess you can check with the service manager.'

'Your friend mentioned something interesting about Kenneth Harper's former *activities*, when we spoke last week.'

Rachel let out a deep, forced sigh.

'Look, I don't want to talk about it. He's dead, right? He won't be *bothering* anyone anymore.'

'But it looks rather suspicious, don't you think? Considering the latest development.'

'As I said, check with the service manager.'

She couldn't believe this was happening. Bloody Olive.

DS Dawson was about to say something, but seemed to change her mind. She laid a hand on Rachel's shoulder.

'It's okay,' she said. 'Thanks for answering those questions.'

Rachel closed her eyes briefly and they went back into the kitchen.

'Hey, Rach,' said Olive. 'Can you believe these guys? Do you think we'd admit smoking dope even if we were?'

Rachel half smiled. They couldn't possibly arrest them for admitting to having a toke from time to time.

'Can't afford fags, let alone skunk,' said Olive.

The way Olive said 'skunk' made DS Dawson narrow her eyes.

'You two been friends for a while, have you?' she asked.

'Since I've been here at the refuge,' said Olive.

Rachel was suddenly wary.

'How long would that be?'

'Going on for two years now, hey, Rach?'

Rachel took a deep breath. Nodded. She'd been there for almost four. Way too long. They'd said they didn't want to lose her voluntary work there, but now she'd set the ball in motion for that flat by the station, she could be moving out soon.

Rachel had befriended Olive when she'd been brought in, beaten badly, one eye black and almost closed. They'd taken her to the hospital with a suspected broken nose, but it had just been badly swollen. The colours had faded to a sickly yellow-green on her cheek. And since then Olive seemed to think Rachel was some kind of saviour. She swallowed.

'You look after each other, do you?' asked DS Dawson. 'Look *out* for each other, I should say.'

'Course we do. Like sisters, we are,' said Olive.

Rachel frowned. She wanted to distance herself from Olive. Were they linking the two of them to this somehow?

'Why did you ask us about whether we smoke marijuana?' asked Rachel.

'Aside from the artwork on the side of Mr Harper's Bentley, which we now know about,' said DS Dawson, looking at Olive, 'The SOCOs have turned up something interesting in Mr Harper's bedroom.'

Rachel heard the gulp in Olive's throat. She was suddenly alert. Why would Olive have had anything to do with his death? The need to know how Olive found out Harper was a rapist was now more than morbid curiosity. She was missing some important information; everyone seemed to know more than her.

'There was an ashtray beside his bed. Traces of cannabis. The thing is, Mrs Harper insists that her husband never smoked.'

Olive snorted.

'Smoking pot is a pastime people like that will always keep hidden from their stuck-up wives,' she said. 'Along with raping schoolgirls.'

Rachel's stomach did a flip. Had Olive already suspected after Rachel's confession in the group all those weeks ago? It would explain the graffiti. She must have been paying attention, and had somehow seen or heard the news. He was a prominent person around town. Rachel didn't think Olive even knew who he was. Why would she have cared? Always so wrapped up in her self-harming little world.

'Seriously, DS Dawson, it's nothing to do with us,' said Olive. 'One of the other girls was watching Corrie with me that night. I can tell you that with absolute certainty. And she'll confirm that Rachel was here too. Our alibi's watertight. Shall I get your coats?'

After a sharp warning to Olive about her sassy mouth, the cops left, saying they'd be in contact if they needed any further information. In the hallway, Rachel turned to Olive.

'I've been wanting to ask you since your little graffiti incident, Olive, how the hell did you know? I never told anyone.'

'Well you've obviously shared your secret with Trudy. I heard you talking about it in the hallway the day she came to the refuge. Rach my darling, you have no idea. Ken Harper? He was mine after he was yours. He's the guy who did all that to me. My abuse. *He's* the reason I'm here. He's the reason we met. *He's* the guy. I worked out you must have been the one who set fire to him in his posh fucking bed. That's why I gave the cops an alibi for you. Much as I miss the bastard from time to time, he deserved what he had coming to him for doing that to you when you were just a kid. I figured it all out. That you must have been the one who snuffed him.'

50

OLIVE

Two weeks ago

Olive wasn't sure about the look Rachel was giving her. It was a combination of shock and suspicion, and perhaps a little bit of disgust. She felt a sharp pang of sadness at the latter. She had thought this knowledge and keeping her secret would bring them closer together.

'I don't understand why you couldn't share this kind of information when we first became friends, Rach. We could have collaborated. With both of us knowing, it would have made it easier to deal with. Together.'

'I don't know what you mean, Olive, but it wasn't me. I didn't kill that man. I'm not sure I'm okay with what you're implying. You never volunteered the information about who your abuser was either, even when we were sitting in that dusty old school hall sharing all our secrets. To be honest, I feel a little stupid, knowing he did all those horrible things to you afterwards.'

'So you should be feeling sorry for *me!* I didn't reveal who'd done that to me for the same reason you didn't.'

'I need to look after number one at the moment, Olive, especially now the shit has hit the fan. No thanks to Trudy, mind. But you should never have written that on the side of his car. I don't think you realise what you've done.'

'I know exactly what I've done. I've told the world the truth about what he was. Because he went and died, taking his filthy secrets with him. And that's just not right. He shouldn't get away with it. Another fucking Jimmy Savile.'

'But don't you see? It doesn't matter which of these flaky residents gives you an alibi, you have just implicated yourself in his possible murder. Christ, I'm still gobsmacked. This is insane! It's so hard to digest. I have to sleep on it. You've got to give me some space.'

Olive smarted inside as Rachel went up to her room. Her heart beat a little faster with the anxiety of having said or done the wrong thing. She didn't want to lose any of Rachel's compassion and respect. Didn't she realise she'd been doing her a favour? But at least now if the police were building a case against the two of them, they would be in it together, and that gave her a grain of comfort.

Before she went to bed that night she took her razor and cut another precise line on her leg, feeling the purity of the pain, purging the stink of wretchedness she always felt when she'd done something she wasn't proud of. It also helped to take her mind off Ken. He hadn't been nearly as bad as her dad, truth be told. He only once, that last time, hit her so hard on her face that it had been obvious for more than a week. That was when the barman and his girlfriend had brought her here to the refuge. Was she grateful for that? Now that Ken was dead, she wasn't sure. If Rachel turned against her, she had nothing left. How could she regain Rachel's respect?

After the bleeding on her inner thigh stopped, she waited a little before climbing under her sheets to avoid them blotting her new wound. She lay with the back of her hand against the sheet, the pale inside of her left arm facing upwards. Thinking of Rachel, she gently stroked the skin with her right hand, her fingers feathering the old scars like a familiar braille, retelling her story. She shuddered with the pleasure of it, the trigger of the nerve-endings a lustrous contrast to the pain still singing on her thigh.

When she woke in the morning, she lay in bed until the pressure in her bladder became too much. She heard the other women in the house getting up, going about their morning business, some of them getting ready to go out to their temporary jobs or to the employment centre to look for work.

When she couldn't wait any more, she removed the chair from under the handle and opened the door to head for the bathroom. Rachel's door opened as she passed and Martha stepped out. She had Rachel's favourite sarong wrapped around her skinny frame and Olive wanted to snatch it from her, tell her she was infecting the soft green and gold material with her bitch's smell.

Had she just spent the night with Rachel? What fresh madness was this? Olive swayed into her on purpose in the hallway, knocked her into the wall and threw the girl a sneer. But Martha wouldn't make eye contact, looked down at the threadbare carpet, deferring to Olive, and pressed herself against the wall to let her pass by. As Olive entered the bathroom she turned to see Martha padding barefoot down the stairs to use the toilet next to the dayroom. She smirked. The tiles would be cold in there.

As Olive sat on the toilet, her oversized nightshirt bunched up against her thighs, she spotted a pregnancy testing kit in the waste paper basket below the sink. Which of the girls had carelessly left this? There was a distinct double blue line across the window of the plastic applicator. How was the girl who took this test feeling about the news? The result of some marital rape. Most of the women there had escaped toxic relationships.

It brought to mind Rachel, who still regretted getting rid of her baby when she was seventeen. What would have happened if Olive herself had become pregnant with Ken's baby? Jealousy streaked inexplicably through her gut. It was a thing Ken and Rachel created that he and Olive hadn't. Of all the times they'd had sex, very few of those were instigated voluntarily by her, and there hadn't ever been the time or sensibility to use protection. Olive had never even taken a morning-after pill. She'd never fallen pregnant. Imagine the tie she would have had to Kenneth Harper then. He would have owed her more than just a set of bruises.

The fact that Olive and Rachel had shared Ken Harper blew her away. Just think of it. Rachel and Olive could have shared his baby too. If Rachel hadn't killed the thing with her gin and hot bath.

There was a loud rap at the door, and Olive snapped out of her daydream. She wiped, flushed and washed her hands. When she opened the door, Rachel was standing in the hallway.

'You're not to threaten Martha in any way, Olive.'

Whoa. Rachel had never looked daggers at her like before. Talk about threatening. Pot, kettle and all that.

'Is she your lezzy friend now, then?'

As soon as it slipped from Olive's mouth, she regretted it. Rachel's chin pointed as she tightened her jaw and drew her mouth into the shape of a cat's arse. Olive noticed Rachel's fist clench at her side, but she didn't raise it. She probably suspected Olive would welcome a smack across her face, especially from her.

Martha was not what Rachel needed; couldn't she see that? She knew what Rachel needed, and she was going to get it for her.

'Look, Olive, I don't know what you think you have on me, or what you think there is between *us*, but our friendship, yours and mine, is just that. It's a friendship. We don't owe each other anything, no matter what has happened in the past that we somehow have this bizarre link to. I'm still trying to get my head around it all – the Kenneth Harper thing – but don't go getting any ideas about an alliance of some kind, okay?'

'What's to get your head around, Rach? Ken Harper's been a naughty boy for years. There's no way he should have been getting away with it. His stupid wife wasn't giving him what he needed so he went looking elsewhere. Simple. It's a small town. Do you think this place is dripping with those guys? Not likely. All I'm saying is, he probably got what was coming to him. The burning, and all that. Someone finally had the guts to waste him, hey?'

Rachel narrowed her eyes. Olive swallowed.

'So let me get this straight,' said Rachel. 'If it wasn't an accident and it wasn't *you* who set fire to Kenneth Harper in his bed, then who the hell was it?'

51

TRUDY

Two days ago

W hen Suzy had called to confirm it was Olive who'd sprayed the graffiti on Harper's Bentley, I pulled Olive aside after the group meeting the following week. Olive admitted she'd overheard me talking to Rachel at the refuge. But I was stunned that Kenneth Harper was the one who'd abused Olive too. Hitchin was a small town, but bloody hell. That was an incredible coincidence. I wasn't sure what the truth was anymore. I could almost have believed Olive made up that story to get close to Rachel. No, that was ridiculous. My befuddled mind was making up impossible scenarios. But one thing was certain, more individual sessions with Olive were going to be necessary.

I regretted Rachel had been dragged into the limelight for this reveal, especially before we'd had a chance to talk to Suzy together about the councilman. On the other hand I was glad the bastard had finally been exposed for his crime, even though it was posthumously.

When I arrived home after the meeting, Harry was already asleep. As usual he was up early the next morning for work, so it wasn't until Thursday evening that I managed to discuss the whole thing with him. I'd had a rough day, Benny grizzling again, probably teething, and the confusion of organising my notes at the clinic after Olive's recent actions. It was public knowledge now, or would be when the press got hold of the police report. They were probably already working on an article about her vandalism.

Over a dried-out dinner the following evening, I told Harry about my continued worries about Olive.

'Don't you think the concerns of your project are preoccupying you at the moment?' he asked.

I was floored. He had always been so supportive of my project. But Harry himself had been looking worn out as well recently. He was spending long hours at the office and on his sites. We were both overworked.

'I know we seem to be coming out of this colicky stage with Benny,' he continued. 'But I'm a little worried you're favouring their presence over his.'

'That's a bit harsh, Harry. It's only once a week.'

'Plus, the reports and your paper,' he said.

'There *was* a point where I couldn't see an end to Benny's sleepless nights, pain and discomfort, and it was starting to do me in. But the group has been a good distraction for me. It's a little unfair of you say I *favour* them over family.'

Harry put his knife and fork carefully onto the plate, his appetite obviously diminished.

'I'm sorry, Trude, I didn't mean to be demeaning. It's just that they seem like such a handful, that bunch. Like they should all still be in full-time therapy.'

I understood what he was thinking. He was coming home exhausted from his own work to find his wife was also simply too tired to function. I should have told Harry I sometimes wished I'd never become a mother. It was hard to separate the two. Giving birth and becoming a mother. Bringing Benny into the world had had an adverse effect on the latter. And that was the last thing I should ever tell Harry. Because after everything, it might somehow destroy the acceptance that he was not Benny's biological father. It might destroy him. It didn't stop me having those thoughts though.

'We should maybe look at getting more help,' he said. 'Your mum's been great. But it's a bigger challenge for my mum as she's a lot older. We can't keep relying on them to lend a hand.'

'I know. None of us could have predicted how I would feel after he was born. Honestly, I think the productiveness with the group therapy is going to help me be a better mother. I really want to make both things work.'

'You worry about these people like they're your children. You worry about them more than your own child.'

'Jesus, Harry.'

He wouldn't let it go, but I didn't need any more of this guilt, even though he had a point. It was so hard to explain.

'I'm sorry. I'm not being fair,' he said, leaning across the table and putting his hand on my arm.

'We'll make this work,' I said with more conviction than I felt.

'I believe in you, Trude. I think we can stretch to paying for extra help for a few hours a week. Don't be the martyr, however much you want to do everything yourself.'

His tone made me hold my tongue. I wasn't going to tell him how I was drawn to the group on Monday evenings, and hated to admit at this stage that I couldn't wait to get away from Benny. That it was an escape. As soon as I thought that, I felt the familiar gathering of tears, the guilt flooding in with the love. I loved Benny. He was part of me. I helped make him. How could I not love him with all my heart?

I recognised the trauma of my giving birth sitting in the wings. It often put pressure on the way I felt about not just Benny, but mainly Harry. Although it was impossible, I was frightened about getting pregnant again. I was terrified about going through another birth. Reliving the trauma hadn't really lessened that fear.

However, for the past two nights Benny had only woken once, at around 2:00am for a feed, and had then slept both times all the way through to 6:00am. This might have seemed like a short night for most people, but for me it felt like a holiday.

The discussion with Harry could have gone one way or the other. I lay tucked into his arm as I imagined him processing the fact that I wasn't going to give up my work, listening to the steady beat of his heart in his chest. I breathed in deeply, my thoughts calming. I took in the muskiness of his body, his strong shoulder flexing under my cheek. I fluttered my hand across his muscular stomach and felt his heartrate increase.

He turned towards me and gently cupped my breast. He leaned down and kissed my nipple, and the electric arrow of pleasure that coursed through me was so much different from the feeling I had when Benny used to latch on. I had no food left for Benny now, so what use were my breasts? This long-forgotten ignition made me smile. That age-old enigma of men's fascination with women's breasts.

'I want to make you feel good,' whispered Harry.

'That feels good,' I said, and smiled. 'It's just... I don't think I can handle you inside me just yet.'

'I can still make you feel good,' he said, and moved under the cover, kissing my breasts, my belly, the insides of my thighs.

I let the feeling wash through me, like a river of rain after months of drought. I raised my hips to the gentle touch of his tongue and succumbed to the release.

I realised it wasn't the sex I'd been afraid of all this time, but the trauma of birth. And I knew, eventually, everything would be alright.

But by 4:00pm the next day, my baby boy had gone.

52

TRUDY

Present day

My body spasms as the flash of another camera brings me out of some weird momentary trance. My heart pounds hard enough in my chest for me to see the cotton of my blouse trembling with each beat. I roll my shoulders and reach to the notch at the base of my skull to try to loosen the tension in my neck. I realise I've been in some kind of brief catatonic state. It's not the first time this has happened over the past couple of weeks. What am I doing in front of all these people? I don't recall being asked to deliver a lecture to the BACP.

And then I remember. I somehow zoned out with the shock of the question from that journalist after I delivered my appeal. The question that was really an accusation.

Where is Benny?

Harry has hold of my elbow. I rise and stumble with him out of the room. I clench my jaw to suppress the sob that threatens to howl its way out of my throat. When we're in the corridor, I turn to DS Flatman.

'Can we go to your office?' I ask him. 'I need to talk about the group therapy members.'

We shove past the last of the reporters crowding the corridor and some technical staff from the *BBC Look East* news team. Once we're inside DS Flatman's office, I breathe out, as though with relief, to get away from the crowd. I still feel sick, though. Benny.

'I'm sorry about that reporter.' DS Flatman pauses. 'So what about these group therapy patients of yours, Mrs Greenwood? You ruled them out, but have you thought of something else since your husband first mentioned them? We've contacted them, to account for their whereabouts on Saturday. But are you having doubts about them? There may be issues we need to be forewarned about, given their medical histories.'

I pick at a pulled thread on my skirt. I don't care anymore whether I'm breaching any kind of therapist-patient etiquette at this point. I need to get the attention away from me.

'One of the members, Olive, is particularly disturbed,' I say. 'But I honestly wouldn't have expected her to do anything like this. For a start, I don't think she'd be capable of taking Benny without my knowing. She's a nervous thing, can't do anything quietly. The stealth required... I am pretty sure it's not her, she has no motive.'

I recall Rachel mentioning recently how she was so worried about Olive's behaviour. There's another kind of jealousy going on there, especially after that weird business with the graffiti on Kenneth Harper's car. There are a lot of things I hadn't realised about Olive. Her snatching my baby seems preposterous. But might she have done that for Rachel?

Then there was Rachel's reaction to Benny in the ladies' loo in the old school building. I never imagined Rachel would have such a strong reaction to discovering that I had a child. Lovely Rachel. Finding her own feet again after the tragedies the world has served her. An image of her holding Benny in the café comes to mind. Her adoring look. The look anyone might give a cute baby. Just the thought that Rachel might have taken him makes me feel sick.

'I omitted to tell a member of the group – Rachel – that I'd had a baby when the sessions started. It wasn't something I was consciously keeping from her. I just forgot. We hadn't seen each other for months. But she reacted very emotionally. Then she held

Benny when we ran into each other a couple of weeks ago.' I don't want to say that we'd arranged to meet.

'What? You didn't tell me that!' says Harry.

I could feel irritation. As though I was handing Benny around to strangers all the time.

'Perhaps that's significant?' he asks, looking hopefully at the police officers.

'She and I became close when she was my patient. I trust her implicitly. Or thought I did. It can't be her, can it?' I feel suddenly guilty that Rachel is on a list of suspects at all. 'But when I think how Olive is so unstable, and how she might be capable of anything to prove herself to Rachel...'

I think of each member of the group, sitting in their circle of chairs in the school hall. It would normally never happen, men and women in the same group like that, unless it was AA or drugs. But no one objected when I'd planned it all. This thing that had become my lifeline outside the chaos of motherhood. As Rachel and Olive are getting ready to leave the refuge and restart their lives on their own, the three of us – Rachel and Olive and I – talked it through and agreed that a little more exposure to the male psyche would help them understand what had been done to them in the past. Rachel especially thought Olive would benefit and said she'd keep an eye on her, feeling safe in a controlled environment. But who exactly has been keeping an eye on whom all this time?

'Daniel Lockyear has had issues about setting the world to rights. He has two beautiful children of his own, and I wondered why on earth he would take a baby. But I think he also recognised that Rachel was pining for the baby she lost. Maybe he wanted to help her, in his obsessive, warped world?'

'Wow, you didn't tell me this either, Trude. This sounds like a lonely-hearts circle.'

I ignore him, stare at the table and swallow. If I hadn't just re-remembered for the hundredth time in the last hour that my baby was missing, I would have laughed.

'The last member is Alain, but I wouldn't have thought he'd be interested in children. He's getting over a relationship. He has trauma resulting from a fire rescue. He just wants to go home to Switzerland.'

'Switzerland... Alain Favre?' DS Flatman asks.

'Yes,' I say carefully.

'The Swiss man who was staying illegally in the music studio on the industrial estate.' It's a statement, not a question. Something seems to click in DS Flatman's mind.

I nod and swallow.

'Jeez. DC Snowden?' he yells, making me jump.

His partner comes rushing through from the outer office.

'Have you got tabs on Favre and the music guy? Did anyone manage to identify any of those kids in the photographs?'

'I'll get onto it, Sarge. You think there's a connection?'

'What photographs?' I ask.

'Yes there could be a connection!' says Flatman.

'Bloody hell, what are you talking about here,' asks Harry. 'Child pornography? Baby trafficking?'

I put my head in my hands while DS Flatman stands up and hurries out of the office throwing orders to his staff left and right.

I don't really know my patients at all. I've been talking about them as though it's not completely impossible that one of these people could have taken Benny. And although he was the person I would least suspect out of the group, it now seems even Alain might have a motive. Would *he* be the one selling Benny to a child trafficking ring so he could pay for his ticket home? My beautiful Benny. A hundred scenarios flick through my mind.

I think of Harry, begging me to keep eye contact with him. To stop the journalists and the TV crew grabbing my attention.

'What did that man mean, trying to compare this to the Madeleine McCann case?' I ask slowly.

Before Harry can answer, DS Flatman comes back into the office. There's a ringing in my ears cancelling out all other sounds around me and I push the chair away to put my head between my knees. DS Flatman moves the waste paper bin over towards me. As the ringing fades and blood returns to my head, the policeman asks Harry a few more questions about his work, about both of our parents, about neighbours, friends in the village. Things he's already asked in our previous interviews.

I squeeze my eyes closed. The notes on DS Flatman's pad must be growing longer and longer. But those top four names are still burning into my mind. It wouldn't be hard for any of them to find out where we live although I've never shared my personal details with them. The four members of my group therapy. The four people I thought I knew, but that I probably haven't even begun to dig below the epidermis.

As I picture the reporter's hand waving around in the heat of that room, I wonder if my own name or Harry's has been added to the list of suspects.

53

RACHEL

Rachel is in the kitchen preparing spag bol when someone calls her urgently into the common room. She slides the saucepan off the element and turns off the water that's begun to boil for the spaghetti. On her way out, she grabs the packet of grated parmesan, knowing it will disappear if she leaves it lying on the counter. She rushes to the room where three women are sitting on the lumpy couch.

'Is that Trudy? Is this live? God, what's happened?' asks Rachel.

'I think it's repeated from last night's news,' continues one of the women. 'Baby snatcher.'

Rachel's mouth hangs open and she's about to ask *what the hell?* when the woman cuts her off.

'Shh. Listen.'

On the top left of the screen is the *Look East* logo. Trudy is sitting next to a good-looking man at a table. Behind them on the wall is a projected image of a baby. It's Benny.

They seem to be getting ready for some kind of press conference. A reporter begins talking over the image of Trudy and the man.

'Little Benny Greenwood was snatched from Trudy and Harry Greenwood's back garden in the Hertfordshire village of Whitwell between three and four in the afternoon yesterday. Mrs Greenwood is a senior psychologist at the Pinewood Clinic and Mr Greenwood is an industrial architect in the City. They are about to make an appeal to the public for their son. Benny was four months old last Wednesday.'

Rachel feels the hot press of tears at the back of her throat. She can't get over the fact that Trudy lives in the same village as her parents.

'Oh my God. Poor Trudy.'

Trudy's eyes are bright with tears and red-rimmed. Rachel's never seen her husband Harry before. They make a handsome couple. It's no surprise Benny is so damned cute. Rachel's stomach lurches.

'Shit, someone took that woman's baby!' says one of the women on the sofa.

'Have you seen Olive?' Rachel asks, narrowing her eyes.

'Haven't seen her today,' says one of the women on the sofa and the other two shake their heads. On the TV screen, Trudy clears her throat and speaks into the microphone on the table.

'Benny is only four months old. Please, he needs his mother. And father.' Trudy puts her hand over Harry's and tries to smile through her teary eyes. 'If you have our baby, please return him. You can leave him anonymously. Please. We just want our son back.'

Rachel wonders whether the police insisted that Trudy say something. It's weird how the world thinks the female parent has more at stake. Trudy is choking up, obviously having difficulty, and these words don't sound like her. She's following some script. A script that might be given to every parent who's ever had their child taken and has been persuaded to do an appeal.

It's over in a moment, so quick.

'Mrs Greenwood, do you see...' It's the voice of a reporter off-screen.

'No questions, thank you!' says the big policeman standing behind Trudy.

'... a correlation with the Madeleine McCann case almost twenty years ago?'

The big police officer who said 'no questions' has a round jolly face belying his status. His hand lingers in the air, held up towards the unseen audience behind the TV camera. The room goes silent. Rachel questions why they'd let reporters into such a room in the first place. That seems so wrong. Something the Americans would do with their glamorisation of cases like this. Now Trudy looks at the man who asked the question with a furrow across her brow and a tear spills down one cheek.

'No... I... not at all.'

Her husband leans across, is whispering something to Trudy. Probably telling her she doesn't need to answer such a ridiculous question. Rachel feels an ache in her throat. The cheek of that reporter. Benny was snatched from their own garden! It's nowhere near the same as leaving your kid in your holiday villa bedroom to go and have dinner at a restaurant with friends. But he has undeniably put the seed of doubt in many viewers' minds.

The flash of a camera seems to startle Trudy out of shock. She blinks a few times, looking out past the camera as though she wants to say something to that reporter, then stands up and walks unsteadily away with her husband at her side. The announcer reads out the telephone and text numbers rolling across a banner on the screen as they all leave the scene.

As the click and whirr of the cameras continue, the blanched faces of Trudy and her husband do remind Rachel of Kate and Gerry McCann. That desperate, unfathomable look of parents who've been kicked in the gut and simply don't know what to do. A horrible thought flits through Rachel's mind. The accusations following the disappearance of Maddie McCann. What the parents might themselves have done to their little girl. Some people will always be thinking the worst.

And Rachel realises the reporter and some of the viewers are now probably thinking that too.

54

TRUDY

I feel like we've been playing a game of ping-pong between home and the police station. I take a deep breath and look around the room. This is nothing like the office I was in before. There's a window of sorts. I'm surprised. I thought interview rooms were windowless. This one is a narrow oblong of reinforced glass, letting in a sliver of light, reassuring me it's still daytime. When they came to our house earlier and said, "You and Mr Greenwood need to come with us," my heart raced.

'You've found...?' Harry had immediately asked.

'No, sorry,' said DS Flatman. 'I didn't mean to either excite you or alarm you, but we need some additional information.'

'Can't you ask us here? In more comfortable surroundings? And in case someone comes back with... news.'

Or Benny, I'd thought. *Why can't Harry say his name?*

'Is my husband answering questions, too?' I ask, dragging my eyes back from the strip of daylight.

'He's next door with my colleagues, Mrs Greenwood.'

I guess that means yes. Why do I suddenly feel like there's a virtual noose hanging above my head?

'Your mother says you'd been having difficulties with the baby. Can you tell us a little about that?'

What? I suddenly feel wary. I guess that's why we're here, and not in the comfort of our home. Keeping us separated to validate our answers. Since that reporter asked the question about the similarity of our case to the McCanns at the appeal, all I can think is: *they never found Maddie.*

'Do you have children, Mr Flatman?'

'Please answer the question, Mrs Greenwood. But in case you're concerned about my parenting knowledge, yes, I do have a three-year-old daughter.'

A hiss unintentionally escapes my mouth. I bite my lip before answering. 'When you're a parent for the first time, it's unclear what's normal. But it seemed to me from all the books and advice I'd been given that Benny was – *is* – fussier than the normal baby.' I feel sick at having used the past tense. 'I meant, he *was,* because he's definitely been getting better over the past weeks. For two months he was colicky, a bad sleeper, quite a fussy eater. Didn't take easily to... me.' I point vaguely in the direction of my chest, weirdly don't want to say the word 'breast' in front of the policeman.

'Your mother has indicated that you might have had a harder time coping than other mothers. Said you'd even considered consulting a doctor, thinking the baby's behaviour wasn't normal.'

Blast my mother's Teutonic honesty.

'Well, you do question that kind of thing, don't you? Especially when you see a little baby in so much pain and discomfort. No one wants to see an infant go through that, especially one's own.'

'Did you ever think you might not be able to cope? That you might have had some postnatal issues?'

How anxious a mother is DS Flatman's own wife? He's obviously been doing his homework since then. Somehow, in this environment, in this neutral grey room, there is not an ounce of sympathy in his manner.

'If you're digging for my maternal mental stability, yes, I did wonder if what I was feeling was usual. But we've passed that stage now. Benny is a perfectly normal baby who needs to be found and returned to his mother and his family.'

What kind of questions is Harry being asked in the room next door? Will he paint me as the angelic mother? How much will he say about his involvement as a father? I swallow. What are the police implying here?

'Mrs Greenwood, during those times when your son was having colicky days, perhaps crying for hours on end, how did that make you feel? How did you react?'

There's that phrase. The one *I* should be asking. *How did that make you feel?* Why do I feel like I'm the patient? Or the accused?

'It's frustrating when there's nothing you can really do. A crying child, especially your own, can tear little pieces of your heart out.'

Flatman tips his head to one side but I can't tell if he's agreeing with me or not. I imagine he had the model daughter. On his long shifts, his wife or partner would have mostly been looking after the baby. I wonder if his wife told him *everything*.

'Did you talk these feelings over with your husband?' he asks.

Ah, so these are the answers they will go away with and compare notes later.

'Some days you know the burden of your partner's work has probably been more trying than taking care of a baby. Some days it's easier to get on with doing the housework and preparing meals as part of the routine without discussion. On top of trying to look after your fussy child.' *If you're in the right frame of mind*, I think. 'And some days those other things don't get done. Those times I concentrated on looking after Benny. Harry would know how I felt, often without having to ask. But he knew.'

I hope, if DS Flatman has never appreciated how much work his wife has gone through to look after their three-year-old daughter while he was working, that tonight he'll go home, kiss her and tell her what a wonderful mother she is.

'Have you ever behaved in a way towards your son that might be inappropriate? Have you ever become angry or reacted physically? Shaken him, maybe?'

'No!' I'm running out of patience. 'What are you implying? Have those stupid journalists given you ideas? Someone has stolen my baby. You think *I* did something to him?'

'That's not what I asked, Mrs Greenwood. You're putting words into my mouth.'

I almost roll my eyes, but resist the temptation. 'You asked three questions, DS Flatman. The first is no, I don't believe I've ever behaved inappropriately. The second, I've never been angry, but it upsets me to hear him in such pain. Tell me any mother who doesn't have a little cry every now and then – no woman is ever completely sure she's doing the mothering thing correctly. And the third is, no absolutely not. I've never shaken him. I know how fragile an infant is. I would *never* do anything to harm Benny. Never.'

'A neighbour of your mother's once saw you parked outside her house, talking loudly to yourself in your car "in a bit of a state". It was only after a moment that she realised your son was in the back. She said she was worried you were getting a little "hot under the collar", as she put it.'

DC Flatman refers to an iPad in front of him where he must have a list of notes from people he's interviewed. My mother would never have dreamed that her concerns would be taken in the worst possible light. And as for the nosy neighbour, there might have been a little more malice in her comments. She's still never forgiven me for throwing a load of rotten apples that had fallen from the tree at the bottom of our garden over the fence when I was six.

'I was having a bad day,' I say weakly. 'I was begging Benny to be good for his grandmother. So she wouldn't begrudge looking after him when I needed some time... in the office.' I'd been about to say "alone" instead of "in the office" but thought that was painting myself into an even darker corner.

I think about those black moments that come creeping in when you least expect it. I'm aware how unpredictable they can be, having had to deal with many patients trying to keep their depression at bay. How honest will Harry be about my concerns? About my own *behaviour*?

The door opens, slicing through the thick atmosphere like a guillotine. An officer leans into the room.

'Sarge, Super wants to see you before he knocks off tonight.'

DS Flatman and I look at our watches simultaneously. I feel the stirring of a meal for Benny in my breasts for the first time in weeks. Benny has now been missing for more than seventy-two hours. I should express whatever is there.

'I'll be right there,' Flatman says to the officer, and turns to me. 'We don't want you to attend your weekly group therapy meeting tomorrow night.'

I'd completely forgotten about the group meeting and almost reply, *of course not. I can't because you've got my husband and I need to be at home to look after...* But Benny's not there. And I'm here. And I'm no longer sure if the police believe that Benny is really missing. I look helplessly down at my arms in my lap, as though someone has only now snatched my baby from me. I think I will go quite mad.

'Have any of the group members been in touch with you?'

'Yes, I... Rachel sent a message asking if I'm okay. Have you talked to any of them?'

'Yes, we've contacted them individually, all except Olive Stanton, but the refuge is onto it. But we'd like to meet with the group together tomorrow. The easiest way is if you could send them a confirmation that the meeting will go ahead. We'd rather not have them all coming to the station together.'

'But won't they think that's odd? My baby is missing. They'll surely assume I'll cancel.'

'They're even less likely to turn up if we tell them there'll be a police presence. I'm hoping their concern for your welfare will mean they'll rally, whether they're involved or not. And of course, if any of them don't show up... well...'

I reach down to my handbag and take out my keyring.

'It'll make it easier if I give you this.' I push my thumbnail between the spirals to remove the old schoolhouse key. 'The library and the admin office at the council have keys, but they're notoriously hard to get hold of.'

My thumbnail bends back alarmingly and a split appears where it meets the flesh. I let out an exasperated sigh and hand over the key.

'Obviously don't tell them you won't be there tomorrow if they contact you in the meantime. After having talked to us and seen the news, they'll be too curious to stay away, certainly if they're innocent. We're hoping to keep tabs on them tonight and tomorrow, though we're short-staffed. But if anyone doesn't turn up to that meeting it'll be a red flag.' DS Flatman leans forward. 'We're doing all we can to find Benny.'

It's like some kind of comical cuckoo's nest scenario to expect the whole group will turn up. Whoever doesn't, though, will take the pressure off the police thinking I might be guilty of anything. If they've already talked to them individually, what do they now intend to ask them? A sheen of sweat on my forehead accompanies a spike of alarm.

'You're free to go, Mrs Greenwood. Don't be alarmed if you see some disturbance in your garden when you get home.'

I frown. 'I don't understand.'

'Your garden has been thoroughly searched.'

I swallow, imagining the entire North Hertfordshire's police force occupied with our case, a forensic digging up of my carefully tended flowerbeds, others observing the members of my group therapy now, at their respective jobs, in their homes, refuges, dodgy accommodations. I imagine if I could look in a mirror right now, I'd see the lines on my face etched as deeply as Kate McCann's in that news conference all those years ago. And because of the one cruel unanswered question posed by that journalist during Benny's appeal, Harry and I have fallen under similar contrary suspicions.

55

ALAIN

Alain knows these guys are cops even though neither of them are in uniform and neither of them interviewed him at the station. It's the smell and the way they hold themselves that tells him they're definitely cops. The senior one is a big guy. Looks like he would be trouble if you met him on a dark street.

'Who the heck are these guys?' whispers Rachel.

'*Les flics*. Police,' says Alain.

'They must be here because of Trudy.'

'I was asked twice about that councilman who was found dead in his bed. I thought this might be more questions about him.'

Alain doesn't say anything about the photos in Ron's studio. They let him go, 'pending further investigation'.

'You didn't hear? Her kid was snatched. From her very own back garden.'

'Yes, they asked me. He's still missing? They didn't find him?'

Rachel shakes her head. 'I thought the meeting would be cancelled. I only came to see if there's anything I could do to help,' she says. 'And to see whether Olive would show up. She's gone AWOL. I hope she hasn't done anything stupid. Again.'

'Well, yes, some money has gone missing from the office at your refuge,' says the cop, as though the refuge is somehow Rachel's responsibility.

'When was that?' she asks. 'Nobody said anything to me. That would usually cause an uproar at the refuge.'

'Saturday, apparently, but we're not here for that,' says the cop.

'Oh, Olive. What the hell have you done now?' Rachel whispers next to Alain.

'Let's wait and see if Ms Stanton comes,' says the cop. 'We'll give her five more minutes.'

'I can't believe someone took Trudy's baby. I didn't even know she had a kid before,' says Alain. '*Mon Dieu*. This is terrible!'

Alain hasn't had a chance to talk to Ron about those photos. He seems to be getting himself inadvertently deeper into a whole series of things going wrong. The baby, stolen?

Out of habit, Rachel and Alain automatically pull five chairs across and place them in a circle. They take two seats on one side of the circle and the officers sit on the other side. There's still one empty. Waiting for either Daniel or Olive. If they both turn up there'll be musical chairs. Alain doesn't get up to fetch another chair. The circle becomes more like a rectangle. A *tribunal*.

'My name's DS David Flatman,' says the larger man. 'This is my colleague DC Snowden. We'll be splitting you up to ask a few questions later. Please, make yourself comfortable until everyone gets here.'

Alain sniffs. This is not *their* space. They don't own this safe place that has grown between everyone in these weekly meetings. He's about to protest, when the door opens and Daniel comes in, saving Alain from saying something he might regret. Daniel pauses for a second when he sees the two strangers, and Alain imagines he's feeling the same thing *he* did when he saw them. Daniel slowly takes off his jacket, hangs it on the hook in the corridor that leads to the bathrooms and walks to the circle. He leans in slightly to read the name badge on the big cop's lanyard.

'You don't look anything like Flats,' he says.

'I can't tell you how many times I've heard those words in the past ten years, sir,' says DS Flatman. 'And you are?'

'Daniel. Daniel Lockyear. Where's Trudy? Has something happened?'

'*Flats?*' Rachel whispers.

'Rugby chap,' Daniel whispers to her as he sits down. Alain is none the wiser.

'We'll wait until everyone gets here to discuss it,' says the big cop.

'Good grief, that doesn't sound good. Is Trudy alright?' asks Daniel. 'Didn't they find her baby?'

'Nothing has happened to Mrs Greenwood, sir. Not directly anyway.'

'Didn't you see the news?' asks Rachel.

'Not really. Unless you count a potential collapse of the US dollar due to the actions of an incapable lunatic president. I've been rather occupied all day.'

'Bloody hell, having your kid abducted is hardly *nothing*,' says Rachel, glaring at the DS. 'The baby *is* still missing.'

'Abducted? Her baby was abducted? That's awful,' says Daniel.

'Who else are we still expecting?' asks DS Flatman, referring to his list, a little late, it seems to Alain.

'Olive,' says Rachel.

'Yes, there was some confusion about her whereabouts. The refuge manager said she was there, and then when someone went to her room, she'd left her radio on, but was absent. There's a search for her going on, but in the meantime we wanted to ask you all some questions.'

'Where's Trudy?' asks Alain.

'Trudy's attention is probably on other things, Alain,' says Rachel.

'Of course. *La pauvre*,' says Alain.

'Her *attention* has been drawn to a few things that have been happening in parallel with this group. I believe you've been speaking to my colleagues about that, Mr Favre.'

Alain leans back in his chair and crosses his arms. He knew they wouldn't be able to resist. This seems unprofessional to say such a thing in front of everyone. Suspicion never ceases from these guys. They're beginning to piss him off. They're so sure he's done something criminal. The Swiss police would be awarding him the "innocent until proven guilty" card, not this relentless desire to pin something on him. If he didn't know any better, he'd have thought they were being racist.

'And, *Dieu merci*, those other *things* were coincidence. I had nothing to do with either fire. I am beginning to feel I am not welcome.'

'Alain, you're a welcome addition to this group.'

Everyone looks surprised that Rachel has said this, especially when she flashes a smile at Alain. He feels a grateful warmth and turns to the policeman.

'I only came tonight as a courtesy to my new friends here, to tell them that I will be leaving them to continue with their... healing process alone, which is obviously happening.' He smiles back at Rachel, the phrase stolen from one of Trudy's introductory speeches a point of mirth between them all. 'But I shall be happy to leave behind your strange methods of policing. I hope to go home next week. And I don't want to appear *insensible*. I really hope you find Trudy's baby.'

A small smile brightens Rachel's face. She's probably happy that he has his wish to go home.

When he turns back, the policeman is giving Alain a hard stare.

'The thing is,' interrupts Rachel, 'if you lot thought any of us had stolen Trudy's baby, where do you think we'd have put the little fellow?'

Rachel sweeps her arm in a circle, as though challenging them to search for Benny in the old school hall.

'First off, Ms...' he looks down at his list '...Headley. Nobody is accusing anybody here of having abducted a child. We're just trying to get a feel for what's been going on in Mrs Greenwood's life over the past few weeks. And that includes this group. My colleague and I have some questions we'll be asking you individually.'

'You think Trudy is somehow at fault? I don't understand, but I certainly don't like what you're implying,' says Rachel.

Alain is surprised. It sounds as if Rachel has suddenly become Trudy's best ally. He admires her for standing up to these men. The depth of defence in her voice gives away a strong emotional bond.

'You'll be happy to get back to your mountain resort after all this crap,' says Rachel quietly.

'Yes, I will,' he replies. 'Sometimes you don't know how much you miss something until it is not there anymore.'

Alain's getting tired of all this. He wishes he could just go. If Trudy's not coming, then he wants to be on his way. He's not sure what the purpose of the police presence is. And then he remembers the photos, and he avoids the eyes of the DS.

'Can we get on with this? Olive obviously isn't coming,' says Daniel. 'In which case I'd rather be helping my kids with their homework.'

Alain thinks back to the questions he was asked on Saturday about where he'd been that afternoon.

'Working at the bike shop on Walsworth Road,' he'd said, though he'd finished at four in the afternoon, but the manager wouldn't have known that as he'd been away. He doesn't have an alibi after that, but lets them believe he stayed until closing time at six.

'I don't even know where Trudy lives,' Alain says now to no one in particular. 'I didn't even know she had a baby. And as Rachel has already said, why would we be here if any of us did such a thing?'

'No one is accusing you, Mr Favre.'

'Well that's a good thing. I've had enough of the English *hospitalité*. And you've probably had enough of me as your guest.'

'I trust you've found suitable and more legal accommodation,' says the cop.

Alain takes a deep breath. *Stay calm.*

'Of course,' he says.

He expects the cop to ask him for his new address, but he doesn't. He probably already knows. There's still the issue of those photos. All those children. Babies. It's making Ron look, well, weird.

'Can we get back to my main concern?' asks DS Flatman. 'I don't think Ms Stanton is going to grace us with her presence. I'd like to ask you all a little about Mrs Greenwood. Her state of mind over the past weeks.'

Then Alain suddenly gets it. The police aren't concerned about the movements of those in the group last weekend. They're not digging for *their* motives. They're worried about Trudy's mental state. They think *she* has something to do with the disappearance of her own son.

He feels the twitch of a relieved smile on his lips.

56

OLIVE

She's had a dream since she met Rachel. They're living together in a thatched cottage in a Hertfordshire village surrounded by a garden full of bushes and flowers. They have to live on Rachel's salary at first. But Olive is sorting herself out and is on the way to getting a proper job. She's determined to contribute. Then they will truly be a family, sisters taking on an equal share of the load.

They grow tomatoes and beans. Olive takes more care of the plants than the ones she let die in the weed-strewn garden at the back of the refuge. They have pets. A puppy and a kitten. Chickens. Like children. And because Rachel is so desperate to have a real child, they decide to get a baby.

And it's perfect, because Trudy doesn't seem to want her baby. She's stressed and anxious and clearly never wanted to be a mother in the first place. So she gives her baby to Olive and Rachel. It's the ideal scenario for everybody.

Martha doesn't come to live with them because Rachel realises it's the baby she's wanted all the time, and the pale timid girl is one responsibility they can all do without. Martha Mouse can get right out of the picture. Now Rachel is the perfect mother. And Olive is the perfect aunt. They are the perfect family.

They change the baby's name. Sometimes in the dream he is Charles and sometimes he is George. Like the rich kids you see getting dropped off from their Range Rovers and Mercs at the nursery school down the road.

They alternate parenting duties. Sometimes they get a sitter when they want to go to the pub, drink chilled chardonnay and talk about how happy they are. They start earning more money and go on holiday every year to the seaside. Charles or George, or maybe even Archie, is a happy boy, loves his mum and his aunt, never cries or whines or gets ill.

Olive has often dreamt about this in the last few weeks. She took the bus to Whitwell and watched Trudy's house for a few days last month when she'd told everyone at the refuge she was starting a new job. Other days she hitchhiked to the village, and sometimes had to get a second ride from the Codicote Road. She was lucky if she got there in one go. She hid in the wheat field on the other side of the hedge bordering the Greenwoods' garden several times. She had to move somewhere else the day they harvested the field. The noisy combine harvester came right up to where she'd made herself a comfortable picnic spot and she was terrified the giant cutter bars would scoop her out of the hedge, its spinning reel ready to deliver her into the threshing cylinder and chop her to pieces. But once the crop was cut and threshed, and the straw baled, she returned to her stakeout. And continued to dream her dream.

If this dream had come true, it would make up for the fact that Ken's baby never made it into the world. She and Rachel would have that connection.

The mild weather has brought out the usual Saturday crowd onto the pavements, beer gardens and courtyards in front of the pubs and cafés. Hitchin town centre is rocking, Olive can't remember when she last saw so many people enjoying the last of the summer weather.

She watches Wetherspoons in Sun Street where people have spilled onto the pavement outside and have to cram together each time a vehicle drives past them down the narrow street. A young woman dressed a little more smartly than the hordes of tipsy teenagers extracts herself from a group who might be celebrating a hen night and walks across the Market Square towards the ATM at Barclays. Olive follows the woman, and watches while she puts in her card, enters her pin and takes a handful of notes and stuffs them into her purse, before slipping it into her handbag and wandering back to join her friends at the pub.

Olive mixes in with the crowd, weaving between a group of young men who look like they've come from a football match and a few couples out for a spontaneous Saturday night without the kids. She narrows her eyes at the latter, perhaps less aware than the former group as they're unused to being out amongst so many people in the open. Olive uses her never-forgotten skills to lift a wallet from the best-dressed and most unsuspecting of the millennial crowd before spotting the woman she saw at the bank. She finishes off her heist with the cherry on the cake.

She wastes no time, goes immediately back to the bank and slips the woman's debit card into the slot and says a little prayer, hoping she got her PIN right. *Excellent!* Nothing wrong with her eyes. She's able to take five hundred quid in one fell swoop. It's her lucky day.

Along with the cash from the other wallet she hurries down the High Street and along Bancroft towards the train station. She doesn't have time to go back to the refuge to pick up her things. Anyway, it would look odd, she'd immediately be questioned. It's time to leave this shithole behind.

Olive picks a seat on the right-hand side so she'll be able to see the sea when they get near the coast up north. Someone told her this when she changed in Peterborough and boarded this train.

The baby next to her blows bubbles while repeatedly reaching for the elastic string of rattles tied on to the handle of its carrier. As the train carriage rocks, the toys swing away from the little one, and he concentrates harder on trying to grab the objects. He finally manages to get hold of a soft blue elephant. As the baby tugs it towards his mouth, the elastic stretches and pulls out of his hand, pinging back against the handle. The baby blinks several times in quick succession and then lets out the squawk of a giggle. Like a tiny Sisyphus he tries again and again, repeating the game without success, but with no less mirth. Olive smiles.

A young man walks down the aisle as the train pulls out of Grantham Station.

'Is that one free?' he asks, pointing to the seat opposite hers. He has an American accent, or maybe Canadian. She can't tell the difference.

She shrugs and he checks there's no reserved ticket along the top of the seat. She nods towards the baby, as though to warn the new passenger of the unpredictable noise level.

'It's okay, doesn't bother me,' he says, and throws his pack into the luggage rack before sliding into the seat.

His pack has a small maple-leaf flag sewn on to the back. Canadian, then. One thing she was good at in primary school was being able to identify the world's flags. The guy is wearing a checked shirt, a pair of those chinos that zip off above the knee and a clumpy pair of hiking boots with thick chunky soles. His hair is short, but looks somewhat scruffy, as though someone in the last hostel he stayed in cut it for him for free, or perhaps in exchange for one too many beers.

'Holiday, or going home?' he asks, pointing at the small case above her on the luggage shelf.

'Moving,' she says and pauses while he sorts himself in his seat. There is luggage in the rack above her, but it's not hers. He doesn't need to know that. 'You a walker?' she asks.

'How did you guess?' he asks rhetorically. He has a warm laugh.

The baby snorts, scrunches up its nose, bares its teeth – two at the top and two at the bottom – matching the young man's laugh with a happy gurgle. They both smile at the baby's cute face for a moment.

'Where are you heading? Moors or Scotland?' Olive asks, not yet sure whether she would prefer him to say the former or the latter.

'Highlands, actually,' he says. 'You familiar with the mountains?'

'Not yet,' she says.

'I hope it doesn't rain too much,' he says.

'Ha. Well, in summer in this country you can't be guaranteed sun either. But someone told me the heather still lights up the landscape whatever the weather up there in the wilds of Scotland.

As he pulls out a paper and starts to read, Olive studies him surreptitiously. She feels strangely liberated. She spent so many months fixated on the fact that Rachel's loyalty and attention, eventually even her love, would keep her grounded. That trying to get her what Rachel truly wanted would make Olive indispensable. Whereas in reality, now that she's here, now that she's *escaped*, she realises that what Rachel wanted was exactly what Olive needed.

After breaking into the office at the refuge and taking a handful of cash, she knew she could never return. Picking those pockets in Hitchin town centre gave her a bit more of a buffer. It was time to leave it all behind. She'd seen the way Rachel and that skinny bitch looked at each other, touched each other, spoke to each other. Olive knew she'd never be able to win Rachel now. She wasn't interested in *that* way.

It's time to let Rachel get on with her life.

Olive closes her eyes and feigns sleep as the train roars into a tunnel. She lets the gurgles of the baby beside her conjure memories of her childhood, a time before people started using her body for their pleasure. She thinks of Rachel in the therapy group who'll never be able to have kids. She wonders, not for the first time, whether the fire that killed Ken was truly an accident.

After Olive's actions led her to ruin the side of Ken's car and it got into the papers, a slew of #MeToo reactions began to emerge. She feels strangely smug about that. As though she set something in motion that might protect those who felt more vulnerable about having been treated by men like Ken.

Incidents were then cited from forced sex in alleyways and violent altercations in seedy motels to a town council secretary who claimed he'd squeezed her backside and whispered inappropriate obscenities. Perhaps these allegations put a halt to the investigation into the fire. Who would want to prosecute that kind of vigilante? The case was declared death by smoking pot in his bed. It was the tamest misdemeanour on his growing list of crimes. Olive would not be held accountable.

Although she was at first torn about her misplaced loyalty to him, Olive was glad Rachel had the guts to reveal the identity of her rapist under the promise of protection.

It seems Alain was also let off. Something about helping his mate with a recording project. He was convincing about his fear of fire – at least to the others, and more importantly to the police, so how could they even think he would have had anything to do with it? She knows he'll find his way home soon. Time to leave the sordid mess behind before people start asking too many more questions.

Olive feels a tiny pang of sadness for the woman who helped her deal with the aftermath of the toxic relationship with Ken. Poor, poor Trudy, who has no idea what's happened to her baby...

Olive opens her eyes to see the woman who introduced herself earlier as Shaz coming back from the loo.

'Thanks so much,' says Shaz as she picks up the baby carrier and puts it on the seat on her side of the aisle. 'Sorry I took so long. Had to change.' She points to her chest. 'Leakage,' she whispers so the young man opposite doesn't hear.

'No worries. He was as good as gold.'

'There's no room in those disgusting cabins and I was loath to take the little tyke in there in the first place. I don't know how they expect travelling parents to deal with everything.'

'I've heard the new trains are better equipped with room for babies, they probably even have baby-changing stations,' says Olive. 'We were unlucky to be assigned an old chugger.'

Olive and Shaz started chatting while they'd been waiting next to each other on the platform for the train in Stevenage where Olive had to change to head north. She'd circled Shaz to put her body between the woman and the surveillance camera mounted above the platform near the stairs. Made it look like they were travelling together. By the time the train pulled out, the kid – Finn – had won Olive's heart and she and Shaz agreed to sit together. Olive looks at Finn now, his fist in his mouth. Shaz begins pulling things out of her bag. Pots of food. Spoons. A bib. A bottle of water.

Olive thinks of Benny, a baby she's only seen in a photo and never actually ended up meeting in real life. She hopes to God the police find him. Such a tragic thing. Who on earth would *steal* a baby? Olive had just begun to enjoy those weekly meetings, but it was time to leave.

She turns to the hiker in the seat by the window.

'How long are you going to the hills for?' she asks.

'A couple of weeks, maybe. I've taken a month off work. Don't have to go back until November.'

Maybe Olive will take up hiking. Those shoes look like they cost a fortune. Perhaps not. She needs the stolen money for simpler things such as food. She only blew the price of the train ticket rather than hitchhike because she didn't want to make it easy for the police to catch her standing at the side of some truck stop on the A1.

But when the train pulls into the station at York, she spots a couple of uniformed coppers on the platform. And after a few minutes, she sees another two walking through the carriage, scanning the seats. And she knows her escape was short-lived; she'll never get to see the sea.

57

TRUDY

I'm lying in bed, preparing to spend another restless night – the third – without Benny in our home. It doesn't help to beg for sleep; the recurring dream of seeing the breeze blow back the netting on the stroller, the mild fear that I've exposed Benny to some insect, something that could sting or bite, and the cascade of terror that sluices through me before waking each time with a pounding heart is enough to put me off closing my eyes.

The bedroom is at the back of the cottage so I don't hear the car pulling up, just the doorbell. It's shortly after midnight. Harry is in a state of semi-sleep beside me. I pull on my dressing gown and rush down to open the door. DS Flatman is smiling.

'Oh God... Really?' I ask hopefully.

I look past him to his car parked in the lane, expecting to see someone carrying Benny towards me. Instead DS Flatman hurries through to the kitchen carrying a laptop. Harry, with hair sticking up in all directions, wearing a tee-shirt and his jockey shorts, follows close on our heels

DS Flatman opens the computer on the kitchen table and clicks open a picture – it's Benny! A recent photo, one I haven't seen before.

'Benny! My baby! He's been found? Is he okay? Is Benny okay?'

'This came through from the Keswick Police Base,' says DS Flatman. 'They received a call from the Community Hospital.

Benny was left anonymously on the doorstep of a couple in Keswick.'

'Oh, Benny. Thank God!' says Harry.

'What? They just opened the door and found him on the doorstep? Was he crying? Hungry? My Benny. But Cumbria! That's so far away. Please, DS Flatman,

you're sure he's not... harmed in any way? We must leave straight away, Harry.'

'He's being checked out by a paediatrician, but first reports are that he seems perfectly healthy,' says the policeman. 'They said the couple who found him were very caring and concerned. He's been well looked after, fed, changed. DS Dawson has been assigned to drive you up there as she was off-duty yesterday and on fresh legs. She's been briefed about the case and can tell you all about it on the way. She's just signing out an unmarked car and will pick you up any time.'

I rush up the stairs to fling on some clothes.

Harry follows close behind and begins pulling things out of drawers.

'I don't think DS Dawson will be here before two, Mrs Greenwood,' Flatman calls up the stairs. 'I think you have a bit of time. Perhaps grab something to eat before you leave. It's a long drive.'

'Eat? I can't eat. Are you kidding? We've got to get to Benny.'

'There's something else I think you should know.'

I look at DS Flatman, terrified he'll tell me something about Benny.'

'Your former patient Olive Stanton has been caught stealing money from the women's refuge in Hitchin,' he says. 'She was arrested on a train in York. She'd been heading to Scotland. Told our colleagues at the North Yorkshire CID that she was starting a new life. A string of CCTV sightings led us to her. She left a trail of very large crumbs.'

'Oh! I'd originally thought there was a slim possibility she was the one who took Benny. But I don't think she'd have the first clue how to look after a baby. Oh, Olive.'

I file my thoughts on Olive. There's no room in my head. My emotions are completely occupied with getting to Benny at this stage. I'm grateful the DS has asked Suzy to accompany us. She turns up in a smart BMW about twenty minutes after DS Flatman has left. I've prepared a bag of things I think Benny might need and put it into the back of the car along with Benny's car seat in case the one he apparently showed up in on the couple's doorstep isn't up to my standards. Suzy navigates the narrow lanes through the villages and round the back of Luton Airport to the M1.

'I'm amazed how far north he got,' says Harry.

'Do they know who took him? Did they find who left him there?' I ask.

'No leads as yet, but they're checking CCTV and asking for witnesses,' says Suzy. 'The important thing is he's safe, and you'll be reunited in a few hours.'

'Do you think whoever took him simply ran out of confidence and left him on that doorstep?' says Harry.

'I can't bear the thought that he'd be ill-treated. Oh, Benny, Mummy's coming.'

I breathe in deeply, a remnant sob of relief still trapped in my chest.

'The hospital says he's perfectly healthy and in good humour,' says Suzy. 'I'm sure we'll find out more information from them when we get there. I don't know much about the couple who reported him and brought him in.'

My eyes sting from the increasing number of headlights from the trucks in the southbound lane and I pray we won't run into a traffic jam as we head north.

'Thank God the couple who found him contacted the hospital. Can you imagine if they didn't do the right thing and kept him?'

Throughout all that long disturbing questioning at the police station in Hitchin I was worried no one was looking for Benny. There was a horrible, sickening feeling that they were trying to pin me and Harry for a terrible atrocity. Whoever took Benny, and the couple who found him, knew in the end that a baby needs its parents. This feeds me an additional seed of positivity that the kindness of people will prevail in the end.

'He's safe, Trude,' says Harry, reaching back to put his hand on my knee. 'Don't torture yourself with thoughts of what could have happened in different circumstances.'

But I can't stop the visions flashing through my mind. All the things that might have happened to Benny: trafficking, child abuse, even death, God forbid. I put my hand on Harry's shoulder, still desperate to evince a feeling of hope, even if I don't yet have Benny in my arms. Until Benny is safely with us, I won't be completely happy.

I bite my lip and look out of the window. My right leg keeps pressing into the footwell, wishing Suzy would put her foot harder on the accelerator and drive us faster up the M1 and onto the M6. As though Suzy has read my thoughts, she turns her head slightly.

'We'll be there in a few hours, Trude,' she says. 'You're going to have to be patient. I don't want to get busted on the motorway, despite the free ticket. It might mean taking more time to get to Benny in the long run.'

'I know, I'm sorry.' I pause. 'Would it be possible to see the family who took him in, who found him, to thank them?'

'I'm sure that can be arranged,' says Suzy.

When we turn off the motorway at Penrith the traffic thins out and the dawn landscape reveals the beauty of the Lake District. Hedgerows and trees bulge over the barriers on the edge of the road. Stone walls, grey cottages, quaint pubs, distant peaks. These things rush past the window in a flash. I study Harry's expression, his brows slightly gathered. What can he be thinking? Like me, he must be impatient to see his son. But there's the question of who could have taken Benny in the first place, and why? Suzy's already told us they have no clues.

We finally pull up to the Keswick Community Hospital and I have my seatbelt off before we've come to a complete stop. Suzy has to jog to keep up with me, pulling up the correspondence on her phone as I rush into reception.

The nurse on the desk looks up, alarmed, glancing from me to Suzy who is struggling back into her jacket after the heat of the car. The woman's face softens when she sees the police lanyard round Suzy's neck.

'You must be Mrs Greenwood,' she says to me. 'Benny's being well-entertained this morning – he's the talk of the hospital! What a fright you've had. You must be so relieved, pet.'

She leads us through a ward to a day room with rugs and sofas, toys and books strewn about. There's a uniformed police officer sitting by the wall sipping a takeaway coffee.

And there is Benny, propped against the pale-blue-trousered thighs of another young nurse, shaking a plastic rattle and trying to shove it into his saliva-covered mouth.

I put my hands to my lips and hesitate a moment; I can't quite believe my baby is playing happily in this strange but sunny room. After a brief static moment, I rush forward. For an instant I worry the young nurse won't relinquish him to me, but I take Benny and gather him to me. He squawks at the abruptness of having been interrupted from his chewing task. But when he realises it's me, he presses his moist open mouth against my cheek and pulls my hair.

'Thank you. Thank you, so much,' I say, kissing Benny's face over and over.

He giggles, probably oblivious that his mother has been away from him at all.

Suzy stands a little awkwardly at Harry's side while I keep saying, 'It's Mama, Benny. It's Mama. I'm here. I'm here. God I'm sorry.' I look at everyone. 'I'm just so happy he's safe.'

Harry puts one hand on my shoulder and the other on Benny's head.

I've been given a second chance. I promise, no matter what the next few months bring, to do my job as a mother so much better this time.

58

TRUDY

'We thought he was a miracle at first,' says the woman, who introduces herself as Michelle. 'Of course, he *is* a miracle. But *your* miracle. You see, I'm not able to have kids. At least, not in the normal way. You can't imagine all the emotions that were coursing through me when I looked down to see his little face in the baby carrier.'

Harry and I are sitting on the floor with Benny lying in front of us on a rug. He's kicking his little legs and revelling in the attention from both his parents and the couple who looked after him before they took him to the hospital.

'He's a gorgeous little boy,' says Michelle. 'It's probably just as well you got here as quickly as you did. Any longer and we would have been begging social services to let us adopt little Benny.'

I swallow, and briefly imagine they'd already picked a name for him. 'Benny' doesn't seem to slip easily off Michelle's tongue.

'Thank you for taking such good care of him for the short time he was your guest,' I say, wanting to yell *why didn't you report him sooner?*

'It was late on Saturday night,' says Michelle, as though reading my mind. 'We weren't sure what to do. Whoever left him had also left formula and nappies. We spent Sunday with him, discussing the best plan of action. We're not big telly watchers. Didn't see the news. By Sunday evening we knew we had to let the hospital or the police know. We imagined something had gone dreadfully wrong for a mother somewhere out there, that there could be a distraught young woman on the streets needing help. The reality that I was looking at a *stolen* baby in front of my house never even occurred to me.'

I take in a shuddering breath, close to tears again. Tears of relief.

Michelle smiles, hunches her shoulders and presses her palms between her thighs.

'Another good thing has come out of all this. We're finally going to try IVF,' she says, grabbing Nick's hand. 'I know it might end in heartbreak, but I feel we have to give it a go. If we don't, then we'll never know. Now we're settled up here in the Lakes I think we're in the perfect place. Benny has encouraged us to make a plan.'

'It's a good plan, Michelle. It'll be worth it in the end,' I say truthfully. 'Benny is also the result of years of trying and many visits to the fertility clinic.'

'I know it's not always plain sailing with children, even once they've arrived. We already saw some of Sarah's challenges with Em and Jas, didn't we, Nick? It will be the start of a tough journey, even before we've got as far as conception, but it might also herald the start of joy in our lives. It's a cliché, but it's still the one thing that's missing from our family.'

A fog has suddenly swirled into my head. Something Michelle has just said. I tear my gaze away from Benny, look at Michelle's shining eyes, her mouth pressed into a line. Seeing how much she wants a child. Knowing how precious the gift of a child is.

I look around the living room. Through the bay window I see a huge lawn and a sprawling garden with the hills in the background. I can see why a desperate mother, someone perhaps with no financial means of keeping a child, would have chosen this house to leave her baby. Or a kidnapper who realises they've made a dreadful mistake. There's a photo of Michelle and her husband Nick on the shelf. I search for more photos, but it's the only one on display.

'It's a lovely house. Perfect for children. How long have you lived here?' I ask. Their accents aren't local.

'We moved up here about five years ago. Originally it was to get away from the stress of the city. We planned to stay for a couple of years. But we found we much prefer the wilds of Cumbria to Hertfordshire, and decided to stay.'

My heart spikes and I catch Suzy's eye. She has sensed something too. I look back at their wedding photo.

'This might sound like a nosy question, but what was your maiden name?' I ask.

Michelle frowns.

'Lockyear. Why?'

I put my hand over my mouth. Suzy holds her palm up and moves to the hallway, already tapping a contact number on her mobile phone.

'What's up?' asks Nick.

Harry also wears a querying frown.

'It's only just clicked,' I say. 'Sarah. Em and Jas – Emma and Jasper. Daniel's kids. Your brother. He's your brother. Daniel took Benny.'

59

TRUDY

When Benny falls asleep next to me in his car seat, I go over and over in my mind how Daniel's instability had escalated without me noticing. There were no signs. He's had two babies of his own, but had surely misunderstood what a mother goes through with a colicky child. What indicators had I given that I couldn't handle being a mother? I'd never brought my problems to the group. I hadn't even told most of them I'd had a baby.

It's tough work, but millions of mothers do it and end up being successful at it. Daniel must have had a misconception about how much love was still on my side, but he couldn't see. What was he thinking? I wouldn't have pegged him for this abduction in a million years.

As the pines and beeches of the Lake District give way to the rolling hills of Staffordshire with a hint of golden autumn colour, I watch Harry in the front passenger seat looking out of the window, his eyes tracking the passing trees, houses and traffic heading back south, his mouth curved into a slight smile. I close my eyes to try to rest, but can't stop my mind whirling about the last few weeks.

I go over the members of the group in my mind, what each of them has seen and suffered. What was going through Daniel's mind when he saw his wife's body fly through the windscreen of their car and land broken on the bonnet? Underneath his brassy shell, and this latest, inexplicable decision, I still can't think of Daniel as a truly bad man. During our one-to-one sessions I'd never managed to get as far as having him entirely describe the accident that killed Sarah. But we ended up hashing it out in the group therapy sessions. Concentrating on the minutiae. Trying not to create a massive return to guilt with the big picture. Threading the small details together to form a story that makes sense and know that every day we make tiny decisions that can go dreadfully wrong. Even if the guilt took a little longer to assuage than I expected, it has partially been achieved. I wonder whether the whole trauma suddenly came back to him, and this bizarre loss of self – I don't want to call it sanity – was the result. This will now be something he will address with another therapist. His alternative reality. I can't now possibly be involved in the remainder of Daniel's healing process.

It doesn't stop the dismay that I was the one who included Daniel in the group therapy.

Suzy's phone beeps and she throws me a look of apology, but it hasn't woken Benny. The motion of the car will keep him asleep for a while. Suzy glances at the message on her phone attached to her dashboard.

'They've arrested Daniel Lockyear,' she whispers. 'He's now in police custody.'

'Bloody good job,' Harry says quietly. 'That child snatcher should be locked up forever.'

I bite my lip. What will happen to his kids? They've already lost their mother. Will they now lose their father to jail? I need to know exactly why Daniel did this thing. Could I intervene and persuade them to register a case of temporary insanity? I won't raise the subject now. Harry is still too angry.

I lean back and close my eyes, allowing the white noise of the car rushing down the M6 to lull me into semi-sleep while Harry and Suzy chat quietly in the front.

I think about the other members of my project.

What can I say about Olive? This patient of mine who has become more complex as time moves on, as though I've done more to hinder than help her. She was the first one I suspected of taking Benny. And now she's lost it again, stolen money from the people who were her protectors.

Apart from Daniel, Olive is the only remaining patient who still desperately needs help. Although after this, how can I be sure I nailed anyone's diagnosis? What will Olive do to herself once the spaces on her thighs have filled with new scars? And there is still a question hanging over Kenneth Harper's death; the investigation is still inconclusive.

I'll recommend a clinic with a caring psychological environment away from Hitchin. Away from Pinehill. The environment at the refuge has possibly done Olive more harm than good, seeing women coming in daily, escaping the horror of coercive and destructive relationships, and actually being jealous of their attention. And lastly, a sisterly friendship gone sour because she's no longer a central figure in Rachel's life.

Rachel sent me a text yesterday to say she'd signed a rental contract for a flat at an undisclosed address. She asked me not to divulge this information to anyone. I'd like to continue seeing Rachel. Not as a patient, but as a friend. But this is against the ethical code of practice. When I held her in the cloakroom a few weeks back, sobbing against my chest, it made me realise that Rachel is still protecting so much about her inner damaged self, and Kenneth Harper's death only opened up and exposed those horrific memories in more senses than one. That man should eternally burn in Hell.

At the thought of burning, I visualise Alain. The one I had high hopes for. I suspected early on that the fire he'd been rescued from in his own flat wasn't the root of his problem. Alain hadn't wanted to commit to our individual sessions at first. But it was a recommendation by the hospital where he'd spent a few days in the burns unit and the police liaison officer who visited him before he was discharged. The doctors mistakenly assumed he was suffering from PTSD resulting from the fire. They hadn't figured his quiet broodiness was part of a deeper connection to fire that I never completely figured out.

He was never found guilty of arson. A forensic examination of the flat he shared with his girlfriend said it was almost certainly a fault in the fireplace. They couldn't conclude otherwise. He was given the benefit of the doubt. His girlfriend Annie was found shacked up with some violin teacher in Paris, which was why they couldn't find her for so long. I'm unsure why the police were so keen to pin something like Kenneth Harper's death on him. Suzy couldn't explain it. Or wouldn't explain it. Perhaps her colleague DS Flatman simply had a bad feeling about Alain. At least the origin of the photos was soon cleared up. Some music project with the BBC of all things. The thought that he might be involved in anything to do with paedophilia or infant trafficking had made me feel physically sick. He'll be on his way back to the Alps any day now, if he hasn't left already.

As Benny begins to stir in his car seat, I jerk awake from the sleep of the relieved, panicking for one brief moment, until I see my gorgeous baby beside me. For once I'm not praying he'll sleep a little longer. I can't wait for him to open his eyes and see me here.

Benny snuffles, but not with alarm, not with the old twist of colic in his gut. He's waking up because he's simply had enough sleep.

'I'll pull in at the next rest area,' says Suzy. 'So you can feed him in comfort.'

I smile my thanks, and allow the relief of having my baby with me to flow through me like cool water.

60

DANIEL

Daniel sits in the police interview room. He's been given an emergency leave of absence from work, but can't imagine what they are saying about him there. He's refused coffee or tea. He doesn't cross his legs, keeps his feet parallel to each other on the floor. He thinks if he takes his feet off the ground, he will do just that – lose his grounding. It's already happened several times over the past six months. He doesn't want it to happen again right now.

The detective's pen hovers over his notepad as he presses the record button and introduces himself – DS Flatman – then announces the presence of Dr Steven Willis, the police psychologist, and gives the date and time. Daniel has waived the presence of a solicitor. He knows how this goes.

The psychologist has less the air of a medical professional, and more that of a car salesman. Next to an untouched plastic beaker of water on the table is a folder with the blue NHS logo at the top. Poking out of it is a pink form. Daniel can clearly see the words *Mental Health Act 1983* in the top right corner. He swallows.

'Mr Lockyear, we are here to discuss the events leading up to the abduction of Benny Greenwood on Saturday July 29th,' says Flatman. 'Dr Willis is here to examine your motive and determine how we should go forward with your... treatment.'

'I admit I took Benny Greenwood. You think I'm not of sound mind.'

DS Flatman frowns.

'First we need the facts, Mr Lockyear.'

Daniel takes a deep breath. They obviously think he was mad to take the baby.

'When I saw Trudy in town a few weeks ago, I was on the point of saying hello. I already knew she had a baby – I'd overheard a conversation she had with Rachel after one of our sessions. I didn't approach her that day because she looked so distraught, and at the time I felt my daughter Emma's presence might have exacerbated an already negative situation. I looked at that mother and child from afar, and told myself that there was one woman who wasn't ready to be a mother and there was one baby suffering the consequences of a mother who couldn't cope.'

'It was presumptuous of you to assess the situation,' says Dr Willis, the psychologist. 'These are feelings commonly felt by mothers. But they overcome them.'

Daniel thinks the man's comment is patronising. He wants to say, *but you weren't there; how can you possibly judge*?

'I was disturbed by that cry of distress,' he says instead. 'And the more I heard Benny crying, the more it set off a memory. While Emma was distracted by a puppy walking past I discreetly took a closer look at Trudy's baby. I was stunned at how much he resembled my son Jasper at that age.'

Daniel hesitates. He's not sure whether what he *could* reveal will have any impact on the charges. But it might have an impact on several people's lives.

'I'm pretty sure I was – am – a good father,' he continues. 'I always helped out with the parental duties. I know all about listening for the signs of when a baby is thirsty, hungry, has a full nappy, or a tummy ache.'

Daniel shakes his head.

'That baby had a tummy ache. I recognised that much. I used to hold Jasper like this on my arm.'

Daniel bends his elbow, holds out his palm, as though there's a towel folded over his lower arm.

'It's important to try and recognise the triggers that led you to do this,' says Dr Willis.

He's using jargon that Trudy might use. The detective holds out a hand, pressing air down onto the table between them.

'We need to get some basics straight, Mr Lockyear,' says Flatman. 'Can you tell us about the day you took Benny?'

'It was the weekend,' says Daniel with a nod. 'The children were both having a sleepover with their respective best friends. Initially I was going to knock on Trudy's door and simply suggest if she felt like she needed a break from her baby, if she felt she couldn't cope and might somehow become a danger to him, I knew someone who would be more than willing to look after him. And that's where common sense stopped. I didn't even know whether Trudy had a partner, a husband. I thought perhaps she was a single mother. I didn't know she was married.'

It's one of the things Daniel hadn't thought through – the consequences of what he was about to do. He's not sure why, but he simply assumed she was a single mother.

'It was so easy in the end,' he continues. 'I knocked quietly at the front door, in case Benny was sleeping. I didn't want the noise of the bell to wake him up, making things even more challenging than they already were for Trudy. When there was no answer, I went around the back. The gate was open. And there they were, together in the garden. It was the first time I'd seen Trudy looking peaceful since she started this whole group therapy palaver.'

Trudy had been in a deep sleep, lying on an Indian rug under the shade of the trees. The stroller was a couple of metres away, the canopy of a hazel tree casting solid shade over the hood.

'I crept across the lawn, lifted Benny out of the stroller and held him to my chest. It seemed so natural. I breathed in the smell of him, surprised that a deep instinct made my shoulders curl around the boy in protection. Like I'd done with Jasper so many times. Benny settled into my chest, and didn't wake up.'

Daniel clenches his jaw before continuing. He's surprised that he feels the threat of tears.

'I walked back across the garden, down the side of the house, putting my hand out so the gate wouldn't bang into its frame. I sat momentarily on the wall at the front of the house, looking around to see if anyone had seen us. The lane was quiet. I clipped Benny into the car seat I'd found in our attic and put in our car in case, in case...' Daniel blows air through his lips before continuing. 'Emma was the last little person to use it. When Benny put one of his fists to his mouth and began to suck his thumb, I knew he would be waking and hungry soon. I knew what to do, recalled the hypo-allergenic milk powder that seemed to work best for Jasper. I'd found a new one that might help more, with an advanced formula. I'd bought a bag of nappies, took some baby clothes that were packed away in our attic.'

The psychologist doesn't say anything, but the sound of a pencil scribbling on his notepad hisses harshly. Daniel continues.

'I already had Michelle's address entered into the satnav. I had a full tank of petrol. It's a bit of a long drive up the M6, and when we ran into a bit of traffic, I wondered whether it would be easier to take the train. But I persevered with driving in the end. I stopped once to change the baby, grab a coffee, then the roads were clearer and I went straight to my sister's door. It was late by then. I knew they were in, I could see the lights, movement through the kitchen window. I rang the bell and ran off down the street, like some farcical game of Knock, Knock, Ginger. I didn't want the baby to be left too long out there in the cold. I never intended to keep him, but my determination didn't waver the entire time we were driving north.'

Daniel looks at DS Flatman to try to gauge his reaction before continuing. He suspects the policeman has more sympathy than the psychologist.

'I felt no remorse until I was driving back down south. And then only because I thought I should have kept Benny. But at that point I didn't know what to do about it. I didn't know how to reverse my actions. And then one of your officers called. He would have heard I was in the car. I told him I was coming back from London. Overtime at work. That's what I'd told my mother. She was looking after the children.'

The psychologist shifts in his seat.

'Often in cases like this, the abductor – excuse the term – feels a strong sense of wrongdoing once they have the child,' he says. 'If you agree to continue therapy, we need to get to the crux of what drove you to continue the journey after the initial act of taking Benny. Meaning your compulsion lasted beyond the usual temporary abandonment of self.'

'Therapy may not be an option if he's convicted,' Flatman says to Willis.

The grain of sympathy Daniel thought he'd heard in the policeman's voice has now gone.

'Unless you implement Section 37,' says Willis, 'He could be hospitalised immediately while awaiting trial.'

'I thought I could bring my family back together, unite us all,' says Daniel. 'I thought I could relieve Trudy's stress. I thought, for a crazy moment, I was doing the right thing.' He presses his lips together and whispers, almost to himself, 'What was I thinking?'

'Can the mind ever really comprehend the mind?' says the psychologist. 'We have only discovered a fraction of what the brain is capable of, and believe me, Daniel, there are people who have had far more mysterious experiences than yours.'

Daniel wants to make both the psychologist and the police, and ultimately Trudy, understand what drove him to do this without further destroying what he already started. He refused a solicitor because he believes he could be absolved of this error if he can make them all understand. He keeps glancing nervously at the pink form on the desk.

It doesn't seem possible that he'd be taken away, locked up. He's responsible for Emma and Jasper. They need a parent too. But even if he tells these people what he believes is the truth, will that lessen the crime, let him off the hook? He could let the powers that be decide whether to dig deeper with their detective work. The problem is, once the secret he's holding is shared, it's no longer a secret. And damage may ensue.

More than anything, he wants this psychologist to assure him that what he has done makes some kind of terrible sense. His decision is swinging. It's probably best for everyone, especially Trudy's husband, if they never learn the truth.

He dwells on the damage limitation. If he's charged, he will have to tell his children in a way that won't frighten them. He'd like to be able to attempt to reason with his own mother who may never understand, even if there is a medical explanation for all this. She's already harbouring doubts, having been called at the last moment to come and look after the children. And as for his sister, she will very likely never speak to him again, despite his wish to try to repair old differences. In her eyes, Daniel continues to make unforgiveable decisions.

He thinks of Trudy and the therapy group and all their different states of mind. Daniel has always had a hard time understanding why Trudy chose them to participate in her project. In what messed-up world did she decide to put suicidals next to rape victims? And self-harmers next to arsonists for that matter? But he realises how difficult Trudy's job must be. To deal with all the secondary problems that have come from the man who killed his wife in a car crash, the girl who was raped, the woman who was beaten to within an inch of her life and a man who was pulled from a burning building.

DS Flatman hasn't said much yet, but has been taking notes as Daniel and the psychologist talk. Perhaps that's a good sign?

'After the accident, losing Sarah, I felt a terrible guilt,' says Daniel.

He won't mention his almost-suicide. The psychologist will undoubtedly find out if he examines his file.

'I was intent on working out how the karma could be redistributed,' he continues. 'How everyone could win in situations that seemed to be going wrong. How I could redress order in the world. I was so sure my decision was the right one. But really, in what world would this ever have been acceptable?'

Daniel hopes the look in his eye shows remorse to both these people.

'It's clear that this was an episode after an accumulation of grief and stress. It had dire consequences – the abduction of a child – but I don't believe it's starting a pattern of psychotic behaviour. You're showing obvious regret.' Willis waves in the direction of the detective. 'He knows what he did was wrong, but not the consequences of his actions.'

'*Psychotic* behaviour?' Daniel asks.

The psychologist's hand brushes over the folder and the pink form on his desk.

'With a few more sessions, we could get to the root of your need to "redress order in the world" as you put it. Mrs Greenwood alluded to your OCD indicators in her file. It could be this secondary reaction has manifested itself in the almost vigilante need to set the balance right for people you perceive have been wronged.'

The psychologist pauses. The detective clears his throat.

'Mrs Greenwood has been trying to convince us not to press charges,' says DS Flatman. 'But I'm afraid it's not her decision. The CPS will decide. It's likely you will be convicted.'

Daniel puts his hand to his forehead, combs his hair with his fingers. He realises he has to tell them the truth.

'I can't tell you how grateful I am for Trudy's kindness. Sorting me out after Sarah's death. It wasn't until I first saw Trudy's baby in town one day while I was with my daughter, that it took on greater significance.'

Daniel pauses. Both Flatman and Willis have creased brows, waiting for an explanation.

'I believe I am Benny's biological father.'

61

DANIEL

The silence is so thick, for a moment Daniel thinks he might have gone deaf. It feels as though all the oxygen has been sucked out of the room. Then the detective blows air through his lips like a horse, and the spell is broken with the comical sound.

'I think it goes without saying that you are going to have to explain yourself,' says DS Flatman, an incredulous look on his face.

'When Sarah and I first married, we scrimped for our future. I hadn't yet had my lucky financial break in the City and we were both working hard to save up for a deposit on a house. When Sarah became pregnant with Jasper, we were just managing, but then she very quickly became pregnant with Emma and the pressure was on. I'd started doing extra jobs on the weekend, mowing the neighbour's lawn, stuff like that. It started as a joke because she conceived so quickly, but I even donated my sperm to the fertility clinic in Cheshunt. It didn't earn me much, really only travel expenses, but Sarah encouraged me to do so because I have such a high sperm count, and I'd planned to have a vasectomy. She said it wasn't just an insurance for us in case we ever wanted to have more kids, but my donation might help couples less fortunate than ourselves. But there are only so many times they'll let you donate, for obvious reasons.' Daniel gazes over the detective's shoulder, a memory coming to him with a sad smile. 'Sarah said I'd likely be able to repopulate the entire world with the sperm count I had.'

Daniel hopes this doesn't sound as if he's boasting.

'There are hundreds of couples seeking fertility treatment every year,' says Willis. 'With the maths alone, I don't see how you could have come to this conclusion.'

'And what about the timing? How long do they keep sperm frozen?' asks DS Flatman.

'Actually, years,' says Daniel. 'And there's a catalogue. A mother can choose which sperm she wants from a list of non-identifying donor criteria.'

Flatman's mouth opens slightly. 'Sounds a bit *Brave New World* to me,' he says.

'Yes, and yet we're several decades on from when that book was written. Huxley was way before his time.' Daniel sighs. 'I know it sounds crazy, but when I saw baby Benny the time in town that I mentioned earlier, I was already shocked by how much like Jasper he looked. Same shaped head. Same hair. Same nose. Even the same cry. And later when Rachel told me Trudy had been having treatment at a fertility clinic, well, I put two and two together and assumed she'd been artificially inseminated. The "maths," as you so put it, made more sense. Really, you have no idea how much like Jasper Benny looks.' Daniel reaches for his phone in his jacket pocket and remembers the police have confiscated it. 'I'm ninety percent sure Benny is mine.'

The detective puts his hand to his forehead and rubs it aggressively, as though he might pull hairs from his brow. It's a sign of complete disbelief.

'Do you have my phone? I can show you a photo. I see you don't believe me.'

Daniel's iPhone is produced from an evidence bag and passed to him. He opens the photo app and scrolls back to the file from eight years ago in his library. He opens the file and flicks through pictures of Jasper. There's a hot sear in his chest as images of Sarah holding his son roll past. He finds one of a close-up of Jasper at six months and turns the phone to face Flatman. The psychologist won't know what Benny looks like, but Flatman must surely have the missing baby announcements imprinted in his mind.

Daniel's feelings are affirmed when the detective raises his eyebrows and tips his head to one side.

'I don't think it's going to help if this information is shared with Trudy and her husband, who I didn't even know existed until I saw the press interview on TV,' says Daniel, handing the phone back to Flatman. 'And that was after I'd returned from Keswick.'

'If you had regrets about what you'd done, why didn't you come forward?'

'Why do you think? I'd be arrested. I had no idea my sister would do what I realise is now the right thing and contact the authorities. I still wasn't thinking of the *what ifs*.'

He feels as if the tables might finally be turning on what they previously saw as an incomprehensible action on his part. He hopes at least the psychologist will see the importance of keeping this secret, even though they are now looking at him with such incredulous faces. The last thing he now wants to do is cause Trudy even more pain.

'I never intended to claim paternity. I just thought I was helping to keep things in the family, so to speak, and to relieve Trudy of what I thought was a burden. I realise now that I didn't read her situation correctly at all.' Daniel clamps his lips together with his teeth.

'Whatever happens, your mental state must be assessed immediately,' Dr Willis says, looking at both Daniel and DS Flatman. 'You've already been charged, but under Section 37,' Willis lifts the corner of the pink form on his desk, 'I propose this assessment happens at Pinehill.'

Dr Willis travels in the passenger seat in the front of the police car while Daniel sits in the back. Something rattles on the dashboard as the young policeman starts the engine and irritation flares in Daniel. He misses the soft purr of his perfectly-tuned BMW.

'Do you think I'm on the spectrum?' he asks.

'You're a stickler for order, so when we've checked you in, perhaps you can create a list of questions to ask yourself about the decisions you make. I'll be wanting to talk about your logic behind them.'

Daniel puffs out an ironic laugh at the word 'list'. He hasn't said anything about the one he wrote in preparation for Benny. He remembers the one for his suicide though, and he hadn't ticked all those boxes. Thank God.

He's already been charged with abducting a child, but he hopes this is a better option than spending a night in a police cell.

He thinks about his parents looking after his children. The police have promised to disperse any journalists still waiting outside his house or his parents' garden gate down the road. He imagines them having dinner together and his mother putting the children to bed. They'll be asking about him, but his parents will probably not yet be ready to tell them about what their father has done. A business trip is the temporary reason for his absence. But they will have to explain soon, before the children learn from their school friends or the neighbours.

For the first time he feels the heat of tears in the back of his throat. His parents can't be expected to look after Jasper and Emma forever. How long will he be incarcerated?

'I still want to be the father of my own children.' His voice cracks. 'Will they be able to visit me?'

'Of course. Perhaps in a few days' time. We'll be starting sessions tomorrow for your assessment. I just need to ascertain that you're no danger to yourself, or them, before we set visiting privileges.'

He already knows he's going to hate this.

The one thing Daniel can't forget, is the feeling of complete control he experienced when he was redressing the balance, when he was driving baby Benny to a new life with his sister in the Lake District. And he's still trying to work out whether that terrifies him or exhilarates him.

It's nothing to do with the fact that he could be the father of that baby. In his mind, he'd relinquished all claims the day he handed over his first sperm donation at the fertility clinic. There's no pang of regret that surrogate mothers must have when they give up the babies they've given birth to. There must be a difference when they've already lived with a baby inside them for nine months. Why he ever thought Trudy would be happy to give up her baby, no matter how fractious and challenging Benny was, is still eluding him. He's now angry with himself that he made a big mistake.

62

RACHEL

Rachel looks up at the foliage of the old walnut tree in the vicarage garden. A few of the leaves are turning yellow. The hard black nuts have begun to fall from the tree and a squirrel is on a frantic mission around the base of the trunk, its tail flicking rhythmically with the excitement of the harvest. Rachel used to collect the nuts with her sister Ruth as children, to stop them getting caught under her father's lawnmower blades. Every year they would try to eat them, forgetting the bitterness of the previous years' experience. They inevitably moved on to plunder the offerings on the pear tree to take away the after-taste.

They're sitting in the well-tended garden, pear and apple trees heavy with fruit, dotted around the lawn. The Virginia creeper is beginning to turn red on the vines draped over the old brick walls hemming in the garden. It was a great place to grow up, apart from the fact that most of her friends at primary were terrified of ever coming back here to play after school. Not because of their magical garden. But because her father was the vicar.

It's an unusually warm afternoon, apparently the last for a while. A cold front is due to sweep in from the northeast, having already blindsided the rest of Europe in early wintry weather.

She's still dressed in black and has worn her favourite DMs, but she's toned down the kohl around her eyes, chosen not to put on blood-red lipstick today. She doesn't swear, tries to avoid subjects that will spark disapproval, apart from the obvious issues.

She thinks of Alain, who sees what she wears as a uniform. And she thinks of all the uniforms she has worn as a child, even before secondary school. The pink leotard of ballet, until she was told she was too tall at the age of nine to ever consider being a dancer. She and Ruthie joined the Brownies, but Rachel only ever earned a badge for foraging in the forest and none of the charitable things that were expected of a vicar's daughter. She was briefly a member of the church choir, with a red velvet cape and a lace ruffle that made her neck itch. But even there she felt a degree of bullying by her fellow singers thinking she held some kind of advantage because she was the vicar's daughter.

Her sister bounced up to her like a puppy when she rang the doorbell earlier. It felt strange to be ringing the door of what was once her home, but it feels as if a century has passed since she walked over the threshold rather than a handful of years. Ruth now sits next to her on the bench, holding Rachel's hand tightly, her arm pressed up against hers. The gesture reminds Rachel of Mouse, and she feels a warm glow in her chest. There will be an opportunity later to introduce Mouse to Ruthie and her parents. One thing at a time. It's something they might also have a problem with, although they would surely understand Rachel's need for comfort.

Her mother sits in her favourite wicker garden chair on the other side of the table from the sisters. Rachel thought she would feel closer to her once all this was out in the open. But her mother made the mistake of asking the one question she should have known the answer to.

'Why didn't you tell us the truth from the beginning?'

'You made it very difficult for me. Tons of accusations flying around before I could get a word in edgeways. I was grateful you took me to the hospital, but I felt you wanted to sweep it under the carpet rather than offering sympathy. And as for Dad, well he ignored it all together. Leaving me there was unforgiveable.'

Rachel has poshed up her accent to soften the exchange with her parents, but it has become such a habit, she finds herself dropping her aitches.

'But if I'd known it was that man, and not some schoolboy...'

'What's the difference, actually? Put yourself in my shoes, Mum. Take yourself back to when you were seventeen. How bold would you have been to talk about things like that with *your* parents? I used to think things were different back then, but perhaps not. Nanna and Grandad would have been just as shocked at the hippy movement as you are with today's wild youth. You grew up in the era of free love. For some young girls, that free love must have come with a terrible price. The ones who were forced to ignore things like this because no one believed that would happen. But some bad men's urges haven't changed in thousands of years.'

Rachel's mother pours tea out of the old silver pot into proper cups and saucers placed on a lace square on the tray.

'I do think the lines were more blurred back then, Rachel. We never heard about men forcing themselves upon women.'

'Damn right they were blurred. Sex had a different label,' she replies, watching her mother flinch first at the word 'damn' and then 'sex.' 'Rape would have had a different connotation. It all came under this ridiculous umbrella of free love, sexual abandonment. I have visions of young people falling over each other to copulate in fields of wild flowers because that's what they were supposed to do. And yet it was likely never all roses for many of those girls, especially if it was their first time.'

Her mum bites her lip, and Rachel lets that little piece of information sink in. Her first and last time.

She studies the dent on the side of the familiar teapot. The one she would spend an afternoon polishing and buffing in her childhood along with the candlesticks on the mantelpiece above the fireplace and an inherited silver tray she'd only ever seen used to serve After Eights on special occasions. All that polishing for a measly 50p of pocket money. The teapot is a cherished heirloom. Dented on one side after Ruthie dropped it one afternoon, but still in use. Forever damaged. Like Rachel.

'I can never have children,' she says.

Her mother's breath catches in her throat.

'With all the haemorrhaging, they had to do a hysterectomy. I still can't believe you just left me there.'

A little sob from her mother this time. The first sign of real sadness. Ruthie squeezes Rachel's arm.

'I just wish you'd told us *who*,' says her mother.

'But that's just my point. It shouldn't matter who. I did nothing to encourage that man. I didn't even know Tim Harper's father was at the party, yet alone who he was. I'd never met him. If it hadn't been for Trudy Greenwood, I would have kept quiet too. But it shouldn't have made a difference to the way you treated me. As soon as Dad knew it was to do with sex, whether forced or not, he blamed me entirely. I'm sure when he thought the village might find out, it was a potential embarrassment for him.'

As she says these words, it makes sense why he simply eliminated her from their lives.

Rachel looks towards her father in the study through the conservatory, dressed so incongruously in his striped rugby shirt, knowing he'll be wearing whatever Sunday colours are the uniform in the religious calendar tomorrow. He's not wearing his dog collar today. The pale shackle of power at his neck that Rachel has always been a little frightened of is missing.

Her mum stands up suddenly. 'Frank! Come out and join us!'

'Give me five minutes,' he calls faintly from the study, his tone friendly but strained.

'Dad was so angry,' says Rachel. 'Without even knowing all the details. I still get the feeling he thinks it was my fault.'

'No, that's not it...' her mother says quietly, almost to herself.

'Why isn't he out here with us, then?' asks Ruth, who has stayed surprisingly quiet until now.

'Darling, he simply wants to get the sermon down on paper before the end of the afternoon. He's not ignoring us.'

Isn't it some kind of sacrilege? To wear rugby stripes instead of a collar while he writes his sermon? She doesn't want to be angry at her mother, but feels something flare in her gut now. Her mother would clearly not have kicked Rachel out of the home if it had been her decision alone. It leaves a bitter taste in her mouth that's nothing to do with the remnants of Earl Grey leaves that squeezed their way through the tea strainer into the bottom of her cup.

'If my identity had been revealed, my name released to the press about what has escalated since Kenneth Harper's death, do you think Dad would have had a better or a worse attitude? He would have been forced, surely, to address the issue with his congregation. Even though Harper lived in the Gosmore parish and not ours.'

'I don't know. But he's going to talk to you about it. It's too late to take back how we reacted, but we didn't know there was more at stake.'

Rachel doesn't understand this cryptic talk from her mother.

'He's supposed to be a counsellor of sorts, people come to a vicar or a minister to seek help when they're going through something they believe only God has knowledge of, being the omnipotent deity, the all-knowing. I'd like to ask him how he would deal with one of his flock coming to him with the same story. How he would deal with a victim who's not his daughter. I guess it's different when it happens outside your family. I'm grateful I never had to go to court, at least not in public. But the shitty thing is, the only people I feel are still judging me are you two.'

She feels tears heating the space behind her eyes, but is determined not to let them spill. Breaking down now will be the undoing of her. She doesn't expect a miraculous reunion with her father, but she would like to mend something with her mother, who has wisely chosen not to admonish Rachel for her language.

Suddenly he is there. His shadow follows him down the path from the French windows to the garden table. Rachel is thankful he hasn't brought his musings with him. Trying out his sermon on his girls as he might have done on past Friday or Saturday evenings. She realises now he has dressed the way he has to avoid Rachel's inevitable scrutiny of his profession.

'I'm sorry, Rachel. I had to finish writing Sunday's sermon today, as we're busy tomorrow with the autumn fair.'

Always putting your flock before your daughters, she wants to say, but keeps quiet. The only thing she really wants from him is his acknowledgement that he abandoned her. The black sheep.

'Ruthie, could you take the pot, go and make some more tea?' Their father directs a look at Ruth that the girls know well. It would be a mistake to disobey.

Ruth pushes herself reluctantly up off the bench and takes the tray across the lawn towards the kitchen. Their father sits down in the space she has vacated on the bench. There's no small talk, no explanation of the gap that has been wedged between them for five years. He simply takes Rachel's hand, and she lets him, tentatively enjoying the feel of the warm dry skin of his palm.

'If I'd known at the beginning, five years ago when you were seventeen, things would have been a whole lot different.'

'But you did know, Dad. You chose to believe it was somehow my fault.'

'I know that *now*, Rachel. But you wouldn't tell us who had done this to you. We thought it was a fling that somehow went wrong. A young lad who you might have led on... Wait. Let me finish.' He says with his hand held up when Rachel tries to interrupt. 'So when we find out only now, it changes a lot of things.'

'I don't understand how it changes anything. Why are you so concerned with *who* did this to me? You didn't trust me back then. What has changed now?'

'Because... I was at Hitchin Boys' with Ken Harper. And afterwards at Royal Holloway. Before I transferred to Durham to study theology at Cranmer Hall.'

It seems the birds have stopped chirping in the verdant garden. The buzzing sounds of the Indian summer have been replaced with a ringing in Rachel's head. He *knew* Kenneth Cock Harper when he was a kid? *Jesus.*

'There were some things that happened at Royal Holloway that I've never spoken to anyone about. A young girl. She was badly beaten. Possibly raped. She was found next to the Queen Vic statue in the North Quad, her clothes torn. She was taken to hospital. Some things Ken Harper said a few nights later when we'd all had too many beers in The Packhorse made me think he had something to do with it. It made me sick to think so. I didn't want to believe it. But I always had my suspicions. Now I know what he was capable of, with my very own daughter, I wish even more that I'd done something about it back then. We live such different lives, in different villages now. I thought he might have changed his ways when he married, had children...'

Rachel has to suck in her lips to stop a cynical snort escaping.

'We can't imagine what you've been going through,' says her mother. 'We're so sorry we ever doubted you. And now all these allegations we're hearing in the press are making it so real, so horrific.'

'It seems to have set a chain reaction in motion,' says Rachel. 'I had to give a long, detailed statement to the police, with my therapist, Trudy. I asked her to be there. I thought of calling you, Mum, but things were still too confused between us. When the papers reported allegations of inappropriate sexual behaviour by that man, Mrs Harper initially tried to sue the paper for libel. But then a few other girls came out of the woodwork.'

'I know you're not a believer, but the Lord does take care of His own,' her father says. 'Harper had it coming to him.'

He goes to take Rachel's hand again, but she snatches it away. She feels a sudden hot anger. His comment has somehow diminished what that man did to her. Like a story in the bible where all the evils of mankind can be swept away with flood or fire.

'There's a crazy girl at the refuge who was one of his victims. She's a wild girl, but even she was shocked at how a monster could have got away with it with so many others for such a long time. You *have* to go to the police and tell them, Dad. You have to tell them what happened all those years ago.'

'Rachel, darling, it's been forty years. Half a lifetime.'

'Dad! There might be someone who needs to talk about this, needs help. That young girl in the North Quad. She'd be your age now. Mum's age. She'll have been living with that terrible memory all this time. What if she...?'

Rachel puts her hand over her mouth. So many things swept under the carpet. She makes a soft growl in her throat. She knows her father won't go to the police. He won't want his name connected to any of this, even as a witness.

Rachel suddenly thinks of Olive. Poor Olive. She was the only one who ever consented to Kenneth Harper's abuse in her own messed-up need.

She feels sick sitting here now, with her father stepping around the ostracism of the past five years as piously as possible without banging on too much about God. He knows her views about him and his profession. Rachel no longer fears him as she might have in the past. If she wasn't so angry about his confession, she would actually feel sorry for him. Carrying that burden. Knowing he might have done something all those years ago, long before she was even born, to prevent the rape of his daughter.

Ruth comes back across the lawn, carefully carrying the replenished tea tray. Rachel smiles as she sees a plate piled high with twice the number of chocolate Hob Nobs as the first round. The danger of allowing Ruthie to bring seconds. She will insist they be eaten as quickly as possible before they melt in the sun.

'What are your plans for the future?' her mother asks as though the past fifteen minutes didn't just happen. She doesn't admonish Ruth for the biscuits.

Rachel sighs.

'They've been good to me at the bakery. No questions asked. But I don't want to bake bread all my life. I've been looking at some evening courses at North Herts College.'

She doesn't remind them that it's where she might have gone had Kenneth Harper not changed the direction of her life so drastically at the end of her first year studying her A levels.

'That's good news. You've always had a good brain on you,' says her father.

'I hope you find something you enjoy studying and something that will help you make a living,' says her mother.

Rachel chews her lip. They are being too nice. Saccharine. She'll never forget that they abandoned her for five years. She was still a child. She hasn't had much contact with Ruth over the years, but she's happy to have her snuggled up next to her now on the bench. Ruthie didn't have anything to do with all this mess. Rachel is wedged between Ruth and her father but she stays where she is for the sake of her sister.

Ultimately the memories from this little tea party are likely to be the last vision of her childhood garden. Her parents were probably hoping to mend the rift between them, welcome Rachel with open arms back into the fold. Not bloody likely now.

Her teacup tings as she places it back in the saucer. She appreciates the strong conviction that tea should only be drunk out of bone china. It's a ritual her mother has stuck to over the years.

Rachel keeps a tulip-shaped Maxwell & Williams mug on the shelf in her room at the refuge. She bought it from a bric-a-brac stall at the market. She drinks tea out of it every day. It's the only thing that's ever reminded her positively of her childhood home. It stands as a kind of trophy. That she was able to survive on her own, and that she doesn't need anyone's support.

As she prepares to leave, parting with cool words to her parents and hugging Ruthie tight, the image of Benny springs to Rachel's mind. Her heart goes out to Trudy and she's thrilled they finally found him. She still can't believe posh Daniel was to blame.

Meeting Benny set the spark of something in her. A spark she knew would quickly burst into flames. Something in her messed-up biology was making her long for the baby she lost. As she promises to keep in touch with Ruth, she feels a curling warmth knowing she's returning to Mouse. They've found a flat together – that one by the station. She hasn't told anybody yet, wants to ensure everything is signed and guaranteed before anyone else can interfere. In yearning for the baby she'll never have, she's ended up becoming so much more than a mother. A friend. A sister. A lover. They will be perfect for each other. She has a family at last.

63

ALAIN

As the cog railway rumbles past the conical roofs of the Château d'Aigle, Alain embraces the anticipation of returning home to Leysin in the change of seasons. The cog engages onto the rack as the train crosses the river. They leave behind the trees in the valley, shedding their red and orange cloaks around their bases. They rise through vineyards which have long since yielded their Pinot noir and Chasselas grapes to the vintners of the region. The train continues up through pine trees laden with cones and moss. Larch needles flutter to the forest floor, winking orange in the shards of fading sun.

The cog train forges through a layer of cloud high above the valley. The first flakes begin falling as Alain steps off at the final station. He throws his pack onto his shoulders and makes his way to the Club Vagabond where he knows at least two friends will offer him a bed for the night and if not, there'll be a bunk free at the hostel.

He walks through the upper village, the rapidly falling temperature stinging his nostrils, the smell of approaching winter a familiar cold comfort. Snow has already begun to settle on the verges and trees, the rapid change in weather a thrilling surprise. As Alain walks through the door of the Vagabond bar and sweeps aside the heavy curtain keeping the draughts out, a cheer erupts. Many old friends welcome him, slapping him on the back. They tell him they never believed any girl could keep his heart away from the mountains, especially in grey, rainy England. A moment of sadness is soon eclipsed by the contentment of being back amongst his tribe. It's as though he never left.

More people come into the bar, stamping snow off their boots and shaking flakes from their hats. Outside a blizzard is now raging, the first heavy fall of the winter season that is not yet really upon them. A lift worker comes in wearing his snow patrol jacket and another cheer goes up when he announces the ski runs will open for the weekend only. They've never opened this early before, but it's been agreed that there are enough employees in the village to operate the highest lifts.

Alain's usual ski gang begins to make plans. They brag about their predicted achievements on the slopes the next day. Each one of Alain's friends claims they will reach a higher, longer, steeper descent. Someone turns up the volume of eighties classics playing behind the bar, and more alcohol fuels their ambition. Beer bottles chink louder with each round, along with their excitement.

Alain is offered the sofa of a friend near to where he's stored his skis during his absence. The gang leaves the bar in the darkest part of the night. The wind whips round their muffled faces, and their boots fill over the rims as the snowplough has yet to clear the roads. They sway and topple as they walk home, the loss of balance in the deep snow a laughable excuse on their drunken, vapoured breath.

The crack of a cannon wakes him at dawn, his mouth as dry as arctic tundra, and his promise an aching regret. He hauls himself from the warmth of the sofa and dresses for the cold. His friend merely grunts when Alain knocks on his door, reneging on their agreement.

Alain fetches his skis and walks to the lift station, ski boots squawking on the fresh snow. The sun rises over the horns of Les Diablerets to the east into a velvet blue sky. He is invigorated by the morning air, as sharp as a shard of broken glass.

His mates don't turn up, but he doesn't wait, wants to be the first on the lift. Their excuses will be a combination of debilitating hangovers and the presence of the hazard lights flashing outside the ski station, telling them to stay on the marked *piste*. Telling them to stay safe. As he steps out of the *télécabine* at the top and ducks under the yellow and black ribbon, the morning sun glinting off the mirrored windows of the mountain restaurant mocks his absent friends as cowards. He clicks into his skis and prepares for the euphoria of the first powder turn.

He opens his eyes and there is a perfectly formed crystal sitting on the glove in front of his face. He thinks of Rachel in the therapy group back in England. He remembers the day she first told her story. Distracting herself with her snowflake. That's what Alain does now, as he studies the one in front of him.

He concentrates on his body, trying to locate each part of himself. He can't move his limbs. He knows at least one of his legs is broken. His ears are blocked with snow. There is a tinnitus roar in his head. He's lost his goggles, and is unsure which way is up. It's not quite dark, but an eerie light envelops him in his blue space.

How many times had they been told in their youth? At school? In ski club? In autumn the earth beneath the crocus-laden alpine meadows still holds the heat of the sun. The first wintry storms arrive on humid air that carpets the ground, thick and deep. But it is deceptive. The earth raises the temperature of the layer of snow touching the smooth substrate where it sucks the remaining water out of the earth. When the snowpack freezes, usually in early morning, its interface with the ground offers no more friction.

Avalanche.

As Alain's breath labours through lack of oxygen, he recalls the stuffiness of the bar last night, the smell of stale beer and overheated bodies. The coffee and croissant Alain rushed on the lift is still acrid in the back of his throat. He remembers the vastness of it, standing on the cornice. An invisible magnet drew him to the edge, tipping him into the narrow gully and spitting him out onto a delta of white. His skis met only the resistance of air, like falling into a weightless eiderdown. The best powder ski of his life.

He stares at the snowflake, his eyes straining in the dim light. Perhaps this is the flake that tipped the scale, grasping the splintered limbs of a hundred million others, chasing him down the gully as his skis carved soft serpentine ruts refilling behind him with the feathers of winter. This snowflake lured him into the vortex of a drunken bet beyond his control.

He recognises the light-headedness, his fuzzy thoughts. He has to get air. He wiggles the fingers on the hand with the snowflake in front of his face. As he twists his wrist, he reaches up an inch at a time, his fingers grappling at the snow above his head. He bores further with two fingers. Slowly, slowly, he pushes the concrete mass of snow upwards, knowing that if he hadn't kept his hand in front of his face, he would have suffocated long ago.

It takes what seems like hours, but he digs himself out through layers of heavy, dense snow with pockets of crystal powder. He screams with the pain of a splintered bone in his leg each time he moves, thinks it might be his knee or his shin, but the pain goes all the way up his thigh to his spine.

As he breaks the surface, grey light floods in with a flurry of fresh flakes. How long has he been under the snow? Another front has blown in and the blizzard has started anew. He takes out his phone. Having to remove his gloves, his freezing finger stabs at the screen but the cold has sapped all the power from its battery. He thinks he hears a helicopter somewhere above him, but cannot imagine it could fly in this weather, and it would be impossible to spot him as the cloud is so thick.

To the left above him on a protected ridge he sees the dark wooden frame of an alpine hut, one of the many refuges the cow herders use during the summer. He thinks of some of the small animals who will be scuttling to find a suitable hole in the earth for their earlier than usual winter hibernation.

By the time he has dragged himself across the gully and has pulled himself up towards the hut, the light is fading. He melts handfuls of snow in his mouth, stops once to pee, fumbling with his ski pants as he is shivering so hard. His urine briefly warms his leg before intensifying the cold with its humidity against his skin. He curses and continues his journey towards the hut.

He pushes open the door and crawls in, his progress slowed by the dry wooden floor and the additional weight of the ski boot hampering his broken leg. There's a table, a few chopped logs in a rough wooden crate next to the tiny iron stove, and miracle of miracles, matches to light a fire. Hopefully the search and rescue team will see the smoke from the chimney when the weather clears and they come looking. His friends will know he's up here somewhere when he doesn't turn up to the bar this evening.

There's no kindling, but he peels the bark from the logs. This is something he has control over. He anticipates the satisfaction of the burn. He screws up the page of an old newspaper, and can't believe his luck when it lights from the first of three remaining matches in the box. The perfect result for the practised fire starter. He will be saved.

He was never found guilty of arson at his flat in England. The final forensic results of the fire stated that it was a fault in the fireplace. Finally, after two months, the police received a carbon report which concluded the beam had already been scorched several times previously. *Carbon dating*, he'd thought with a smirk when the police told him. It doesn't mean that the latest burn wasn't on purpose. Annie might have given the police a clue if they'd found her, but by the time she was found shacked up with some violin teacher at the Conservatoire de Paris, the case was closed. Ironic that she'd returned at least halfway back to the Alps.

One of the old newspaper pages next to the stove has a photo of a group of young children, a choir or a scout group. He recalls the photos of those children at the studio. Ron really was making a music score for the BBC's *Children in Need*. But even the police had put a doubt in Alain's mind when they talked about the abduction of Trudy's baby. He had wondered for a moment about those innocent little faces. But they were genuinely being gathered and sorted for an animation set to the music. Sometimes something so innocuous and philanthropic can turn into something else that's sinister and menacing.

Alain keeps blowing the flame in the little nest of fuel he has carefully formed in the firebox – he is an expert after all. Every puff out of his lungs sends shooting pains down his leg. The pieces of dry bark catch and he smiles at his prowess. The comfort of flames. When they begin to smother with what he assumes is a backdraught, he leaves the door of the stove open so it can draw.

The wind picks up outside the hut in the thickness of night. The only light in the hut is from the flickering flames in the stove. As its iron belly warms, his shivering ceases, but the throbbing in his leg ramps up. He pulls himself closer to the fire, sits up and props himself against the wood crate.

It's not until he feels a familiar caustic burn in the back of his throat that he looks up and realises his fatal error. The pitched ceiling of the hut has disappeared in a ghostly grey curtain of smoke. How stupid of him! Of course! The roof is covered in more than a metre of snow. The chimney will be blocked. Any rescue helicopter won't see the hut from above and certainly won't see the smoke, as it's all inside with Alain. There is no escape from the fumes.

He can barely move, pinned to his position by the throbbing in his leg, and a lack of oxygen. He considers his choices. The pain is now at a level he feels he can't sustain. Even if he could pull himself across the floor to open the door, he would surely be dead by morning from exposure, whether he crossed the threshold or not.

This could be the last of hundreds of fires he will ever set. Back in England, the one before this served two purposes. It satisfied Alain's desire to exert power that gave him that familiar euphoric thrill in the pit of his stomach, and the power to eliminate a dirty piece of vermin who shouldn't be allowed to walk free on this earth.

Alain recalls the weeks he scouted the house in Gosmore, and the satisfaction when the wife finally left on a Friday night with an overnight bag. Harper pulling into the driveway in his car that would have looked right at home on the streets of Geneva, but was ridiculous on the narrow lanes of Hertfordshire. Harper's arrival was announced with tyres crunching on gravel like the distant roar of spectators at a ski race.

Harper entered the house, keyed off the alarm, and walked down the hallway to the kitchen without locking the door behind him. Alain had shifted so he could see him through the window and the open dining room door. Harper hung his jacket on one of the bar stools and disappeared for a moment out of sight. He came back to the bar with a plate and some items from the fridge. He ate messily and scrolled through his phone. Leaving the plate on the bar, Harper went back through the hallway. He still didn't lock the door.

He continued to the living room, poured himself a large glass of whisky and sank into the armchair that was obviously his regular place, reaching for the TV remote on the table beside him. No matter, Alain had time.

After his third drink, all triples, no ice, he left his empty glass on the table, turned off the TV and the lights in the living room and went upstairs. There was a moment where he paused on the stairs as though remembering something – the door perhaps – and Alain was ready to bolt across the lawn. But Harper simply regained his balance against the bannister and continued upstairs.

When the light went out, Alain waited another half an hour before moving towards the front porch. He removed his shoes and left them on the step – an exemplary Swiss habit – and quietly opened the door. He listened for a moment at the bottom of the stairs. He heard a faint snoring from the floor above and crept up to find Harper's bedroom.

Contrary to the characters in most crime movies, most people in real life are incapable of killing another human being. No matter how angry they are, it still remains repellent to take someone's life. Even if that man has raped, beaten, or abused a string of women and managed to get away with it.

But take a man who's been deeply affected by the stories of a woman he had come to respect and even love a little. Rachel. A kind of replacement for his sister, Françoise, who died so young. Even Rachel's crazy friend didn't deserve what Harper did to her. It didn't take much research to find out the name of Rachel's rapist. She probably thought no one was listening when she told her story in that early group meeting, but Alain absorbed everything, the outrage building like a pyre in his mind. Take another look at this man Alain, hungry for the spark of a flame, whose legs have been honed to a muscular strength through years on the ski slopes.

Harper wasn't drunk enough to be trusted to stay in his bed once the ensuing smoke asphyxiation began to steal his life. Alain had to be sure. He removed his backpack and laid it on the floor next to the bed. He climbed onto the mattress and sat astride Kenneth Harper's body. His strong thighs clamped Harper's arms to his sides, stopping him from moving. Harper's body jerked in shock, but Alain held fast. He lifted the pillow next to Harper and without hesitation, pressed it down on his face. As shouts muffled into the Egyptian cotton, Alain strengthened his hold against the squirming body below him.

That man who was respected by society should know better. A man for whom a few years in jail would never be sufficient justice for his sins.

He sat on Harper's chest and waited five minutes beyond the point he'd first stopped moving to make absolutely sure he wasn't faking it. When he was convinced Harper had gone, he shook the pillow in his hands and placed it next to the body on the bed. His face looked slack, drunk, but it was his absolute stillness that was confirmation. Alain reached down to his backpack and took out two items: a foil disposable ashtray – the kind often found in the smokers' area outside a pub – and a rolled joint. He placed the ashtray within inches of the bed and arranged the quilt to hang over it. He said a silent thanks to the youths on their social bench on Windmill Hill from whom he'd bought the marijuana. He lit the joint with his Bic lighter, taking one deep victory puff, and blew the smoke into Harper's face as he climbed off his chest. Then he put the joint in the ashtray and held the lighter under the edge of the quilt. It took a while to catch, but once it was fully burning, he took his pack and left the room, closing the door so the smoke would take longer to reach the detector on the ceiling in the hallway.

He's filled with a yearning to stroke Rachel's shiny jet-black hair, wipe away her kohl-streaked tears, erase all the sadness and guilt and wasted time she feels, try to make her feel better. She would have loved his snow-clad landscape, the dark granite gullies dusted with white, the drama of the Alps. But it's too late now.

The popping of a log in the burner brings him back to the hut. They say that dying in the cold is the least painful of all the ways to go. Alain lies down on the floor, to take advantage of the last clear gap of breathable air. His eyes are stinging now. Smoke or tears, he's no longer sure. In some ways, this is only right. Fitting.

He looks upwards, at the upside-down ebb and flow of the smoke approaching like an ocean ready to drown him, and he readies himself for a very long sleep.

64

TRUDY

Ask any mother what the hardest thing she's ever done in her life is. Most will say childbirth. It's a wonder there aren't more specific groups dealing with this kind of trauma. I've already made notes to upgrade and modernise the leaflets on how to deal with postnatal anxiety I saw strewn about the midwifery unit of the hospital where I had Benny.

As a psychotherapist, I may not have been my own best patient. But in retrospect, I now recognise the signs I should have been looking for back then. Things no one tells an expectant mother might happen after giving birth. My journey has been turbulent and often one of denial. But I have come out the other side with a new perspective.

Benny slept last night for a full seven hours for the first time. It's a beautiful autumn Saturday morning. The sun, now lower in the sky as the days shorten, shines onto the alphabet frieze lining Benny's bedroom walls. Antelope to Zebra.

He's been playing quietly in his cot, and I return to our bedroom and choose some casual clothes for myself for the day. I'll shower later after I've done some work outside. I return and stand by his open door, enjoying the golden warmth of the sun flowing through the room as it does only at this time of the year. After a minute, I go to him while he's still in a good mood.

When he sees me, his mouth opens in a bubbly grin with his two lower front teeth perched like little pearls in his mouth. I reach out and hold his foot in his Winnie-the-Pooh onesie.

We dress and go down to the kitchen where Harry, who has decided not to play tennis, has prepared breakfast. Today we are playing happy families. Benny gums his way through three eggy bread fingers while Harry and I enjoy a full English. A rare weekend treat.

After breakfast we go out to the garden. Harry brings out the tools to replace the temporary bolt he put on the garden gate at the beginning of August with a sturdier bolt, and I put Benny, dressed in a smart new Tigger fleece, on a rug in the old wooden playpen I had as a child. He clings on to the top rail with his chubby little hands and grinds his new teeth on the age-old smooth wood.

I'm deadheading flowers when my phone buzzes with an incoming message. I figure it must be someone I know, as it's the weekend. It's from Suzy. Daniel will remain sectioned for the foreseeable future.

A small part of me had felt the tug of something maternal while we were discussing his motives on the way back from the Lake District at the end of July. What will happen to Daniel's children in the absence of both their parents? Perhaps Daniel will be released in a couple of years. At least the environment of the clinic will be better than them having to visit him in jail.

There's a second part to Suzy's message. Olive Stanton is being admitted to the Pinehill psychiatric facility. I'm relieved. I think the environment will be far healthier for her than the women's refuge, given all her issues. I guess while I was digesting and dealing with Benny's abduction and recovery, the authorities didn't want to burden me with what I might see as a failure on my part in the healing and repair of Olive. I haven't even been back to the clinic since Benny's return.

I'm not really sure I have the words to acknowledge either of these pieces of news. I reply 'thanks for letting me know.' and pause before adding 'thanks for everything.'

I note an unread email that came in on Friday evening that I must have missed. The pilot study I submitted for the PTSD group therapy back in July has been approved and funding will go through from the council in the absence of Kenneth Harper. But in light of what developed at the end of July, the fact that two of the case studies have committed crimes during the research, the project will undoubtedly be made null and void on ethics grounds. Instead I shall concentrate on providing more information to mothers who've experienced birth trauma.

Benny chuckles at a flurry of leaves floating to the ground in front of the playpen which he can only see with one eye. I reach up to put his wonky hat on straight and am overwhelmed with a sudden rush of emotion. I take off his hat, pick him up and bury my nose in his fine blond hair, smelling his sweetness, placing my lips against his soft cheek.

Harry pauses in his task of screwing a hinge to the gate to watch us. I feel a swell of love for my husband. But the most wonderful feeling is that I have finally fallen completely and madly in love with my son.

ACKNOWLEDGEMENTS

A novel involves a collaboration of many people. My heartfelt thanks go to the following people in no particular order of importance: Michael Loveday for helping to round my characters originating in a piece of work long-listed in the Bath Novella-in-Flash Award, Zoë Apostolides for her suggested edits in the early stages, Dr Stéphanie Carty for her psychotherapy advice, Scott Pack for his structural editing prowess, Diane Jeffrey for her keen grammatical eye, Vicky Newham for her support and suggestions, Antony Dunford for his keen line editing, Jayne Farnworth and Graham Bartlett for their police procedural guidance, Bridget Walsh for her honest critique, Julia Gibb for her proofreading, and the members of my book club in Aegeri who supplied the last critiques before the final edits and proofread. And lastly, much love and gratefulness to my husband Chris and our two sons Max and Finn for their continued support of my writing.

ABOUT THE AUTHOR

Louise Mangos writes novels, short stories and flash fiction, which have won prizes, been placed on shortlists, and have been narrated on BBC radio. Her short fiction appears in more than twenty print anthologies. She holds an MA in crime writing from the University of East Anglia in the UK.

You can connect with Louise on Facebook —/LouiseMangosBooks, or Twitter @LouiseMangos, and Instagram as @louise-mangos, or visit her website https://louisemangos.com/ where there are links to some of her short fiction. If you'd like to receive information about new releases and be in with a chance of winning the occasional giveaway, subscribe to her newsletter on her homepage.

Having grown up in the village of Whitwell in rural English Hertfordshire where Trudy lives in the novel, Louise now lives at the foot of the Swiss Alps with her Kiwi husband and two sons. When she's not writing, she enjoys an active life in the mountains.

Dear Reader,

I'm lucky enough to live in the beautiful Aegeri Valley in central Switzerland at the foot of the Alps, but I grew up in the village of Whitwell, the setting for the home of Trudy, Harry and Benny. I attended Hitchin Girls' School in my teens, and for a couple of years played badminton in the old school building on Queen Street where the group therapy sessions take place in the novel, which is now the British Schools Museum.

The most important people in an author's career are you, the readers, whether you're a blogger, a reviewer, or someone who simply enjoys a good yarn. A fellow author once told me that reviews are like coins in a busker's hat. I'd like to use that analogy and encourage you to leave your review on the platform of your choice. Each of those coins contributes towards an author's bread and butter.

If you enjoyed my writing, you might like to try one of my other psychological suspense novels, or if you enjoy historical fiction, perhaps you'd like to read my medieval mystery. Details of all these are on the following pages.

I hope to bring you many more tales for your enjoyment in the future.

Cheers,

Louise

MORE BOOKS BY THE AUTHOR

Strangers on a Bridge

How far would you go to protect your family? While Alice Reed is on her morning jog in the peaceful Swiss Alps, she unexpectedly saves a stranger on a notorious suicide bridge. But could her Samaritan deed turn out to be the first of many mistakes?

Adamant they have an instant connection, Manfred's charm gradually darkens and his obsession with Alice grows stronger.

In a country far from home, where the police don't believe her, the locals don't trust her and even her husband questions the truth about Manfred, Alice has nowhere to turn.

And she begins to think she should never have saved him that day on the bridge...

FINALIST in the EXETER NOVEL PRIZE

LONG LISTED for the BATH NOVEL AWARD

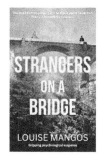

The Art of Deception

She must prove her innocence to save her son... but time is running out.

Art school dropout Lucie is on a backpacking trip across Europe when she arrives in the idyllic Swiss Alps. A holiday romance with ski instructor Mathieu takes a crucial turn when Lucie discovers she is pregnant. Spiralling into a relationship of coercion and dark domestic abuse, Lucie is powerless to escape her marriage without losing her son.

Seven years on, Lucie is serving a sentence in a Swiss prison for a murder she insists she did not commit. Surrounded by an eclectic group of inmates, Lucie must summon all her strength and intuition to uncover long-kept secrets and fight for her freedom to be reunited with her son before he is abducted by her husband's family.

The clock is ticking . . . but who can she trust?

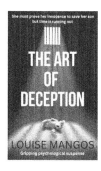

The Beaten Track

After her stalker takes his life and she's jilted by a holiday lover, Sandrine comes home from her round-the-world backpacking trip perturbed, penniless and pregnant. She meets handsome Scott, who offers her love, security and all she and her new baby could ever wish for. But their dream is about to turn into nightmare...

FINALIST in the Page Turner Awards

Writing historical fiction as L.S.Mangos

The Secrets of Morgarten – a medieval mystery

A young nation in peril. A web of deception. A triangle of forbidden love.

The year is 1315. The fledgling nation of Switzerland – the Confederation Helvetica – is under threat from the Habsburgs. In France, the Knights Templar have been disbanded and declared heretics by the king. Magda, a beautiful weaver living near the alpine village of Morgarten, befriends Walter, a messenger and tracker who is the son of the legendary Wilhelm Tell. Walter and Magda's budding romance is threatened by the arrival of Sébastien, a French fugitive. What secrets is this foreigner hiding? Can Walter solve the mystery of a murder and a stolen religious artefact before a mighty battle with the Habsburgs ensues? And who will be the victors in their turbulent triangle of love?

FINALIST in the Page Turner Awards

Printed in Great Britain
by Amazon

44700960R00189